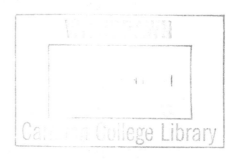

YOUR NAME HERE: _____

Other Books by Cris Mazza

Exposed

How to Leave a Country

Animal Acts

Revelation Countdown

Is It Sexual Harassment Yet?

YOUR NAME HERE: ——

A NOVEL BY CRIS MAZZA

COFFEE HOUSE PRESS ☕ MINNEAPOLIS

Acknowledgments are made to the following publications, in which portions of this novel first appeared: *The Iowa Review, The Santa Monica Review, Colorado North Review,* and *West Wind Review.*

The publisher would like to thank the following funders for assistance that helped make this book possible: Dayton Hudson Foundation on behalf of Dayton's and Target Stores; The General Mills Foundation; The National Endowment for the Arts, a federal agency; The Lannan Foundation; The Andrew W. Mellon Foundation; Star Tribune/Cowles Media Company; and The McKnight Foundation. This activity is made possible in part by a grant provided by the Minnesota State Arts Board, through an appropriation by the Minnesota State Legislature.

Coffee House Press books are available to the trade through our primary distributor, Consortium Book Sales & Distribution, 1045 Westgate Drive, Saint Paul, MN 55114. Our books are also available through all major library distributors and jobbers and through most small press distributors, including Bookpeople, Inland, and Small Press Distribution. For personal orders, catalogs, or other information, write to:

Coffee House Press
27 North Fourth Street, Suite 400, Minneapolis, MN 55401

Library of Congress CIP data
Mazza, Cris
      Your name here: a novel / by Cris Mazza.
           p. cm.
      ISBN 1-56689-031-4
      1. Women—Crimes against—Fiction. 2. Rape—Fiction. I. Title.

PS3563.A988Y68   1995
813'.54—dc20   94-45779
                                                              CIP

10   9   8   7   6   5   4   3   2   1

To Harold
Maybe now I'll shut up

Thanks, Diane

Half her face was blue, but her skull wasn't fractured. Her eyes were not closed, although the moment they had opened is inexact. What was the first thing she saw? She was dopey with pain killers, clenching her teeth because her jaw was wired shut. Did she really see him there? She didn't move. Technically she could've—there was no paralysis. But everything below her iceberg head was just a lump covered by a sheet. A bouquet of faces and flowers and probably stuffed animals surrounded the foot of the bed. Family, friends, about ten people—did she know that many people? Whose voice came from which mouth? Then her mother—never the tearful worried type— taking charge:

"Now's not the time to try to describe what happened, Corinne. Just rest. There'll be plenty of time to say who did it and why later."

Her eyes closed, then opened again, touched his face for a second. He didn't flinch. She looked away, looked back, settled her eyes on his, then blinked again, stared up at the ceiling.

"Some people came while you were out cold," her mother said. "I have a list of them: some girls you knew in college, one of your neighbors, a Mr. Warren Kyle, Aunt Deb, and Uncle Bobby. Tell you what—I'll get you a pad of paper so you'll be able to write instead of trying to talk."

A nurse's head through the door: "Visiting hours are over." The little crowd of people shifted, forming a sort of receiving line as each person came to the bedside, kissed her cheek, and left. But he moved behind the line, going the wrong direction, went into the bathroom and shut the door. She might've fallen asleep for a second or two. The room was empty when she opened her eyes again, empty except for him. He approached the bed, stopped near the end. He touched her toes, held her foot through the sheet. Then what did he say? Anything? But her memory must have been scrambled by one of the blows to her head: it was like several stacked layers of transparent photographs—all pictures of him speaking to her, at a restaurant, in the studio, in a gloomy apartment (not hers), in his car, in her car, on a swingset at the park, and—like the bottom of a double-double-double exposure—in the hospital room, at the foot of her bed, where he might not've ever been, except she could still feel him holding her foot. Were any of his mouths moving in any of the memories? His voices, all talking at once, coming from somewhere:

"Why didn't you stop them, just leave—just walk out the door?"

"Something was telling me not to let you go out that door at that moment. You were blind angry."

"It was never my intention for you to get involved, Corinne. I kept you out of it for a long time. But . . ."

"Dammit, when someone thinks you're a thief, does that make you steal? So when someone thinks you're a whore, did you have to turn into one?"

"I thought I knew Haley. But after she lost her show, she wouldn't even fight back, she just cleared out and disappeared."

"Why bother yourself with it, as long as you're not involved, be thankful that you're not."

"Maybe you saw me land the first one, maybe not, your back was turned, you went down to your knees. I hit you again and you folded over on the floor. Then I hit you again. Someday maybe you'll understand. . . . But I hope not."

He touched her jaw with a single finger, then put the back of his knuckles against her cheek.

The beating might've really made me stupid, daft, barmy, addled. I hardly remember anything about it. There's a computer printout from the hospital: hairline fracture, right mandible; mild concussion. The charges include three days, three nights. This information is in a folder, filed under B in my file cabinet. The index on the folder says The Beating. It's in my handwriting. The other thing in the file folder is my mother's list of people who visited while I was unconscious. His name is there, almost exactly in the middle, including the Mister, first and last names. Is that how we were? *Mister?* No nickname? Not even in quotes? Every time I think about this, I ask the same old fifty questions and add ten new ones. When was the last time I saw him—in that group of people in my room that day? Were *that* many people really in my room? Did he or anyone tell Haley I was in the hospital? Did she say, Corinne *who?* Did I ever tell the police anything? Did anyone ever ask any questions? Show me a lineup? Take my statement? Was he really there? Did he just stand there? Or did he touch me? Or say something? What happened? What happened *before* I was hit?

And every time the questions wander through my mazed mind, I've thought about these journals—the same ones I went and hid as soon as I left the hospital.

Since I don't recall much except how difficult it was to eat and speak, what I do—often without meaning to—is see the hospital scene from somewhere else in the room. Not like an out-of-body experience, even more removed than that—as though I had never been me, maybe knew my name and where I worked and could see, just from standing there and looking, that I'd been beat up.

But if I'm watching as someone else, who could I be? No one else was there, except him, if—as the story I've told myself goes—he managed to be the last one to leave. And we can't both be him. Only one person at a time can be Warren Kyle, though he had lots of names: *Kip,* the nickname he told me he liked to be called; *Champ,* the one Haley made up; and *C.K.,* which was Cy Golden's invention after Champ, which made Kyle wince the one time I heard it. But, the thought occurs to me, if my memory *could* let me be him—or better yet, if only I could slip into and borrow *his* memory (*if* he remembers), maybe I'd painlessly know everything I need. I'd know why he was at the hospital—an obligatory visit? Concerned friend? Angry acquaintance? Why angry? And I'd know what had been going on for the previous six months. Or if nothing had happened, I'd know that too and wouldn't be haunted, ten years later, by the feeling that something's not finished. I would know what he thought as he stood there and saw my fat purple lips, my blackened eye, the Frankenstein stitches along my jaw. And I would know why just once he'd insisted on taking me home after the show and making lunch for me—peaches, string cheese, grilled Polish sausage, green salad—and why he smiled at me crookedly over his wine glass, but never made a move on me, spent a lot of time suggesting different desserts we could have, from instant pudding to flaming cherries jubilee, then let me have the last swallow of his seventy-five dollar bottle of Rothschild wine. I just suddenly remembered that lunch. What else will I suddenly remember when I open these dire little notebooks?

Knowing any one of the answers would certainly tell me something about the rest, tell me something about whatever happened before, up to and including the day in my hospital room. But I don't know. So I only remember it as though I'm not either of us—I've been pushed three or four steps farther away, demoted to a bit part, a nurse or intern or scrubwoman watching through a peephole in the door:

The man at the foot of the bed looks at the woman—the body—in the bed. The man touches the woman's foot. It seems logical—the foot is there, handy, within reach, sticking up under the sheet. And he uses her foot like a handle, to pull himself closer, so that maybe, if for some reason he needs to or wants to, he can touch her face where she got the beating. And he can say something, anything he wants, because she can't say anything back, because he probably won't see her again afterwards. It looks that way from here. So he can confess, if there's anything to confess to. He can explain a lot of things. He can cover a lot of ground, like: how would he define their relationship, and how would or could it be resolved? Or why on two separate occasions he'd told her he liked to be called Kip, but in between those two times suggested that she call him Mr. Kyle. He can—but why would he?—describe how he'd felt about Haley. But he can't explain how SHE'D *felt about Haley. He can't explain why she would think about Haley when she chose what clothes to wear to work, or why she used to imagine Haley in the studio introducing a song or giving the weather report while looking at her through the glass window of the booth with her eyes all lit up, sticking out her tongue or waving, which Haley had never once done.*

Instead of bringing up Haley at all, he can explain to the woman in the bed why he never touched her when she cried, yet often tickled the backs of her knees with a feather duster or put her in a half-nelson or pretended to choke her if she was angry, though they laughed together from different corners of the room. Or what he was thinking all those times in the studio when, while doing his humorous bit on the show or taping a silly commercial, he stared at her grimly? Or why, as she lies in this white bed, barely thinking, has it hit her like another fist ... that maybe she's lived through a hailstorm or overnight frost and thinks she's survived . . . but an entire ice age is on its way.

Maybe he did say something in my hospital room. And whatever he said is still sleeping in my unhinged, whacked-out memory. I see myself like a little paralyzed nerve in the middle of a knotted, novocained mass of gristle. No, I don't remember the beating, but for some reason always picture it the way I've thought he might've described it: *Your back was turned, you went down to your knees. I hit you again and you folded over on the floor. Then I hit you again . . .* What crazed part of my imagination tells me he did it?

San Diego, California
12 February 1989

Dear Mr. Kyle,

Shouldn't I be calling you Warren by now? After all, believe it or not, pretty soon we'll both be ten years older than when we met.

I'm writing to let you know I'm back in town. I heard you on the radio this morning. No, I didn't really hear you. I figured the news would be on at eight, then I turned the radio off after the reporter said, *Now back to Kip Kyle,* or *The Kip Kyle Show,* or something with your name—your nickname, that is, which you never used professionally in the Golden-and-Kyle days. Progress, right?

Let me catch you up on me. After my jaw healed, I moved back to Arizona and went to one of those two-cent broadcasting schools. That, plus my experience with you (and the old journalism degree you used to laugh about), got me my first job as a TV news reporter in Pine Bluff, Arkansas. I was married for a while in Pine Bluff. Long story. Moved from there to Billings, Montana, then to Las Cruces, New Mexico. I might have those last two mixed up. I got my first news anchor job last year in Redding. And you stayed here all along. Different station, I know. KIAM doesn't even exist anymore, does it? Well, for that matter, neither does Corinne Staub. Terrible name for a TV personality, they said. Now I'm Erin Haley. But before you start to grin, I *know*: I took Haley's name. Where is she, do you know? I've often thought I should tell her I took her name—borrowed it. A tribute to her. She might get a kick out of it. She might not care. Or she might not remember me at all. And if she saw the review I got during my first month in Redding, it might seem like a coincidence—or less than that—for the Redding news anchor's last name to be the same as her first name. Excuse me, her *only* name. She dropped her last name, whatever it was, didn't she? I thought she might've liked what the reviewer said:". . . exudes a grim sexiness even while delivering the worst news."

What do you think he meant? I'm still puzzled by it. It can't be because of my appearance. I have a short unisex haircut and my face is thinner than it was nine or ten years ago, same broad shoulders for my size, but I've lost weight. They make you do that. I wear a few more earrings in each ear. Four on one side, five on the other, I forget. But not on the air. I fill all the holes but two with makeup, wear matching pearls or some dull thing. Sweaters with shoulder pads, V-necked dresses, suits with high lace-collared blouses. You know the uniform. During my days off it's a different story—they wouldn't even know me if I won a tattoo contest and they interviewed me for the evening news. Maybe you wouldn't either.

So, anyway, they've given me time off. I *took* time off. I'm right here in San Diego in the Cresmoore Hotel downtown with all my old journals, which have been in storage here in town all these years since the day I left the hospital. I do remember that frantic cab ride to my apartment—which my mother was in the process of clearing out—followed immediately by another breathless excursion to an impersonal downtown bank to stuff the notebooks in the safe-deposit drawer.

I haven't kept any journal since my three days in the hospital. There are some questions I have to find answers to. Too many questions to list now. Suffice it to say, I don't really know what happened. No, I'm not just claiming amnesia from the beating, even though I don't remember much about it. I mean before that, I never really knew what was happening, did I?

Why now? I don't know. My jaw still aches when it rains. It might not all be the fault of the fracture, though—I started having to wear a hard rubber guard in my mouth at night because I clench and grind my teeth in my sleep. Had to get my teeth capped. I've always had problems with sleep. And I became a lucid dreamer—although I'm not lucid at the same times that I'm grinding my teeth, or I probably could stop myself. But I'm not a completely lucid dreamer—I can't decide what to dream, then be in the dream as long as I want, directing it, rewriting it, rerunning the best parts. What I do is become aware and almost conscious, stay asleep but *know* I'm dreaming—at least know it while it's happening. The problem is afterwards. Besides feeling like I got no rest at all, it feels like the dream, whatever it was, really happened to me. I remember it, dwell on it, it buzzes in my head all day, puts me in a funk, my pulse bumps in my fingertips, makes me feel worried or guilty or abandoned or betrayed, depending on the dream, and always strangely, profoundly lonesome. I'm beginning to think that maybe what's been happening is—months or years later—I can't tell the memory of a lucid dream apart from the memory of something that happened while I was awake. I suppose I could just write some of these mysterious memories down, send them to you and ask, did this one happen? How about this one? Do I have the details right? Or I could ask you face-to-face. Except you'd laugh. Not out loud, but that smile that is a laugh anyway. Sometimes a shared laugh. That was only okay if I was the one sharing it. If not . . . I felt like someone who desperately wants something, deprived of it over and over and over. But what *was* it?

Well, I just wanted you to know I'm in town. It finally became time I knew I had to come back for these journals. A gnawing apprehension suspects I'll find something in them— just not sure what. But I'm going to stay here to read them. I

may want to talk to you afterwards. I plan to read slowly. Not
sure why. Maybe that same apprehension. And I'm also a little
afraid to call you or visit. Not until I know more. Because *you*
might not remember me until *I* remember.

Anyway, what would I say? Is Mister Kyle in? Mister Warren?
Mr. Kip? Mister Champ? Choosing what to call you means
choosing the distance—I can't *choose* the distance but I do want
to know what it really was. I'll know what to call you if I ever
remember or discover that you really did kiss, kick, bite, or
screw me.

So, Kyle, knowing now that you'll never see this letter should
make me quit writing it, but I'd like to pretend, for a while at
least, that I could've just called you or walked right into the studio. But even if you did remember me after this long, you
would only want pleasantries, a joke or two, maybe a light-
hearted remembrance. Anything more, you'd cut me off. Your
eyes would get hazy, drowsy, bored, looking over my head or at
someone passing by, bland smile, and: "Well, nice seeing you
again." Maybe: "Keep in touch." Maybe not. Probably not. It
would be the type of thing that can make me spend the day in
bed. I don't drink. Much. Maybe I still take too many sleeping
pills. Usually only at night. But I need them sometimes in the
middle of the day too . . . then I lie in bed, drowsing and waking, always trying to dream a better scene, where at least if you
knock me down, you're the one who picks me back up. But, as
I said, my lucid dreaming isn't *that* controlled. I might dream
about you, but you'd be cutting my hair or touching my eyelids
with your thumbs or balancing me as I walk around on the
handrail of a balcony or tickling me with a live microphone and
making me giggle while you ask, "Are you *mad* at me?" or
counting my fingers and toes, or . . . well, I don't want to talk
about that most recent dream right now.

So, anyway, I'm absent a little too much from work. They think it's PMS. They think I'm very irregular. The guy I married used to say no one could look at me cross-eyed. He wasn't very original. A fairly normal tree surgeon who saw me as a sophisticated girl from Southern California. How could I pass *that* up? He slapped me a few times, rattled my eyeballs, that's all. Trying to snap me out of it, he said. Out of *what?* Well, I moved on, to Las Cruces, and he stayed behind. We're probably divorced by now. Maybe annulled. I got something official forwarded to me after I'd moved to Billings. I wasn't afraid of him, even though he was the first person I knew who had a gun. He'd take it out of the dresser drawer every night, load it, then put it on top of the nightstand, butt toward the bed, barrel pointing diagonally away, toward the window. Then he practiced—lay down on his stomach, facing the center of the bed, away from the nightstand, eyes shut, one leg straight, one bent, arms cradling his pillow. Slowly, with his right arm, the one closer to the nightstand, he reached out and without fumbling around in the dark, without having to feel his way, he put his hand on the gun's handle, wrapped his fingers around. He lay there holding it, no other part of his body moving, like a race starter who'd gotten trampled by the runners before he got the shot off to start the race.

I tried not to come to bed until he'd already let go of the gun and curled on his side. But I wasn't afraid of his gun . . . or his love of motorcycles and chainsaws. Of course he used a truck for his tree-trimming business, but I think his fantasy was to be able to roar from job to job on a Harley-Davidson wearing a leather jacket with a chainsaw strapped to his back. I have a halfway nostalgic memory of him doing it, too, at least a soft spot in my heart for him so innocently wanting it. It's a fonder way to remember him than the time he lay beside me, the second month out of the six we were married, both of us naked, one of his legs across my body, holding my shoulder, careful not to touch any of my erogenous zones for fear I wouldn't have an orgasm. Again. I knew it wasn't his fault. I'd been with some men since leaving KIAM but every time it was the same thing, as though I'd taken one of my sleeping pills or something even stronger, something that creates a temporary coma. A coma without brain death. While my mind whizzed out the window—planning human-interest stories or a hitch-across-the-country vacation—my body was motionless deadweight. Not a totally unpleasant state of relaxation, I guess. Like being buried in warm sand on a cold day at the beach—nothing can move, but nothing wants to move. Nothing itches, so you don't need to scratch. I've never been stupid enough to tell a quadriplegic that I know what it feels like . . . but I think I do at least for twenty or thirty minutes at a time while a sweaty man groans and works like hell over me.

So Alex asked why I don't come and I told him I didn't know how.

He said, "You don't have to *know* anything. Just do it, let it happen."

I said, "But I don't know what it is I'm supposed to do."

He rolled to his back, freeing me, so to speak. He said, "You're too aware of everything all the time, reading into and investigating. Shit—just *feel* it."

I explained how it was a vicious cycle—if I tried not to think about it, I'd be lying there being aware of trying not to be aware.

He got mad. But I still wasn't afraid. "You're so full of bullshit excuses," he said. "Haven't you ever really wanted—*needed*—to get laid? You know, jumped out of your skin with lust?"

I told him I did want to get laid.

He said, "Only because you think you *should* want to." He got out of bed, then stood there, well-muscled, no fat, with his lean, almost gaunt, face. I remember these things because to picture him soft and refined would be an invention. But I don't remember details—the color of his eyes or hair, the length of his nose, the shape of his lips. "Admit it," he said. "I don't turn you on. What does? *What ever has?*"

How could I answer him? That's when I first remember the trembling—not shivering on the outside, nothing he could notice. But suddenly I was a coward. I wasn't afraid of him, though. I wished he would hit me, god, pound me with a crowbar or get out his chainsaw. Give me something *else* to be afraid of. I didn't take anything from the marriage except his question.

I left him to move up somewhere else. Just like after I left the hospital: I never tried to go back to KIAM, just left San Diego altogether. I wanted to become a new person in a new place where no one knew the old me. There've been so many changes since then: a little plastic surgery, weight loss, different colored contact lenses, the clothes, the walk, the posture, the voice, the name. . . . I *made* it, Kyle. I made it. So why should all this old stuff still be with me, why should it all follow me around? The sleep disorder, the aching jaw, the druglike paralysis during sex, the unexplained trembling, the unanswered questions. And the dreams. They've become more frequent. For a while, I have to admit, I might've occasionally had a good dream—like flying, my favorite dream—then looked forward to the next like a vacation . . . until I started to realize I wasn't always sure if I was remembering a dream or something that really happened.

Sometimes I sit at the anchor desk, in the moments before the finger points and the camera lights go on, and I say, *Look, you're here now, what difference does anything that came before make* NOW? Obviously, if I'd talked myself out of it, I wouldn't be back in San Diego. Despite the production and editorial meetings, the news writing, the location shots, the feature stories, the private office, the studio lights, it's been harder and harder to keep myself from continually dwelling on things I both can't remember and want to never have to think about again. *Be glad you can't remember,* I say, *that's one way of putting it behind you forever.* But I was forced to realize: answers don't linger and haunt and distort themselves; questions do. So dreams must be made from questions. At least mine are. It seems I couldn't've slept enough to dream as much as I apparently do. Yet at times it has felt like everything I've remembered *could've* been a dream. How do you get a glass jaw from a dream? Something had to be real. But there are things that've *only* existed during my scanty hours of sleep. Like lust. I can come in my sleep. Sometimes I really know the man but sometimes it's someone I only know in my sleep; sometimes I never saw him before in my life and sometimes don't even see him at all—he might not have a face, or the dream might be too dark. Sometimes I know exactly what he's going to do and sometimes I can be surprised . . . both are okay. Sometimes it may start out tenderly although sometimes, I admit, it's rape, but I don't mind. How can I be saying that? But maybe it doesn't matter because soon after it starts, the me who is just a mind finds itself not in the female body but in the man. I don't know when or how it happens. And after that, I don't know who the man is anymore, if I ever did. Just thinking about this, I get that same quaking, cowardly desire to be beaten with a hammer.

Believe me, Kyle, I never dreamed I was you when I was a man doing the screwing. Whenever you're there—until recently—all we did was talk, look at each other. You sat on my bed or on the ground beside me, leaned against my leg, or tucked my hair behind my ear. You know, I'm not sure . . . but I don't think I've ever dreamed about Haley. Maybe once. . . . No, I'm not sure. But sometimes when I see myself in a dream, I look like her. Did I ever look a little like her? Her hair was lighter. She had freckles and I don't. She was thinner—maybe thinner than I am now.

I never tell these dreams to anyone.

I don't think just a dream could chase me away from my job to come down here and sit in a fleabag hotel with six or seven frayed journals and a laptop. Why now? I was doing the news one night last week and the copy was shaking. It had never before been visible in the studio when I had one of my cowardly days. My speech may be slowed because it's my brain that's rattling. My pulse may be thick in my tongue and lips. One eye may twitch, but someone would have to look close. My jaw and teeth may throb. But this time it was all out there on the surface. They cut to the co-anchor and got me off the set. I was breathing like I'd been stopped short in the middle of a race, my rubbery legs unable to figure out why we weren't running any longer.

Well, the night before that, I did have a dream, or several dreams. I wonder if you would remember that time you took me down to the lunch room and bought me a soda. I think you had a beer. Did they sell beers at our lunch room? You were on your way home for the day. We sat on opposite sides of a sticky brown table, on benches. So far this doesn't sound like any specific time, I know, but *this* particular time I'm talking about is when you told me that Cy Golden had said that I'd better stop looking at you so much in a certain way. *That* wasn't a dream, right? It really happened? You might think it was too insignificant to remember. Now I'm wondering if what I remember is real, because that's where we were in this dream: sitting there, your fingertips holding the beer mug like a crystal ball, saying, "One member of this station has expressed the opinion that a certain other member should stop looking at a third member in a particular way . . . so much." Was I dreaming it or lying awake remembering? Or both? My heart started beating, as though it had stopped somewhere along the way. I knew you were waiting for me to answer or respond, but I was confused—didn't know if you meant I shouldn't look at you, or Haley shouldn't look at you, or you shouldn't look at Haley, or *I* shouldn't look at Haley. Did you see the fear in my eyes? What was there to be afraid of? You were suddenly beside me, putting your arm around me, putting your warm cheek against mine, saying, "What's the matter, you never going to look at me again?"

"I don't think so," I said.

You laughed, but just a little later, although my cheek was still warm, you were back on the other side of the table, saying, "I have a rule about life that I've decided is 100 percent accurate: In either case, if someone seems to be having an affair, or if it appears that someone might be gay, they are."

Why did you say that?

Then we went home, and, naturally, we lived together—along with Alex, my Pine Bluff husband, and I think several others, although I never saw Haley and no one even mentioned her name. I had to climb through a window because I couldn't find the door. You were already there. I was wearing pants and suspenders but no shirt. You held me in front of you, your hands on my waist, not my shoulders, while you babbled excitedly about something. I gathered finally that you were directing a play and I was in it and we'd been great. But I got the feeling I wasn't the star. Who was? I didn't know where to put my arms: Cross them over my chest? Let them hang stiffly at my sides? I finally clutched your forearms and stayed there, not looking at you or at my naked upper body, until you were no longer holding onto me. Then I went through the room picking up Alex's clothes, lying where he'd stepped out of them.

I don't really remember how we got from there to standing in line for a ride at a theme park. It was a whole group—maybe an outing for the KIAM employees—but again Haley wasn't there. Maybe it was after she'd lost her show and left the station. Even if she had been there, though, I didn't have a buddy to pal around with. My eyes felt like they'd been open all day without blinking, or like I'd gone to sleep wearing my contact lenses. But when my turn came, it was a private tour, by horseback, through a purple forest, stage-lit, dim in some places, floodlit in others. You were leading the horse. I said, "I've never been here before," even though I've been to Disneyland dozens of times. But I wasn't lying. Suddenly, or finally, I felt like I could really relax and rest. I didn't even have to hold onto the horse. I closed my eyes and lay down, put my cheek against the back of the horse's neck, right behind his ears. I could feel the horse walking tranquilly and I knew you were there, holding the halter, but I was no longer seeing or hearing anything. Dreaming about resting. Dreaming about total darkness and total silence. Just the warm movement of the horse, knowing you were there, and my lucid self telling me: *Keep your eyes closed, he'll finally kiss you.* My eyes stayed shut. Continued dreaming without seeing, feeling your hand move from the halter to the back of my neck, lifting my head up, your warm mouth covering mine, sucking softly, your tongue strong but not any less gentle. I still didn't open my eyes. You lay my head back down on the horse's mane and went on leading us along the trail. But I was slipping. I wasn't holding on, relaxing too much—each step rocked me farther and farther off the horse. I knew I was going to fall. I don't think I cared, though. Because you were there. When I landed, the horse stepped on my face. Like a jarring punch in slow motion, took forever to finish happening.

I don't remember waking up. I was groggy and groaning, still felt the kiss on my mouth and even had one surge of adrenaline, as though you might come back along the trail looking for me, pick me up, hold my stepped-on face. But I was also cold and sweating, and repeating in my head: *A dream, a dream, only a dream, it never happened, you can only pretend it happened . . .*

The sweats came back again and again all that day. And I started to wonder hysterically, unable to catch my breath, how much of the you I thought I remembered was really just one of those dreams? But I *know* you really existed . . . because Haley really existed. It's little comfort, but since I never seem to dream about Haley, I know that everything I remember about her must be something that actually happened. Maybe it's my fault you lost Haley . . . and that's why you did it.

And all day, that last day, buzzing like a tapeloop in my head . . . all the same old questions, around and around, except this time as though asking the questions directly to you. And asking: *Are you, by now, just a creation of my imagination? If so,* WHO BEAT ME UP? *Why do I hope it was you?*

When they pulled me off the air, I was soaking wet all over again, thinking about the hidden notebooks, knowing it was time to find out.

AUGUST 20, 1979

Is it disappointing for my arrival to be so unspectacular? Well, face it, who's going to give a fanfare for a new intern or gofer or writer or whatever it is my job title would be here, if it had a title? They're apparently too lazy to do their own background research like most talk jocks do. I've never heard of a job like this. Doesn't mean I'm first-of-a-kind. Anyway, this is more than just my first day at a job . . . more important than the start of my career in broadcasting . . . the best part is that none of the people here knew me the past three years at State, there are no carryovers, no one to know Corinne Staub, who lived in her bulletproof bubble, sending out invisible warning rays: *Stay the fuck away from me.* (And it worked, which didn't even make me feel better.) But I can break the cycle now because no one here saw me that way. Now's my chance to change. The same chance I had when I *started* college. *No* one in San Diego knew what (or who) I'd left behind in Arizona . . . a clean slate . . . and I did it wrong . . .

One of my first tasks: a stack of *National Enquirer, Star News,* and other pulp to go through, searching for possible schtick. I'm going to have to get a feel for the show quickly because ideas have to fit the personalities.

That's what this notebook is for and that's what I'm really doing right now, what looks to them like I'm taking notes from these newspapers — I've got to take notes on *them* too. They're just sitting there, one on the phone, the other reading a letter, drinking coffee. The stereo speakers are carrying the FM side — they came in and switched over after their show. And its one reason my arrival and first day have been so unheralded: a new FM jock, a husky female voice that cracks on certain pitches, certain words, like when she said "Oh baby!" after a song that vamped out with a lot of "Oh baby, yeah baby." The one reading letters, Kyle, looks up whenever it's her voice and not music. He just stares at a wall. Earlier there were two other guys in here. I don't know who they were—news guys or weather guys or engineers or something. They were saying they heard this new chick—their word—used to be the program director's girlfriend. They wanted to know if Golden or Kyle had met her or seen her or anything. You can't see the FM jocks while they work unless you go to the other end of the building. Golden thought their question was a laugh riot. He said sure he's seen her and called her a juicy piece and said Al wasn't the only one she came on to like a bitch in heat. That made Kyle look up. But Golden didn't even glance back at him.

Kyle's mouth was this flat line across his face and his eyebrows were practically a V over his nose, except they flipped up, like evil-stepmother eye makeup, at the ends. At my interview, where Golden did most of the talking (and when Kyle asked a question—what did I think about being the only Indian with two chiefs? I never answered because Golden interrupted with another of *his* questions) . . . anyway, at the interview, before the questions, Golden introduced Kyle as his "token former-jock partner." And he called him "Jocko" a few times. Kyle was a baseball player. He's not much older than me, so it must've been a short career. He does all the voice characters on the show.

The ideas I'm supposed to be searching out and helping develop are mostly for little plots for the lives of these characters, who supposedly do the show with Golden and Kyle. Before I can be of much use, I'm going to have to learn all those characters and their personalities. But I have to learn the real people too. That's the other thing I remember Kyle saying at the interview, that their intern had to be very perceptive and know what kinds of things they would want and what was right for them without waiting to be told. I think I can learn Kyle just by watching him.

Golden is another story. All you see is a short guy, verging on pudgy, with white Julius Caesar hair or a wig. And watching him I see a guy who thinks he's acting eccentrically Jewish—like one of his phone calls was trying to get a shoe store to donate shoes to him because when he wore them for special guest appearances, the shoe store would get free promotion. But, really, it's just bad-taste self-importance. Like when the new female FM jock came on a minute ago doing an ad for motor oil, full of words like hot, friction, and looooobricate, with her husky, low, cracking voice, Golden held the phone away from his head, let his jaw go slack, started dog-panting and shaking his hand in the air like he'd just touched something scalding.

Kyle rolled his eyes, glanced at me, then went to the Coke machine out in the hall. He doesn't walk like a jock—no strut, no muscle-bound swagger. How am I ever going to get a single idea for these two?

Golden had already decided on his part of a new opener: "This is the Golden-and-Kyle . . . Golden for the color of the sunrise over America's Finest City . . . and Kyle because . . ." Then Kyle's part would come there. Golden kept repeating his part over and over as though really brainstorming a perfect line for Kyle, his voice trailing away, holding a hand out as though to cue Kyle every time he got to the end of his line, but staring at the ceiling, then starting his line all over again.

Finally on one of those cues, Kyle said, "Because it's my name."

Golden acted like he hadn't heard him.

The next time through, Kyle said it again, louder, with more of an on-air voice quality. Golden pulled in his cueing hand and put his knuckles against his mouth, apparently thinking. So I said, "It's great. Use it!" Kyle smiled at me. The laugh lines at the corners of his eyes seemed part of the smile, like they were for me as much as the smile was. Golden said, "Hmmmm." I said, "Except the sunrise isn't golden. It's orange and pink and red." He didn't look at me. Kyle still was, though, the smile gone but only because the corners of his mouth were fighting to *keep* it gone. The laugh-lines were still there. Maybe that's what encouraged me to go on: "So why doncha change your name to Pinky?" Kyle looked down and bit his lips and his eyes seemed to be nearly popping out from trying not to laugh out loud. But Golden shot me a glare, then picked up the phone as though this discussion about the color of the sunrise had made him forget to make an important call.

LATER

I'm supposed to be concentrating on learning the show, not the off-the-record stuff Kyle said . . . which can't help but seem more important. They had some sort of meeting with Al, the program director, and another guy, the station manager, so Kyle gave me a bunch of tapes from old shows to go listen to in a special booth. I remember some of the characters now: Mrs. Olsen, the coffee lady from TV. He just does a Swedish accent in a falsetto voice and calls it Mrs. Olsen. She's the official caterer of the Golden-and-Kyle. Peter Pepper, the diction coach; Jack Spratt, he's the health and fitness

expert. There are some others from nursery rhymes: I
think Jack-'n'-Jill made a guest appearance, but I only
heard him—them?—once. And there were more.

Kyle is really good at the voices, but he's himself
sometimes too. They do ad-lib ads, but I know they're
not *really* ad lib. Planning them is one of the things I'll
be working on. Could be fun, if only Golden weren't so
uninspiring. His persona on the show is supposed to be,
I think, Mr. Old-Time Radio Announcer who is having
trouble adjusting to these new styles, a guy from the old
school where only voice, not personality, mattered. No
wonder Kyle gets more fan mail. No one's supposed to
know that. When I came back from listening to the
tapes, Golden had left already, but Kyle was still reading mail. Another of my jobs is to help answer it, he
said, and—his eyebrows came down, not to a glare, just
making a point—to never count the letters. I asked if
that was an order from Golden. "No," he said, "a rule I
made up by myself." I asked why. "It's one of those
things," he said, "when you just know what's best." And
I'm going to have to learn things like that too: "You'll
learn not to suggest he change his name to Pinky," he
said, "but I wouldn't've wanted to miss that!" Then he
got serious and said, "I don't think you'll have to worry,
but just be careful. I'm glad you're starting now while
he's got this new FM girl to occupy his mind. You were
obviously the best we interviewed but might not've gotten the job if she wasn't here to take the pressure off."

How does she take the pressure off me? What am I
supposed to be careful of? Even his background story
and stuff about Golden's ambitions didn't explain, but
he kept saying "I'm talking too much, I'm saying way
too much." Then he would say some more. "Didn't you
notice before Golden left," he said, "What happened

when the station manager came down? Let's test your initial perceptions."

Well, the manager, what's'z'name, I don't remember, Adcock or Shelby, came down to thank Kyle—more like congratulate him for being honorary chairman of the Special Olympics. And Golden got chummy and jovial, joining in the congratulations, saying how worthwhile it had been. Apparently, according to the message I was getting from Kyle, Golden had never said a word about Kyle's Special Olympics gig before this.

But I wasn't able to come up with all this on my own. Kyle had to point it out. At the time to me it had just been another bigwig talking about business in front of me as if I was an ashtray within reach but not exactly needed right then. Well, that's not an entirely fair thing to say. Kyle did introduce me, called me their new valuable asset. Cy jumped in and joined the introduction too, echoing that indeed I was a valuable *asset*, and Kyle shot me a funny, forlorn look. That's what I remembered, but I didn't tell Kyle.

So I definitely have work to do—And I have to learn all these names! Joe Adcock and Gene Shelby . . . owner and station manager . . . or station manager and owner. Let's see . . . okay, it says here Mr. Shelby's the owner. The station manager is Mr. Adcock. Al What's'z'name is program director for just the AM radio.

STILL LATER

Is someone getting screwed? Golden came back a while ago. Up to then I'd been alone after Kyle left, answering mail, taking phone messages. It's true, Kyle *does* get more fan mail—I didn't have to count, it was obvious—

some from men, just wanting to banter as though
they're old friends, giving suggestions for the characters, like have Peter Pepper going through impotence
problems. Women sometimes enclose a photo. Nothing
nude or anything. So far. Anyway, Golden came back.
He wanted his phone messages. There was only one for
him, from Al. I had Kyle's messages in a different stack.
Kyle's agent had called—he'd said, "This is Warren
Kyle's agent," no mention of being Golden's agent
too—and had a gig for Kyle to MC an awards banquet
for the Hall of Champions. If Golden had instead noticed that Kyle's stack of mail was bigger, I was prepared for that. I was going to say I'd already answered
all of Golden's first. What I wasn't prepared for was
Golden grabbing Kyle's phone messages. I said, "Those
are Mr. Kyle's."

He said, "That's okay." I started to say something
else, but he cut me off with, "I'll take care of it, bye,
Colleen." I corrected him, but he was already dialing
the phone and swiveled his chair so his back was to me.
It took me a minute, but I realized who he was talking
to! He called him Bob, so maybe they do have the same
agent. But I wonder if Golden was lying to him. If so,
should I tell Kyle? Then again, maybe Golden and Kyle
really *do* have an arrangement to only do guest appearances as a team. If so, wouldn't their agent already
know? Unless it was only Kyle's agent. In that case, I've
helped get Kyle in trouble with his partner. Wait, how
could there be any agreement about always working as
a team if Kyle did the Special Olympics thing without
trying to hide it?

13 FEBRUARY 1989

See how I get real things mixed up with dreams? Kyle, I had always remembered that you told me stuff about Golden while you were sitting on the edge of my bed. I would be sitting propped up, under the covers. Your hand on my knee. You held on very tight and told me to stay on Golden's good side, but not *too* good. You moved farther onto the bed, almost straddling the mattress like a horse, wrapped both your arms around my legs, propped your chin on top of my knees, and talked so I could feel the movement of your jaw grinding against my kneecap. But I don't remember what you said—either in that dream, or on my real first day. All the stuff I was ever told about Golden or stuff I unfortunately found out on my own is already in my head, sort of instinctively there, so I don't know exactly which things you told me on the first day and which came later. It doesn't seem likely that on my first day you would tell me how hard it was for Golden to get in serious hot water because he and the program director were such good buddies from way back. *Eventually* I knew that he had ambitions to be program director and his-pal-Al wanted to be station manager, but that didn't mean Golden was going to give up his spot on the Morning Show. Sometimes Golden even carried his tendency to kiss-ass the station owner onto the show, so I had to be careful not to think up ideas that would make that too easy for him to do.

You'd only been on the Morning Show for a year, Kyle, but already a big hit. I think one of the things you did tell me that first day was to make sure I remained aware that Golden had been on the Morning Show at KIAM for fourteen years, *solo* for thirteen years, then when morning teams started to be so popular in the biggest markets, the owner wanted one on his station, too, so Golden had no choice. Golden may've licked the owner's butt, but he also maybe had hated him. So, makes perfect sense, they hired a baseball player with a burned-out arm who had a month in the major leagues to his credit. No broad-casting school, no experience. You did show me that tape of your TV ad which you'd done in a minor league city for a local restaurant—the ad got noticed and got you a chance to do a national ad although you were a no-name nobody, but you could already do all those voices. You were just in the right place at the right time, the old story, that's what you said when you told me how Golden had to change from his own show to having a partner.

God, Kyle, I can picture myself . . . I mean Corinne Staub, a different person, wasn't she? I can see her hunched over the table or curled in bed with that journal. *This* journal. The girlish handwriting with open circles making the dots under question marks, slashes underlining a word five or six times. I can see the girl with heavy eyebrows, flat cheekbones, and hair falling into her eyes, no makeup, thumbing the worn edges of the pages. *These* pages. Now I talk to a laptop. Almost as compact as the stack of journals, its own leather carrying case with shoulder strap. Aren't I the consummate contemporary professional woman? Believe me, they've known it everywhere I've been since I left KIAM. That's why my last day on the air in Redding came as such a shock. Even to me, because—I hate to brag, Kyle, but it *has* been true—I am a professional success story, always with sights set on moving on to bigger and bigger markets. Not an overnight sensation, but steady progress. How did that curled-up, watery-voiced girl-in-the-shadows learn to walk into a newsroom or studio with the unmistakable sound and authority of high heels on tile? Know what else? You certainly can't find it on my résumé, but I went into radio/TV journalism in the first place as some sort of perverted rebellion against my pathetic attempts to be noticed and heard in high school. Yes, rebellion *against,* because in this high-visibility profession, *I* was going to sit mutely at the dials or behind a camera and never be

seen or heard from. Look at me now. *Exudes a grim sexiness . . .*
But with you, I was exactly where I'd sent myself when I'd run
from Arizona at 19—definitely background research was the
only job for the girl-in-the-background. Even when you talked
to me, I was somehow in the background. Because Haley's voice
was on the radio. It was always there, Kyle, always. Well, until
she left.

AUGUST 27, 1979

I didn't look. Tried to wait in the car in the parking lot,
but Kyle was holding the door open for me. Tried to
just shake my head and stay in the back seat, but he sort
of widened his eyes at me, a pursed smile barely showing, and I slid out. Watched my feet walking. My new
leather shoes with crêpe soles, can't hear my footsteps
except on a polished floor, where they squeak. Didn't
look up. Crashed into Kyle's back when they all
stopped just inside the door. He steadied me with a
hand. I was the only female in the place. At least the
only one in pants. The second week and already I'm in
pants. By tomorrow it'll be jeans. Probably never wear
a skirt again. I'm supposed to be starting over, not
going backwards.

Their voices and laughter weren't specific words.
Someone wanted to sit nearer to the front. And Kyle
said he wasn't hungry. We all sat down. Some guy between Al and Golden. A fat guy with a shiny face, kept
wiping his brow with his napkin. Golden said, "Welcome to the big city." Golden trying to act nonchalant,
like it's a typical lunch in a strip joint, joking about up-
coming contract negotiations, "How about having negotiations *here!*" then some serious financial shit, then
he got even more serious when it came to rival radio

stations copying format, and the call-in contests he's
going to refuse to mess with. "You can take care of that
shit," to Kyle. But all the time his eyes, about the color
and depth of an old penny, darting toward the girls.
The fat guy asked if I was Haley, without addressing
me: "Is *this* Haley?" Al and Golden both rushing to assure him I was not.

Who's Haley?

Then, finally, after only about ten minutes, Kyle said,
"Let's play baseball," indicating with his head a side
room—pool table, pinball machines. Followed him
over there. Didn't look. Didn't see anything. Kyle was
kind of mad and wanted to play the machine first.
"Need to hit something," he said, and pounded buttons
with his fists, losing quickly and easily. I told him to go
ahead, take another turn, feeling the opposite of him:
not needing to hit anything, just glad to lean against the
machine and let my eyes glaze over, staring at the silver
balls and flashing lights. It could've been an opportunity for me to tell him why he didn't get his phone messages from last week, but I think he knows anyway, I
think Bob-the-agent called this morning, right after the
show. And while Golden was laughing out in the hall
with Al, Kyle said to me in an undertone, his brows
arching above his eyes, after he got off the phone,
"What is listening, *real* listening? It's getting the whole
message besides the direct words. It's an important
tool—"

Then Golden came in with the lunch plans. The fat
guy, some guy he and Al both knew, was visiting from
somewhere, and Golden wanted to take him to lunch at
Les Girls. It was already a plan, not an inquiry, Golden
just said, "You come along, Warren. Bring her too.
Looks better."

I looked at Kyle—I was closer to him than to Golden—and he was saying, "Okay, sure," while he wrote on a used envelope, behind his hand but where I could see it ". . . to his wife." I might've been able to figure that out before he told me, but I hadn't known Golden was married. Found out later this isn't the first time they've had lunch there. Oh yeah, it was when Kyle said, "You should've seen the time he and Al took the old station manager out to lunch here."

I said, "Well, *I'm* not doing this for lunch again, I don't care what his wife thinks."

He said, "What? You mean you don't want to go in there and relax and enjoy the show?"

I said, "I don't enjoy admiring other women."

Him: You *do* it, you just don't enjoy it.
Me: What?
Him: All women do. Don't they?
Me: No!

I haven't really thought about stuff like that for over three years. But when he said that, I felt like my heart was shooting a geyser of blood to my head. He may've noticed . . . he must've, because he changed the subject. I don't want to think about it. There are enough other things to think about. Like some of the stuff Kyle was saying about Golden and Al.

They're pals from way back, Kyle doesn't know from where or when. And he said, "No one's sure just *how* close they are." He said he was talking too much again. He'd had a few beers while we were in the pinball room. It'd been about an hour.

Golden paused in the doorway and whistled, time to go. Kyle grabbed my arm before I left the room. He said, "But don't chide me about being a follower. I can't

cross him, he's number one, I'm number two, I prom-
ised myself I wouldn't do anything to change that. I'm
tied to him in a funny way that I just can't do anything
about right now." Then he gave the machine a shove
with both hands and his body, a pelvic push, raised the
thing off its front legs.

15 FEBRUARY 1989

How could you talk for an hour and a few hours later I could
only remember five minutes of what you said? Maybe in an
hour a person only says five minutes worth of anything of value.
Maybe that's when you told me about Golden's ambitions to
move into management, but I'm not sure you ever really told
me that point-blank, or if you told me in a dream and it just
happened to also be true. With a few beers, I think you were
talking about several things at once, but I do remember how
you compared them to a herd of lowing cattle crowding in from
the parking lot to chew their cuds and roll their eyes at some
bare udders. . . . "But that's just what they are," you said, "Steers.
Know what a steer is? Goddamn steers." Oh yeah, some of it's
coming back to me, because you brought up Haley again, saying, "All that fat ass had to do was think you were Haley and his
horns were ready."

But I wasn't thinking about them. I never told you about
Libby, did I? It was supposed to be an act at a feminist rally, Lib
was going to do a parody of a striptease, to show exploitation of
women's bodies in beauty contests. A parody, a political statement, for God's sake! But when she was practicing, a creepy
feeling turned my stomach over because suddenly she didn't
seem like a parody, she meant it, and I was the only one in the
audience that day.

I've got to get out of here for a while.

LATER

Maybe I should tell you what I've been doing the past few days. I bought some clothes. Tight pegleg black jeans, ankle-high black leather boots, a white silk shirt with long full pirate sleeves, another white shirt that easily slips off either shoulder, black leather jacket with silver chains, a new unisex earring for each hole: a lightning bolt, a moon, a woman sign, a man sign, a sun (or star), a safety pin, a heart, and several others. Got a haircut, short and spiked. And I've been going down to the station. I've never been to my station dressed this way. I wouldn't've been noticed if it was one of Alex's biker bars, but at the station's cafeteria—a roomful of suits and heels—it was easy for Garth and me to notice each other. So we met today. He said he'd seen me the other times I went to the station. I don't know why I've been going there. To find you? I know you never hung in the cafeteria, and you probably still have your own coffee machine—maybe a much better one now, so complicated that someone else has to work it for you, but that's okay, who's going to care *now* if someone gets your coffee for you?

Anyway, both other times, and today, I stood just inside the door for a while. Same round tables and plastic chairs. Maybe they're not the same chairs as when I worked there. You and I, Kyle, the few times we went there, we used the longer tables and benches along the sides of the room.

Well, they don't let you stand in a doorway long . . . without meaning to, I got moved along over to the counter where everyone fixes their coffee or their hamburgers, gets straws and napkins. Empty sugar envelopes and squeezed-out mustard packages, drops of cream in a line, the little cream cups ripped open and rolling on their sides, salt sprinkled like snow here and there, a smear of ketchup like the scene of a crime.

That's where we met. He came over for another napkin.

But . . . I didn't recoil like I normally would've to a suit with silver hair leering at me with a crumpled napkin in his hand.

Well, *Corinne* is the one who would recoil. She kept it up for six or seven years after I left here. What does Erin Haley do? It doesn't happen to Erin. And I guess I hadn't given her a chance before this to find out. Maybe it was different because while he *could've* been a suit with gray hair—he does have gray hair—he wasn't wearing a suit. Thick, wavy gray hair, as though it should've been brilliant chestnut or sun-streaked brown, wind-blown, like a pool lifeguard's or a tennis instructor's or a whitewater rafting guide's or the lead rider's on a pack train at Yosemite. *That* kind of hair, except gray . . . streaked with black. And no suit. Khaki pants and a V-necked white pullover shirt . . . not tucked in. And blue tennis shoes. You might even know him: Garth Nelson, the temporary consultant. Did you meet him, Kyle? Did you notice his eyes? They're small, as though they prefer to be closed, like a mole's. But even when you look, you wonder what color they are. Sound familiar? How many people in the world have eyes in between two colors? Garth's are brown or green. Brownish green, greenish brown, faded, like pond water, like an overcast sky. But you probably know how alive they are. Like after he asked if I worked at the station and I said no, then he said, "Want to?" his eyes were like the color of the moon, maybe, on a very bright night.

Just think—I could've gotten a job, in a major market, just like that. And dressed like this!

"If I wasn't temporary," he said, "I'd nab you for an anchor *here*. They want a startling new image? They'd have it!"

Would I have accepted? Could I have worked here with the ghost always hovering? That ghost, Corinne Staub . . . you know, I've only been able to make myself read a few pages a day in these journals, maybe for fear she'll rise out of the blurry pencil words and come back to some sort of life again. She *has* been dead or I wouldn't've made it as far as I have. At least she's *dormant*. My rise may not've been meteoric, but still—*success*. And even more impressive, considering I've been The-Zombie-Who-Never-Sleeps . . . for how long now?

Maybe the problem is Corinne hasn't been dormant *enough*. Maybe that's the reason I've been skulking around the station these days—trying to see how dead Corinne really is. I could probably keep you from recognizing me, Kyle. Maybe let you feel nothing more than an unsettling déjà vu. Maybe you wouldn't even know *who* I might be reminding you of. Maybe, for some reason, you'd think of Haley. I'm different from her, though, and different from Corinne. Yes, I drink more now, take more pills. But I don't serve coffee to anyone . . . and I don't flinch at sudden movements anymore. Wait, I'm getting mixed up . . . It was *after* I left here that I started ducking . . . you never knew I was like that. I remember when I first left here, I couldn't stand to look at anything that reminded me. I threw away everything. Even clothes I'd worn, clothes I'd put on while thinking that you, or Haley, would be looking at me some time that day—those were clothes I could never bear to wear again. I did pack them, but could never unpack them, threw whole stuffed suitcases into dumpsters behind McDonald's. Was there ever some unsolved crime in Phoenix where they thought the packed suitcases found in a dumpster were evidence? I can see those clothes spread out in a police lab. But I was still *Corinne* after I left here. Corinne, ducking and flinching. But no one cowered today. Meeting Garth makes me . . . I don't know . . . I feel *optimistic,* can you believe it? When Garth asked my name, I didn't hesitate, and I wasn't afraid . . . just said, "I'm Erin Haley." And it felt true.

How did it move so fast? From "Do you work here?" to having coffee together at one of the round tables where he touched my wrist to emphasize things he said—put his whole hand over my arm when he said he'd take me to be an anchor here on a dime. His hand on the back of my neck as we walked out to the parking lot. What did I say . . . all that time? What did *he* say? All I remember is his hand on my neck, his fingers slightly under my collar, and the stab in my stomach—which I still feel now when I remember, only worse, or better, every time, so I have to double over, lay curled on the bed, as though in agony . . . but smiling. *What* am I smiling about? It's not as though my life is here, it's not as though I don't realize there'll be a time when I'll be leaving again. . . . And how temporary is Garth at the station? He already has his return ticket to Chicago . . . four months from now? It doesn't seem to matter. The only important thing, Kyle, is that I want him to touch me again.

SEPTEMBER 5, 1979

The famous Haley, FM jock. Cold handshake, the limp feeling of a woman's hand. She banters with Kyle and Golden, mostly Kyle, her voice cracking every other word, it seems. Her laugh has a squeak in it. Kyle just told her that we plan our show while being serenaded by the inspiring sound of her voice doing FM DJ. But her voice is hardly different live. She's a natural. Kyle told her that too. She's beaming. She hasn't glanced back at me since that hasty introduction. It was Golden who introduced us. Did he call me by my right name? Will she know me as Colleen or Corinne? I don't remember what he said. By the time he said who I was, the handshake was practically over, her interest, what there was of it, already gone. And here I am scribbling while they talk.

> H: I hear you're a jock! That's great. Adds a little class to the station.

K: Except I'm not a jock anymore.

H: You know what they say, once a jock . . . [*Laughter, voice crack*]

K: Have I been insulted?

H: No, I think it's great. You work out, don't you? Looks like it. Is there a gym in this building? I mean besides the spa and one lousy piece of equipment upstairs. [*Giggle, glance at Golden*]

K: Upstairs?

G: Haley got the grand tour.

H: You know—that penthouse at the top.

K: The owner's office?

H: Cy, you bastard, you said it was Al's!

G: It was Al's that night.

[*The phone's ringing. No one wants to answer. I guess I'll have to get it even though Golden is closest.*]

It was for Golden. He could've gotten it himself but instead looked at me, nodding toward the phone, and Kyle said, "Corrine, get in gear." As I picked up the receiver, I heard Haley saying something about her interview being a real party, then silence—they were maybe waiting to see who was on the phone. But Kyle staring—glaring?—at Golden . . . staring back.

When Golden got on the phone and I edged past them back to my place at the table and my notebook, she was saying, "I'm sure everyone's been talking about it already. I'm not afraid to discuss it. Go on, what've you heard?"

But he never answered directly, just said, "That your ratings are good."

She laughed. While she was laughing he said, "We'll have to talk."

"Sounds great," her voice cracks.

Golden's still on the phone. I wonder if she would make that tiny hoarse edge, that squeak, if she said my name, like if she saw me across a restaurant or down the block and called out to me. While coming toward me, would her face have that light—some sort of happy eagerness under her skin and the string of freckles across her nose, and her almost black eyes, almost almond shaped, which laugh without the crinkles and lines that Kyle has?

They're almost exact opposites and they're both ignoring me. I thought I was starting over here, that things would be *different*. Now it's agonizingly noticeable that he never said, "We'll have to talk" to me. He never suggested lunch. Just like she won't. She'll never come radiantly into our room, take my arm, pull me into the hall saying, "Corinne and I have to talk." We'll never exchange meaningful glances across a crowded room.

Golden suggested lunch before they could make plans that didn't include him. He saw it coming, he intercepted. Why didn't I do that? Well, it's easier not to. It's less confusing to sit here calling myself names than to sit in a restaurant hoping he'll only talk to me and ignore her. Of course I would want that. I can admit, I like to look at him—the width of his shoulders, the flatness of his stomach, the way his pants fit, the color of his neck just before it disappears into his collar, the tightness of his cheeks when he smiles, the creation of the laugh lines, the dark-lightness or light-darkness of his gray-then-blue or blue-then-gray eyes, and his eyebrows arching up and out, out and up, the saucy flip at the ends when he's teasing, and the weird way his eyebrows do nothing at all while he's on the air doing silly voices. Of course I'd want all that just for me. So why do I also want *her* to pay attention to only me and leave *him* out? Her eyes that just washed weakly over me while we were introduced—they're probably the kind of eyes that can go from playful to a sigh to intense seriousness and make you feel you're invited to come along. Like L. But Haley doesn't look like L. Ever-so-slightly crooked teeth, small pale mouth, straight dark brows almost too heavy for her alert little freckled face, her tiny waist and hips and well-muscled but not bulky shoulders and arms. Nothing like Lib. Why'm I even comparing them?

16 FEBRUARY 1989

Libby. I never told you about Lib. I never told anyone. I was at KIAM, my first job, trying to start a new life. It was three years since I'd seen Lib. The college years had been a marathon obsession with studying. Why? To prevent any chance that my mind would wander to anything other than the symbolically mute career I would someday have in radio or TV? Did studying do the trick by itself? The ever-present sleeping pills did their share. So then the new job with you, Kyle, *that* was supposed to be it: my fresh life, my new start, a little delayed, three years after leaving Arizona. . . . But there was Haley . . . to make it that much harder, or impossible.

SEPTEMBER 11, 1979

Haley, how come you never come in here after your show and ask *me* what I think? Only Kyle. Your voice is in the background of all our discussions. Sometimes the foreground. Like foreplay.

What am I doing? Stop it. It's something Golden would say. No, it's too subtle for Golden. Kyle thinks he's crude. Golden stepped out when his-pal-Al came by, and Kyle muttered something, not to me, about refusing to go along. Golden's favorite thing to say is "sit on my face." The first time was after Haley did an ad for some tanning lotion, "C'mon [*crack*], you'll love sitting on the sand, soaking up rays, while he or she smoothes [*Whatever*] lotion on your shoulders," then Golden said, "You can come sitting on my face any time, baby."

Kyle grabbed a letter and tore it open. I wonder if Haley were putting lotion on someone's shoulders, would her hand seem tiny and inefficient and you'd have to rub the lotion in yourself after she was done? But she's got muscles, not those sickening round, tube-like smooth arms most girls have. I can picture some guy grabbing one of those sickly arms and leaving five fingerprint bruises because it's so fragile. Haley is small but anything but fragile. She was arm-wrestling with Kyle the other day—not winning but not getting smacked flat right away either. She was wearing a tank top and I could see the muscles flexing in her back.

Golden actually tried to pat her butt, like for encouragement, during one of the arm wrestles, but she must've seen him coming because she suddenly shifted her weight and her butt swung two feet in the other direction. Golden's hand was hanging out there patting nothing. Strike one.

I think Kyle started to laugh but was hiding it, and she started laughing too, so he pinned her. They didn't suggest I could wrestle the winner.

By the time she comes in here after her show, our planning discussion is over. I've been here since nine, listened to the last hour of their show. I don't listen to the first three hours anymore. All week Golden's been asking what we can think up for Peter Pepper. He wants him to marry Liz Taylor and call into the show for advice while on his honeymoon. Kyle kept saying Peter's too shy to ever even ask Liz Taylor for a date. I suggested Liz Taylor could get a crush on Peter Pepper so he's always trying to avoid her. Golden doesn't like it. Kyle said, why do we have to have *Liz Taylor?* Haley, on the air, said, "Oh baby, we have some hot tunes for you this hour." Golden said, "She *is* a hot tune." Kyle looked down at his half-eaten sandwich. Seemed like his eyes were closed. I wonder what he looks like asleep. Anyway, Golden hasn't mentioned Liz Taylor yet today. Haley's show is almost over, five minutes after that she'll be here—it's been our signal that the session is truly over: Haley comes in with a crooked-toothed smile for Kyle, not a glance left or right. Yesterday, as she came in, Kyle motioned with his head toward Golden, who wasn't looking, so she shrugged with a smirk, then turned to Golden to say something to him first, like he's some sort of king you have to genuflect to before doing anything else. "Hey, Cy, how's business?" Kyle didn't tell her she had to say anything to me, so she didn't.

LATER

Something interesting just happened. They've all gone. I don't know where. It's like: Haley appears, and Kyle starts packing up, finishing his last sentence if he's been saying anything, putting on his coat, and they go out the door like their plans are already set. I think they may decide what they're going to do at the last minute, as they get close to their cars in the parking lot. That way they can avoid having to include Golden. He has some VIP parking spot inside the building. I don't think

Golden has gone with them often, judging from the things she says to him. You don't ask somebody "What's new" in a sort of obligatory way if you've been going to lunch or out for drinks with him after work. I thought she was dating him or had dated him . . . or had dated Al, or something.

Anyway, today she didn't even stop for the customary first greeting to Golden. She was kind of laughing, her voice cracking more than usual, went straight to Kyle, and said, "How about this, I got a call to be the featured speaker at some journalism society dinner at the college. I'm not ready for that kind of thing. But I told them I could get you—they really went for that."

The awkward silence only lasted a second. Then Golden went over, actually stood beside Haley and put his arm around her, and told Kyle he shouldn't do it, that it was small stuff and not worth it. I think Haley tried to get out of Golden's arm by sitting down across from Kyle at the conference table.

She said, "Aw, c'mon, a free dinner *plus* they pay you. They said I should come too if I got you to do it." Golden had kept his hand on the back of her neck even though she sat down.

Kyle said it might be fun, and ironic, since he never even went to college. "Yeah," Haley squeaked, "Like a nose thumb: you *fools*, wasting four years here."

Kyle knows *I* went to college. He may've glanced at me once out of the corner of his eye.

Golden was calculating, hand still on Haley: "The dinner takes at least an hour, the speech another hour, then afterwards they all want to talk to you, that's another hour. If they pay $150, that's only $50 an hour."

Haley got up and edged around the table to Kyle's side, finally getting Golden's slimy hand off her, and said, "They need you to tell them about the real world."

"That's for sure," Kyle said. "It's a good cause. Like charity."

Golden sort of laughed snidely and said, "Jesus Christ, don't let yourself get the label of being a good-cause champion—they'll *all* be calling wanting freebies."

At the same time Haley, who was kneeling beside Kyle, her hands flat on the table and her chin on her hands, was saying something I couldn't hear all of. When Kyle said, "Okay," Golden kind of made a sneering chuckle, shaking his head, said something about a couple of kids invited to their first birthday party. But when he turned his back to go get his coat, Haley stood, patted Kyle's back and said, low but fairly clearly, "Atta boy, Champ."

Meanwhile I was there, slitting open envelopes, taking the letters out, stapling each letter to its envelope.

20 FEBRUARY 1989

I guess parties don't make me nervous anymore. Parties used to feel like races, like the swimming races at Girl Scout camp. With my childhood tomboy confidence, I was sure I would win. Then on the sound of the whistle, we all jumped in, splashing and kicking, gulping air . . . except I was splashing and kicking without going forward. The waves made by all the bigger kids jumping into the pool and digging for the other side were too much for me to swim against. I was working like hell, but I only managed to tread water. Sometimes parties also remind me of how I met Alex, which was at a bar, not a party, but half the people in the bar that night worked at the same TV station, so it was like a party too. But Alex and the girl he was hitting on didn't work in TV.

Well, last night was different than a party at a bar, and different from any other party where I splashed and kicked or stayed clinging to the side of the pool while everyone else swam the race. I didn't know anyone but Garth, and I didn't care. They all knew I was with him, noticed us, and looked at me long before being introduced. Maybe Garth and I look funny together. He was in his usual khaki pants and blue sneakers, but had tucked in his shirt, a dark blue wool Pendleton with leather breast pocket. If you'd showed up at the party, Kyle, you'd've seen me in a short denim skirt, black lace stockings, ankle-high leather boots, and the other white shirt I bought last week, the one that rides off one shoulder. And all my pierced ear holes had the same earring: a silver chain.

Because Garth is new and he has some special temporary position—some sort of consultant to figure out how to boost ratings—everyone wants to talk to him, to get to know him, to invite him for lunch or a drink. They're possibly jealous or envious or idolizing me for being with him. Maybe some of them know he's married—that would make them look with new eyes at the girl who's letting him put his hand up the back of her shirt as he stands talking to some bald station executive. His hand made me feel I was made of silk, like I loved my skin, and also made me fold in half . . . his hand on my back, my hand wanting to clutch my kinked-up stomach. Luckily I didn't have to take care of myself. He kept my glass filled, he steered me around the room. People in Sunday slacks, loose ties reporter-style, mid-length dresses, sandals, thin bracelets and necklaces with a single pearl, holding wine glasses, nibbling grapes or shrimps on crackers. My stomach didn't want food, it wanted Garth's hand to explore farther inside my shirt.

Over half the people were gone by ten, the ones with kids and babysitters to pay, so by midnight there were maybe four or five people left, and two of them must've lived there. We were all sitting on the floor by then, leaning against the sofas, I was digging my fingers into the soft plush carpet, Garth's arm around me, his fingers moving sleepily back and forth on my neck, peeking now and then under my shirt and onto my shoulder, and once I think I groaned, just loud enough for him to hear, and he chuckled, very softly, and we both knew . . .

It's something I've never *known* like that before, Kyle. A primal knowledge welling up like laughter from some other place. Laughter that never breaks the surface except as a gentle, secret smile. As we drove to my hotel, we didn't say anything to each other about what we were going to do. And there, on the bed, it was as comfortable as being alone . . . no strangeness. As though his hand had touched and known me since I was a baby—he was welcome anywhere. But the welcomeness wasn't blasé. There was also that surge of energy just under the surface wherever his hand was, and in the pit of my gut, so I was relaxed and supple and excitedly quivering at the same time, none of which is my usual response. If there was ever any anxiety—early on, for a second—it was that I might do my usual fall-into-a-coma routine. No, it wasn't even anxiety . . . I just wondered, briefly, in the car: Would it happen? But the question was calmly answered by someone in my mind: *Are you kidding?* It was an innate, instinctive knowledge, like a pulse from a new heart, answering me.

It was late, maybe 2:30, we were just lying there on our sides, facing the same direction, he was holding me against himself, curled around me. Still fully clothed, both of us, except for our shoes. No secret that he had a hard-on pressed against my butt, but no pressure, no humping, no insisting. I liked feeling it snug against me. But we hadn't spoken for a long time. Then he said, "Thanks for being so nice to me."

"Nice to you?" I said.

"Well, you know . . ." he said. "It's nice to be able to get turned on again. Slowly, without any hurry. And without guilt."

Is that a strange thing for a man to say?

His hand was stroking my stiff hair, his mouth against the spiky back of my head. Then, after a while, I said, "Maybe *I* should thank you."

"Why?" he asked.

Again, though, I didn't say anything right away. He pulled me closer, his voice even more of a whisper: "Why?"

"It's hard to explain," I said, my voice sounding easy, but muted and slow. "For . . . being good for me."

"How do you mean?"

I didn't even know I was going to say it. I'd *never* said it before. But there I was saying, in the same calm but slow murmur: "I think I was raped once."

"You *think?*" I could feel him smile. Not laughing at me. Not taking it lightly or trivializing it, just smiling because we were together and whatever had happened was a long time ago. I smiled too. And that's probably why I tried to tell him. I've never tried to tell anyone else. I never even really think about it specifically. In fact, truthfully, I don't remember it . . . that's why it was so hard to explain.

I said, "I say *think* because I don't *know.* I probably just had sex with someone I didn't want to have sex with."

He was sort of tugging gently on my ear, then said, "So you knew who it was?"

"I *never* think about who it was. I *never* think of it that way."

My voice had gotten sort of hard and stayed in the air too long, especially with the little silence that followed. He was still listening, though, and waiting. I could tell from the way his breath felt against my head and the way his body was . . . not stiffened, but careful. Like when you're lying in bed with someone, eyes closed, and he lifts his head off the pillow to listen to a noise outside . . . you can tell his head is being held up and you can't relax or go back to sleep until he puts his head down again.

"I honestly don't think about it, Garth," I said, my voice effortless again. "I don't remember it. I was probably so drunk or zoned-out at the time . . ."

"Then why'm I good for you because of it?"

I couldn't make sense. I hardly knew what I meant. I told him, "I don't know why I said it. I honestly might've expected myself to tell you any number of other things . . . that you were good for me because I was married to an asshole . . . or because I've been celibate for years. I don't know why I said what I said. I should've said . . . that you're perfect for me because I'm usually no good at this."

He rolled me to my back so he could see my face. I thought he was going to kiss me, but he didn't. He hasn't kissed me yet. Is that strange? He said, "You're wonderful at this."

"But I'm usually not. Usually . . . well, there hasn't been enough lately to call it *usually* . . . but, it's like, suddenly, I'm all doped up. Like serious hospital medication. Dead weight. Numb and paralyzed from the hair down. Really. Without taking anything, I mean."

He was sort of pinching my tit through my shirt and my back was arched and I was humming in my throat when I wasn't talking, all of which makes talking that much more difficult.

"You may be a little drunk," he said, "but you're sure not acting doped-up."

"I know . . . I'm not. Not with you. And I wonder why. No, I don't wonder why. It sounds stupid, but . . . I'm a different person with you. I don't mean I'm acting phony. I'm real—I think I'm the way I'll always be from now on."

And, you know, Kyle, it also makes reading the old journals easier. It's strangely exciting to see myself as I was, someone else, then immediately afterwards watch who I've become . . . and am *becoming*.

SEPTEMBER 15, 1979

It's not even Saturday night anymore. I don't know if I want to think about the party, but I can't sleep. Haley's welcome party. Maybe I should've worn a dress too. Not that she was dressed fancy. Just another of her tank tops, white this time, and a yellow skirt, almost like a sheet, thin like that, all the way to her ankles. You'd think in a tent like that her tiny waist and tight ass would be hidden away. Her bust is too big, though. So she's not perfect. God, but I felt fat anyway. I don't mind being flat, but I hate these muscular thighs. She had lipstick on tonight, and a little extra makeup, and she was almost like a flower—not an exotic or gaudy one, but like a yellow and white daisy someone was carrying through a crowded bus station filled with identical people in gray business suits: You always knew where she was, could locate her easily moving among the dark shapes of other people. And you could hear her too. Not really louder than everyone else, certainly not louder than Al. Just a different wavelength. Golden was kind of glued to her for a while, with Al along as usual, and they kept calling her "our discovery." I wonder if Golden ever got drunk enough to believe he was the center of attention. He probably managed to interrupt every group of people, in every possible combination, to tell his guy-with-a-duck-on-his-shoulder joke, or the one about gay men's farts that he got such a yuck over when he told Kyle last week. Kyle just gave one of those sick-faced "heh-heh" laughs, then muttered "Hadda be there, I guess." I laughed at that and Golden said, "Sheesh, takes her long enough to get it." Kyle laughed at *that,* and so did I, and Golden, poor sap, joined in.

Quiet and not mingling a lot, Kyle was actually more noticeable than Golden and his leisure suit. And Golden was calling Kyle *Champ!* I saw Haley and Kyle exchange glances the first time Golden said it, then later they were laughing together in a corner. Only the three of us would get that joke. I thought he might introduce me to a few people, since I'm supposed to be having an effect on his show, but he didn't. All I got was, "Having fun, Corinne?" God, why did I *stay* at the damn party when I felt so terrible . . . just so I could watch who he talked to and who *she* talked to, and who she talked *seriously* to, and who she left with? I never found out, and why did I need to know—did I think I was going to change her mind? And Kyle—I kept waiting for him to wander off to another room where nobody else was, so maybe I could follow him. But there really wasn't any other room in the owner's famous, or infamous, penthouse . . . except the bathroom. I'd actually halfway thought he might follow me there and sit on the edge of the bathtub while I stared at myself in the mirror, then ask me what I was looking for . . . even though he should know: He'd heard what Golden said after bumping into me: *almost* said excuse me, then noticed it was me and laughed, "Why doncha at least get your ears pierced so we can tell you're a girl!"

I know I don't look like her. Am I jealous of her? Then explain to me why I want some of her enthusiasm directed toward me . . . why would I have been happy and content with the whole spectacle if she'd just edged up to me once and muttered, *Let's get out of here and talk later.* Or is that something *you* said to *her?* I wasn't in the bathroom crying. Maybe you thought I was. I kept waiting for a knock on the door that never came.

How long did I stay in there? I could've taken a bath in the huge tub. I don't even remember much about that bathroom, I know it's big, but I can't remember its colors, was the light off? All I can clearly remember is hearing the voices right outside the door — Golden and Al, right where I'd left them, still talking through their noses and laughing. I kept trying to hear if you were still there too — you'd *been* there, Kyle, but I couldn't hear what you were maybe saying. Perhaps you were talking to them about me in a low solemn voice before turning away to almost knock on the bathroom door, then changing your mind? All I heard was Golden and Al getting drunker. God, Haley, how did you manage to hook everyone in the room? Even people's wives were asking where you got your hair cut so they could go there too, wondering where you went for aerobics, showering you with invitations: "We'll have to have you over sometime." I could've slipped up beside you and said something too. Like to ride bikes? Like to go to the beach real early in the morning? Like to go to espresso bars late at night? But I didn't. I didn't.

21 FEBRUARY 1989

Maybe I should finally apologize to you, Kyle, after all these years, for the way I acted at *that* party. Sniveling, useless, watery thing that I was . . . always running off. Can't believe this girl I'm reading had the kind of grit it takes to not only tread water but swim upstream in TV news. Obviously now I'm okay at parties. Of course how would everything have been different if I'd had someone's hand under my shirt, on my bare back, at Haley's welcome party? And what if it had been you?

That's a very feminist, mature and professional thought, Erin.

I can't help it: The whole day, yesterday, after Garth left at 3:45 and I slept till ten, every time I remembered his hands on me, his body against me, his voice in my hair and ear, I shuddered and had to double over. Delightful sharp pains I might've never known about till now . . . yet I can tell I've been waiting for them my whole life.

And I've probably also been waiting my whole life for this: how I had one of those power surges that allows people to lift automobiles to save trapped children when he called my name from the sidewalk at about 5:30 yesterday evening. I phoned down for them to let him in, then practically danced on all four walls until I heard his footstep on the stairs, the same sound he made leaving the night before, but this time coming *back* . . . with a bottle of wine and two deli sandwiches from the station lunch room, which I ate one of even though I haven't eaten meat for at least five years now. He was tired from having to get up so early after leaving me so late, and, after eating, leaned back on my pillows with his eyes closed. He was talking about how comfortable he was, how he wasn't ever going to move again, he thanked me for keeping him sane, and I think he even dozed for a moment . . . but then he jumped up, scary in a thrilling way, grabbed me in one arm, scooped me off the bed, violently shook the sheets, saying "I hate to make love on crumbs," then tossed me back onto the mattress, fell after me, sighed, breathed heavily for a moment, seemed to calm down, unbuttoned two middle buttons on my shirt, spread the space open so my breast showed, and gently took the nipple into his mouth.

Is he different from other men or do I just not know enough of them to know? There was no silent, unemotional moment that says *now?* when the guy's ready to position himself for penetration. Maybe that was always me positioning myself for penetration, like a dog hearing or seeing a silent command. Garth's hard-on was happy to just press against my bare butt, his fingers were happy at how they could astonish me over and over, his mouth happy with my breast. His sigh had the hint of a laugh in it, his groan was smiling. And when he said "Touch me," it wasn't greedy or selfish, but just . . . natural. I hadn't known what to do with him, but when he said, "Touch me, please," his voice kind of smoky—the sound of dusk, which had been steadily dimming the room—again, I just suddenly *knew*. Like I'd always known. Not that I hadn't touched a man before, or hadn't jacked Alex off a few times with my hand or mouth . . . because that was easier than getting mounted and losing consciousness for ten or fifteen minutes, and hearing about it later, what a dud I was.

But all in that instant yesterday, I knew that touching a man was something I wanted to do, and I did it . . . so differently than I'd ever done it before . . . until he grabbed my wrist and held my hand away from him, rolled me over onto my stomach but didn't lie on top of me, stayed beside me, maybe one leg across the backs of my thighs, and he said things I'll never forget. . . . His finger was teasing me on the outside, moving in circles, and he said, "Tell me you like me."

Is that a funny thing for a man to say?

Later after everything calmed down a bit, while I rubbed his back, he said, "You don't know, you have no idea how much I think about you all day."

"Then," I answered, "you understand what I do all day also."

He rolled over and pulled me down beside him. "The work I have here is important, and I consider it a big opportunity. But you've made it an even greater opportunity. I'm allowed to have this timewarp with you, try out a whole new life for a while."

Some sort of relief flooded over me. "That's what I'm doing here too."

"When you go someplace where no one knows you," he said, you can be anyone you want." He reached under my shirt again."You're always hard, you know that?" he said, "Your little tips are always ready—can you feel it against your shirt?"

"It must be part of the new me," I laughed.

He laughed too, and said, "Have you ever felt this comfortable this quickly?" He wasn't looking at my face right then, sort of staring, with a crease on his brow, at my shirt, and his hand was underneath, his fingers spread, touching one breast with his thumb, the other with his little finger.

It was already 9:30. We went for dinner. Had some wine, sat across the table from each other holding hands. There was a shaded light suspended above each table, and ours seemed brighter than all the rest. The waitress checked and said for some reason our bulb was a higher wattage. When she left, Garth reached up and unscrewed the bulb a little, so the light went out and we sat in the dark.

I wonder if this is uncommon: we went back to my room and got in bed *again*. As though it hadn't all happened just three hours before: as though it'd *never* happened before. As though we were the first two people who were figuring out what to do with each other on a bed.

We must've dozed for a while. It was around 1:30 or 2 when he got up and buttoned his shirt, zipped his pants, came around the bed and sat beside where I was still lying. I said, "I'm lying here with my jeans still completely on just *one* of my legs."

He laughed softly. The room was dark. He put his hand on my back and said, "You know I can't stay all night."

"Yes, because you'll have no clothes for work tomorrow."

"No," he said. "Because of the phone. It might ring. My wife in Chicago."

I didn't move. It felt good to be sort of drunk and lying in the dark with him sitting beside me, his hand warm and heavy on my back. "Oh," I said. "And she can't just think you're not home yet?"

"At three in the morning?"

"She wouldn't call then."

"She might if that's when she thought would be the best time to catch me home."

What could I say to that? Yes, I already knew about his wife in Chicago. He's staying in an apartment-hotel in Hillcrest, sort of across the park from me. His wife couldn't leave her job—a nurse or doctor or whatever she is—for as long as he'll be here in his temporary position. He went home and I went to sleep, still wearing one leg of my pants, one shoe, and an unbuttoned shirt.

SEPTEMBER 17, 1979

Haley: Sleep it off yesterday, Cy? Hey, Champ.

Golden: That wasn't drunk. You haven't seen blitzed.

Haley: Oh no? Hey, Warren, you said you'd tell me how to get to that riding stable?

Kyle: Okay. Why don't we drive out together. You could give me a lesson.

H: On a rent-a-nag?

G: Talking about my wife?

H: Yukedy-yuk. [*Back to Kyle*] Hey, I liked that thing with Peter Pepper getting a fan letter from a secret admirer. The way he does that wobbly moan when he's nervous . . . the way *you* do that moan. I can hardly imagine it's the same you I know. Then when it sinks in that it *is* you, it's like this cosmic crash and I get chills. I'm not kidding.

K: Thanks. I think.

H: [*Laughing, squeaking*] No, it's a compliment!

K: Well, I'll return the compliment.

H: No, really, what do you think of my voice on air, my style, is it different than right now, what do you think, really, when you hear it?

K: [*Carefully controlled face, laughter in his eyes*]
       This girl's a real pro, a complete profes-
       sional.

H: Liar!

They're getting too fast for me, but I like to play
steno for them. I don't know how I keep coming up
with ideas for the show. My idea about Peter Pepper's
love letter has more mileage than I first thought. A different celebrity can call every day, claiming it's them
who wrote it, but then they make some big blunder, obviously not even knowing what the letter says. And one
day have someone like Frank Sinatra call and say *he*
wrote it. That'll *really* make Peter moan. Kyle said he'd
buy me a drink for that idea, but so far he hasn't.

Haley's getting a haircut today and she's describing
how she's going to get it cut. She's going to have it dark-
ened too—she doesn't like the red highlights. Don't,
Haley, I *love* those highlights, and your skin is too light
for darker hair, except when you wear more makeup.
What if *he* suggested it? Or if he suggested you shave
your head bald . . . would you do it? You might, because of the way his laughlines creep out for you even
before the laugh comes into his eyes; because of the curl
of his eyebrow, the one closest to you; because sometimes when he smiles, it's only on one side of his face;
and because his voice can vibrate your breastbone . . .
makes you dizzy if you listen to the radio and imagine
he's doing it all for you. Is that what you meant? You've
got no room to talk—if just once your voice had
cracked over something you were saying to me . . .
I'd . . . God, this can't be happening again.

   What's that they're talking about? He's been leaning
back in his chair, listening seriously, his brows drawn
down, his face intense, listening, like no one ever listened to anyone before, to her problems dealing with

the old-fashioned engineer who does her show. Suddenly he comes forward, his face breaking, not a laughing smile, but just a smile. He taps her wrist with one finger. They're getting too far ahead again —

K: . . . you're just a puppy.

H: You'd be surprised.

K: We all have surprises.

H: Some time we'll have to get together and get drunk so we can share our surprises.

What surprise could I tell? That it's happening again? It was a triangle last time too. Started out as one kind, ended up another. But this time it's a triangle that's *only* happening to me.

23 FEBRUARY 1989

Lib, you knew me as a fake and a coward. And Kyle, do you only remember this powerless, ineffectual shadow on the wall? Obviously, when I ran from Libby, I left the fake behind but remained the coward. Just remember, Kyle, at least with you I didn't run away until *afterwards.* Wasn't that *some* progress? And this time I'm not running at all. I'm not afraid. The nights after Garth goes home late, I don't have to sleep with my mouth guard. I don't grind my teeth. And my dreams are about flying—that *I* can fly. Not fly *away.* Every day I'm eager to astonish him and myself all over again. I wish Lib could know this about me now.

SEPTEMBER 20, 1979

This isn't written in red because that pencil's broken, the sharpener is over there, and I'm over here, newspaper and tabloids spread in front of me, marking good stuff. Hard to concentrate with the hissing whispered conversation at the other end of the table. I can almost hear them. Do I want to? Got to stop *looking* like I want to hear them—that's when they change the subject abruptly, a smoke screen, probably. Like when I got up, without a cue or request, got the coffee pot and re-filled Kyle's cup. He didn't stop talking to her but looked directly into my eyes while he spoke, "Because I think we're all ultimately responsible for what we say, *that's* why." But if I'd stood there waiting for more, for some further connection or explanation, I'd've obviously been butting in, so I came back to my newspapers and red pencil.

This isn't the first time. Yesterday, Golden on the phone, me with a red pencil, Kyle and Haley muttered a conversation. Golden, on the phone: "Yeah, no, that's not what I said." Both my eyes focused on the tip of my red pencil, marking an article about Olivia Newton John making secret trips to an island to visit the cells of JFK they're preserving to create a future clone; Golden listening to a phone, his eyes on Kyle and Haley. They felt it and stopped talking, just stared at a spot on the table between their coffee cup and Coke can. Then it was Golden's turn to talk again: "Yeah, I made that clear, now you listen to me one more time . . ." Haley, barely loud enough for me to hear, said, "Maybe he's making a date for the penthouse to-night. You know about that, don't you?"

K: What?

H: How he uses it.

K: I don't like to hear those stories. I don't listen.

Today it's different. But the same. Her voice even cracks sometimes while trying to whisper. I closed my eyes and leaned on my red pencil until it snapped.

Golden just left a minute ago. They're planning a new radio partnership, Kyle and Haley . . . I think. Golden's departure is like turning off background white noise, their conversation still muted, but easier to hear. She said, "You don't show it enough—don't you get really mad?"
"My wrath has no boundaries." Smile. I watch them like a movie. If only it were that simple. I could rip the screen with a knife to prove they're just an illusion.

Except an actor on a torn movie screen wouldn't have suddenly turned to me like that, pushing his coffee cup toward me, smiled and raised eyebrow pointed right at me, then another quick smile when I brought his coffee. Too bad she doesn't drink coffee. She usually comes with a can of Coke and leaves half of it here. A few times, if it was still fizzy, I finished it on my way home. I never used to like Coke. It's growing on me. They *both* said "bye" when they left, hers an echo of his.

SEPTEMBER 24, 1979

Yes, I can imagine her: tight blue jeans and pointed-toe cowboy boots, fringed leather vest, big hat that flies off as soon as they let the bronc out of his stall. It would all be in slow motion, the twisting, powerful grace of the animal and Haley's body fitting perfectly, molded to the horse or bull, her thin legs, all muscle, gripping the horse's heaving rib cage, her back arching forward and back as the animal's body jerks up and down, spins, rocks, thrusts back and forth. Her hair short like a boy's, straw texture from the dirt, her face solemn with the effort, but not tight, no grimace, dust mask around her eyes and half covering the reddened skin around her flaring nostrils, sweat on her neck, under her vest her plaid shirt stuck tight to her skin, the arena lights cheap and harsh, pickups in a dirt parking lot, a tinny drawling announcer's voice saying things like "Way to go little lady! Give'r a hand, folks. " And the cramps already starting, ripping through her, blood dripping out the bottoms of her jeans and smeared on the horse's flanks, turning pink and foamy in his sweat. Was that your secret surprise, Haley? When did you two have a chance to share surprises? What was his? Is that how it happened? Did anyone notice or were blood-soaked jeans the usual after riding a bull? I wish you'd told me about this yourself, or maybe you think nothing I could possibly say about it would make any difference. What did he say? I know, he probably didn't say anything for a minute, looked down at his sightly red knuckles, the peace-sign ring he wears on his middle finger, perhaps rubbed the ring with his other hand, with the tip of his index finger, then maybe looked up without raising his head much, looked up from under his eyebrows, looked at you silently, then said something about building character—no, something about now you can face anything. And he wouldn't've touched you. Not then. But maybe when you left . . . where were you, a restaurant? . . . he put his hand on the back of your neck, under your hair.

Was he not supposed to tell anyone? Maybe you said, Don't spread it around. And he said, *What about Corinne? Corinne should know.* Did you raise your eyebrows? Glare? Or nod okay? Maybe you wanted me to know, without having to tell me yourself . . . ?

Really, though, why *did* he tell me? Something had happened, was happening . . . a news break in Haley's show, she came all the way to our conference room for some reason that never came up. Kyle and Golden were having their conversation in code, which I wasn't supposed to understand.

G: Why not, Warren, just go talk to him and see what he has to say.

K: It's not necessary.

G: Improvement never hurts, a step up can't hurt.

K: It's not more money, I already know that.

G: Status, boy, he's got the papers all written up. It's a great opportunity.

K: I'll think about it.

G: Might not be available tomorrow.

K: I'll take my chances.

G: Use your head, boy.

Haley: What's this *boy* shit?

She had come in, a little out of breath from running all the way from the FM side, and put a deafening pause in their conversation. She only had a few minutes. But Golden ignored her at first. Kyle was staring at the wall, no expression.

G: C'mon, Mr. Champion Jock, you had to work with a GM, you were owned like a prize pig, you know this kind of thing is an opportunity to jump at.

H: Let people figure out their own careers, Cy.

Golden was putting letters and stuff into his thin briefcase. He said, "Stay outta this, sweetheart. Who'd've figured out *your* career if Al and I hadn't been there to—"

There was more silence. Kyle shut his eyes for a minute. His eyelids bluish or transparent. Haley grinned, sort of pretended to slap Golden on the cheek but just patted him and said, "Pow! I know people who'll take care of you for me."

The weather report was on. She took off. Her footsteps tapped up the hall. Golden left right after her.

Were we finished? Charlie's Angels are calling Peter Pepper tomorrow, all the plans are typed out for Golden to read before the show in the morning, as usual. I asked Kyle, "Does she really?"

"Really what?" He smiled at me. He stood up and stretched. It did seem easier to move after Golden left.

"Does she know people who'll take care of him for her?"

Haley's voice came on the speakers, couldn't tell if she was out of breath: "Tickets for the Bee Gees in Los Angeles sold out at 9 A.M. this morning, one hour after the box office opened — but here's a little incentive for the rest of us to keep 'Staying Alive.'" He listened to her, then said, "I wouldn't doubt it, she's a pretty tough girl." Then he told me her story. He sat on the table. At first it wasn't like he was telling *me*, just retelling it to himself, but he said, "Maybe I shouldn't tell you, but it might help you to understand her."

Why does he think I need to understand her?

24 FEBRUARY 1989

Do you remember what you told me about her? I'd forgotten that she grew up, lived and traveled as a rodeo rider, as was her father, who screwed her regularly until she got pregnant, then kicked her out. She never had the kid, though. Went on riding and lost it somehow. Haven't thought about it for a long time. Was she the only one of us who shared a secret? Or did I have one for her too?

SEPTEMBER 28, 1979

Kyle said it didn't seem like I was ready to work. He's right — my mother called this morning. The usual. Asking had I met any new interesting people? She hated L.

Only mother on earth who was glad her child ran away from home.

Why didn't I just come out and tell him? Because he wants me to pour Golden's coffee first? Because of how I answer half of Kyle's letters at home so Golden won't know they exist? Because of how Kyle's characters aren't "allowed" —we never even discuss the possibility—to interact with each other because that would prove the show could exist without Golden? I know what he'd say if I said *that* out loud, he'd say, "Look, this show *won't* exist without Golden."

Haley came on a few times, doing ads, a Barry Manilow concert next month, a health club called Slender Lady. After a jingle, Haley came back and said, "Ten-fifteen and it's Haley on your radio," I guess her new ID tag, but he made a face and said, "I suggested she not use that."

In a way, though, it fits. Rodeo—radio. Change a couple of vowels and she has a new career. When I thought of that and said it to him, he smiled, the kind of smile where you'd like to laugh but for some reason you're too worn out. He said, "But it wasn't really that easy." He started talking about the rodeo being this sort of little closed-in world of its own, worse than professional baseball because you grow up there, you eat, sleep, live there, your family's all there—at least in her case it was—and no matter how tough this little world makes you, you're still, in a way, cloistered, so when you leave, like she did—out on her own in new unfamiliar territory for the first time, you can still be very vulnerable even though you survived the rodeo.

So I said, "So that's what you have in common? Is that how you felt coming from baseball to here?"

He said, "You've been listening too much to things you shouldn't."

Haley's voice said, "Paul McCartney and Wings, another great song. You know, my little niece said the other day, *The Beatles — wasn't that the band Paul had before Wings?* What's this world coming to?"

Haley doesn't have a niece, at least not one that she would've talked to the other day. Kyle read that comment aloud from a column in the newspaper last week. We looked at each other. He said, "So someone will write or call saying they read the same story in the paper. She'll learn."

We both watched the coffee maker like an audience as it spit out the last drops of a new pot. Haley gave the time and the weather, the calendar of local events, which included an amateur rodeo in Lakeside, but her voice didn't change, didn't go hoarser or softer or slower, as though to her it was just another boat show or quilting demonstration. My stomach burned for a moment.

Then I told him about yesterday, when someone called for him, maybe his agent, but Golden answered the phone and said he didn't think Kyle was available for an appearance on that date.

Kyle didn't say anything for a minute after I finished. He had some paper, today's notes he'd used on the show, rolled in his hand, walked around the table, took a batting stance, then just one practice swing with the rolled paper as his bat. Haley did an ad for a restaurant and the act that was singing in their bar. Kyle said, "Just let it go."

"You're not going to do anything about it?"

"I'm going to let it go."

But why? Why do you let him keep his thumb on you like that? Pacifying him for now because you're planning to leave soon? With Haley? What about me? I could find material for her, I could write her ID tags and openers and closers and make her the hottest thing on radio. I could. The three of us would be good together.

OCTOBER 3, 1979

How can I even dare to wonder if they'll ask me to join them for a cup of coffee, let alone move with them to a new station? I thought I was being so outgoing, actually inciting a conversation, I thought I'd get them to move forward, from "we ought to get together" to an actual time and place.

I didn't know how to bring it up smoothly, so I just stammered into it, quick, before Golden got here, but continued listening for his scuffy footsteps in the hall or his "sophisticated" bored chuckle, or Al's nasal whine. Haley was already on the air — she didn't say "Haley on your radio," instead something like, "I'm Haley and I'll be with you till two," so I gestured toward the speaker with my *National Enquirer* and said, "Uh, that thing about the rodeo and her father, I, uh, is *that* what she was talking about when she said we should all get together and share secrets?"

He smiled. "Were you there when she said that?" And then: "Must not've been what she meant — I think I knew about the rodeo before she said that."

At least I got my answer. I got two answers.

LATER

This isn't an excuse, more of an explanation. When you asked — *told* — me to leave . . . I was, literally, combustible. I knew damn well what you and Golden were talking about. You've *always* talked in front of me . . .

sometimes in code, but . . . what's it been, five weeks, and *now* you're kicking me out? So I won't know you're being walked on by his step-on-your-face jealousy? You think I'm goddamn stupid? I know Cy had his lawyer fine-comb your contract and concluded you "weren't allowed to do private gigs anymore." Were you afraid I'd say something when I caught Golden lying through his cheesy teeth . . . would that be so awful? So I left mad! As mad at myself—crashing my chair under the table—as at anyone else, so you needn't have issued your order: *Don't react like that, Corinne.*

I wish you knew I was right there in the hall when Golden came out and stalked away without a word to me. I knew it was time to go back in. But I didn't. Not right away. I sat and flipped those newspaper pages. Flip, flip, I couldn't actually *read* them.

You wouldn't have had to say a word. If I were you, I would've ignored me, just listened to Haley chuckle and groan over her own bad joke . . . like someone carrying on a lively conversation in a room of grumpy, silent people. I would've just sat and listened to her with you, and let you be mad at me, and watched your rapt attention on her and taken my punishment that way. But no—

"I have something to say to you, Miss Staub."

I slammed myself into a chair. "What." My last word before my voice would start to wobble, so I had to keep quiet, just let you talk, and Haley talked at the same time—I couldn't understand her through you, except she said Doobie Brothers once, and something about Pepsi. Your words I remember, though.

"In our interview, I don't think we discussed the issue of authority—who has most of it. There are going to be some things you don't understand, but you're going to have to accept them without reacting. I'm not going to undermine anybody's seniority. That's all. I already decided that. You don't have to understand, just follow the procedure."

I felt like a bird when my uncle would take me hunting: suddenly pelted with shot, falling, fluttering, bones shattered, killed without being dead, waiting on the ground for someone to come pull your head off.

Then a hand on my knee made my bowed head go even farther, but a finger against my forehead pushed me upright. I stood to get away, but you stepped onto my foot, pinning me in place. Then just touching with your fist—my shoulder, my other shoulder, my gut—barely touching, and, "I won't let you go until you smile."

Your weight still on my foot . . . I sat, I stood again, knee-to-knee. "Okay, I'm smiling." The words like ripping cloth in my ears.

"Oh no, you're not!" But the weight was gone from my foot and I backed away, heard Haley's voice returning through a song like the sound of someone's voice reading to you as you wake up from groggy sleep.

25 FEBRUARY 1989

Well, she almost had a spine for a minute there—albeit not a very mature or professional one. And it sure didn't last long. Did these people ever *work?*

You'd probably ask the same of Garth. In a way, dinner last night was a familiar scene. A business discussion that I mostly ignored but still heard the same old words: contract, audience share, sponsor, counterprogramming, personality, air time, affirmative action. . . . Well, no one was getting their contract analyzed by a private lawyer, but the buzz words were all the same, and those absent, as usual, took the short end of every stick. Garth did introduce me as an anchor from Redding, but I sat there like an airhead sucking the peppermint stick they put on the tray with the bill. He doesn't have anything to do with content—writing, reporting, interviewing aren't in his repertoire. He's going to evaluate, then experiment with whatever ideas he comes up with to try to make local shows look better, have more contemporary and visual pizazz . . . including the dynamics of the personalities and ideas for non-news fluff or even new locally-produced shows . . . basically anything and everything to spruce up their act here. I have some ideas for him. Maybe he'll give me a subcontract and I could add a notch to my résumé.

Anyway, after a while I did become aware of Garth watching me as he talked to the others. He didn't have his hand on my leg under the table, nor his leg touching mine, not even his feet. I caught his eye as I slid the peppermint stick into my mouth. So I took it out, offered it to him, slid it into his mouth until the tips of my fingers touched his pursed lips, then pulled the candy slowly out and put it back in my own mouth. I sucked that stick into a very sharp white point and showed him, testing it gently on his knuckle. He took my wrist and brought my hand, holding the peppermint, back up to his mouth, closed his eyes, then opened them and watched me as I slipped it out of his lips and back to my mouth. Again I realized he's never kissed me. Then the bill was paid and we all went out to our separate cars in the lot. By then the peppermint was only about an inch long, my fingers sticky. Garth watched the road and said, "I've never been much for oral sex, at least I haven't had much experience with it, but watching you with that candy cane . . . I wanted to fuck your brains out."

I'm not sure if he saw me smiling in the dark. I wonder why we haven't kissed yet.

OCTOBER 12, 1979

Why'd you two invite me if you didn't want me to be there? I mean you obviously had a date of some sort. There was no sitting around, doodling, arm-wrestling, joke-telling. She came in and stood in the doorway, waiting, tint of smile on her lips, tint of lipstick too, denim skirt and flat sandals. And *you* immediately got up, put your coat on. Golden stopped mid-sentence. Or was he finished? Were either of us listening to him? Haley doesn't have to shave her legs. There's almost-white hair sprinkled over her like sugar. How can she have white leg hair and such dark hair on her head? You've been dyeing it, haven't you, Haley. Let it grow out, okay? I'll bet it's light brown. I'll bet those red highlights are your real color.

This isn't what I wanted to be talking about. Get back to having dinner with them at Aspen Mine Company. Okay, I was invited at the last minute . . . *Please take me with you* . . . is that what my face looked like as they prepared to go?

No, it was his idea.

But if you wanted me along, Mr. Kyle, why did you turn and say outright that I wasn't allowed to listen to her story about her date in the office penthouse a week before she got her job here? Did you think I would really plug my ears and hum? Three in a booth, her in the middle telling you the story, her back half turned on me anyway. She has about five freckles on one shoulder, two or three on the other, a few moles on her neck — not the kind with black hairs growing in them, just soft brown spots, slightly raised. She's been to the beach, I swear I smelled Sea-n-Ski, it smells like the beach, not like cocoa butter or coconut oil. But, anyway, with her back half turned on me, I guess she could pretend I wasn't listening.

He glanced over at me now and then. When he did, I met his eyes, but I would've rather he asked me to take over for the waitress than be there and not supposed to listen, so finally I turned my back on them, sat sideways, swung my legs to the open end of the booth, leaned one arm on the table, and stared around the restaurant, which is fabled as a pick-up spot, but all I saw were suits and dresses eating heavy meals early in the day, and lots of tall thin beer glasses catching the light so that the room seemed to be lit by the beer. In the background the tinkle of dishes, laughter, dull pulsing conversations, piped-in Muzak, and Haley's voice, almost like back in our room at the station except that she was a little more high-pitched or harsh, excited, talking a little faster, but not as upset or angry as *he* seemed after a while when he told her to stop because he didn't want to hear any more.

It sure didn't seem like she was talking about the same place where the party was. I never noticed a hot tub, sauna, waterbed, or exercise equipment. Okay, there *was* a bar. But she wouldn't just make the rest up, and why would he be angry? Maybe it turns into a different place in different situations, like with only two people up there. Or three, as the case may be. Probably you're right, Haley—you'd have to be stoned to appreciate it. Did you ride the weight bench like a bronc? Lift more than you thought you could? Slip like a seal from the hot tub to the sauna then strip the sheets off the waterbed and roll there wet and slippery like on the surface of Jello? I don't know why he cut you off. You could've told me and I'd have listened.

2 MARCH 1989

I do remember being there, and I can still close my eyes and clearly see the heavy wooden decor and greasy menu and thick yellow lights and massive vinyl booths . . . and hear the dainty tinkle of glasses. But only now have I realized that you must've invited me along so Cy Golden wouldn't get mean-jealous of you having a date with Haley. But *you* were the one getting mean-jealous, Kyle. Or just mean. Angry enough to tell her to shut up, then sit there staring at your beer. She picked at the fried potato skins, humming. My memory, especially since last night, feels like a recently burned hillside—after all the over-grown weeds and bushes are gone, you can see the stuff that was there underneath all the time: The image of her fingers picking at the potato skins, your scowling stare, my stomach growling, draining the last drops of liquid from the ice in my soda glass for the twentieth time, the sound of her voice describing her date with two admirers, and how as she talked about it, it evolved from romantic to exciting to "well . . . it was different, at least." That was after you told her to shut up. She had to say one more thing, putting a microscopic piece of potato skin on her tongue.

Maybe it'll turn out to be a good thing that I exercised my memory with Garth last night. Maybe it was the weed we were smoking. Whatever it was, I didn't feel like I wanted to feel. Where was that person I'm supposed to be, the one with her shit so together? I was *trying*: rummaging around inside myself for the cool, suave anchorwoman. . . .

It was a small party, six or eight people, three men, the rest women. They called me Erin like they knew me. They had the stereo on an oldies station and one of them put the TV on— Johnny Carson. The conversation changed to favorite TV shows, half my mind dredging up material that I never bothered to share, another half of my mind saying, "Hold on, you can't be threatened by this."

I couldn't concentrate because while the favorite-TV-show conversation took its course, a couple of other women were giving Garth a foot rub. He was beside me on a sofa, his arm around me. They took his shoes off. He slid off the couch to lie on the floor. One started on his shoulders. He rolled over so she could work on his whole back, then he sat up and they formed a back-rub circle, each one kneading another's shoulders, while favorite old movie titles were tossed into the room like someone holding a stack of trading cards and flipping them one by one toward the center of the circle. I turned toward the window behind the sofa, parted the blinds. Outside it was raining its ass off. *You're the one he'll leave with,* I told myself. Someone said *A Man and a Woman,* and everyone groaned.

I'd taken my shoes off when we first got there because the rug looked so new, almost white, and the ground had already been wet outside. They were starting to try to describe *Far Side* cartoons. Garth leaning back against another sofa, getting a scalp massage. I watched, couldn't watch, knowing what I was *supposed* to feel—detached and unaffected, confident, fearless— but holding my ears because one girl's harsh laughter was louder than the TV and stereo combined. The rest of me probably looked okay, laughing at another man's impersonations of Sylvester Stallone as a news anchor, Madonna doing the weather. Then I looked at my shoes. And it felt like one of those dream-scenes in old TV shows where a see-through image of a character gets up, climbs out of the real person who stays lying in bed or asleep in a chair, and the see-through person goes and does something that would've been a complete surprise to the person who stayed behind if she were awake to see it. In just that way, I got up, moved over to the love seat near where my shoes were, and started putting them on. I must've been doing it slowly, a little clumsily. I hadn't even gotten the first shoe on when Garth was beside me on the chair, watching me fumble carefully with the laces, as though afraid I'd make a knot by mistake. "What're you doing?" he said.

"Going out to walk in the rain." That's what I was doing but hadn't known it until I said it. I didn't even know I was going to say it. I didn't know what the hell I was doing.

"Everything okay?" he said.

"Yes, I just want to see what it feels like to go out in the rain."

He watched me tie my other shoe, then said, "Please come back, okay?"

I said I would. My voice was reassuring, I think, clear and sensible. I'd never intended to leave for good . . . I think. I don't think I intended anything except to get up, put my shoes on, and leave the room. So that's what I did.

I liked the way he said, "Please come back." I wanted to be able to keep it, but you can't keep things people say. Remembering isn't the same as keeping.

The rain didn't drench me all at once like I expected. I walked backwards with my face tilted up, could see the parallel lines of water falling from way up there, felt it dripping down my collar, making my jeans heavy and darker, and it was cold. I walked to the corner, sat on a curb, then got up again and went across the street. I shook my head like a dog and hugged myself. Then I turned around and Garth was on the other side of the street. He held one arm out for me. I wanted to go back to him, but my reaction time was very slow, probably the grass—it felt like several minutes that we just stood there before he crossed the street and held me, what seemed like another interminable stretch of time, our damp clothes getting warmer where we were touching, our backs and heads getting wetter. Down that block a few yards there was a covered bus stop, and that's where I started telling him a little about Libby.

Why did it take a rainy night, abandoned party, wet clothes, bus stop bench . . . and Garth to get me to start talking?

He said, "Don't you ever feel . . . not uncomfortable exactly, but. . . . You keep trying all sorts of things to get rid of some weird feeling?"

I said, "Sometimes a sleeping pill works."

Then I wanted to just sit there, with the rain and gurgle of the gutter and the sound of his breath and his heartbeat in my head, and listen to myself, as though the story was coming from a tape recorder in my pocket that I'd forgotten about . . . fourteen or fifteen years ago.

It started with Marcus, of course, the usual thing in 1973: two high school hippies with our long hair parted in the middle. It was so typical that the typical old farts would typically call after us: "How do you tell which is the boy and which is the girl?" We slid our hands into the back pockets of each other's jeans, carried our books in backpacks, wore wire-rimmed glasses. Both of us virgins, until Marcus tried it with the school whore behind the stage in the cafeteria after drama club rehearsal. That set the stage, so to speak, for a dramatic break-up and reconciliation, promises of faithfulness . . . but he said we should try it together. So we did. I think Marcus is probably a necrophiliac by now. That's how it was with him. Except this wasn't a case of *me* going into a coma. *He* wouldn't've noticed if I was alive or dead as long as I had a hole. I didn't say that part to Garth. I didn't think of it then. I was still sort of stoned . . .

Eventually Marcus had another girlfriend. Not instead of me . . . in addition. She went to another school and he poked her about once a week for a year before I let myself admit to knowing. By then the three of us were going to the local junior college together, Libby no longer hidden in the background and me no longer knowing-but-pretending-not-to-know. With Libby in the foreground, it was hard to pretend it wasn't happening, so we were kind of a trio. I wasn't the flimsy, insecure thing who wrote these journals, but . . . on my way, I guess. I don't remember thinking how hip it was of me to share my boyfriend. A trio of *friends*—at first it was still unspoken among us that we knew he was sleeping with both of us. How did he do it, what was so fascinating about *him* that allowed it to happen? Nothing. *She* fascinated me, though. Her long, straight, parted-in-the-middle hair seemed more intense than mine, her level stare more mysterious. Her unusual and not-often-heard laugh more acrid, more sarcastic, more damning than mine. The books she carried around were more heavy in content, more politically relevant. The chain she wore around her neck had more meaning than mine. So the chain that connected her to Marcus also seemed more significant, more mature than my connection to him. I was scared of her, my heart leaped and stomach flopped when I saw her approaching. I wanted to be like her—so Marcus would prefer me, yes, but it was somehow more than that, bigger than that. It was important that *she* recognize *my* hipness, *my* intensity, *my* dramatic mystique. If it ever was "What does he see in *her* and why doesn't he see it in me?" it wasn't that for long.

Marcus was still around, poking each of us in our turn, but Libby and I were circling each other without Marcus in the center any longer. What book should be on the top of my stack when I see Libby today? What underground newspaper can I discover that she's never heard of . . . so I can turn her on to it, and it'll be *me* who pointed it out to her? What news item can I comment on with fresh hippy sarcasm? What protest button can I wear when Marcus and I meet Libby for lunch today? And from her side: "Are you going to the feminist rally tonight?" "Did you know *King of Hearts* is playing at the Strand?" "Want to submit a poem to this new magazine some guys I know are starting up?" "Shall we picket the homecoming queen ceremony?"

Those are the things we started to do without Marcus. I

couldn't let Lib read more relevant newspapers, go to more rallies, see more foreign movies than I did. . . . I would've said it was all to make Marcus' choice between us more difficult, although he saw no reason to ever make a choice, but did I realize that it was actually more complicated than Marcus making a choice? Would *Lib* be able to make a choice? Marcus started to seem silly to us . . . we talked about him when he wasn't around. How he cared more about his job delivering pizzas than he cared about the environment; how bourgeois was his desire to be an architect; how little we got out of his screwing.

Then one night there was a benefit spaghetti dinner at the women's center which I had to go to alone, and on my way, found myself thinking: *I wish Lib wasn't getting fucked by Marcus tonight so she could go to the dinner with me.* As though I'd walked into a gong suspended across the sidewalk. I stood and vibrated, blind and deaf, for a moment, then turned around and went back to my car, drove home, went to my room, and took my first sleeping pill. Just one. But the first of thousands more to come. I just had to stop thinking.

I sort of stopped talking about it right there. I was shivering so deep in my stomach, it was shaking the whole bench. Garth tried to hold me still, finally turned sideways on the bench and circled me with his legs as well as his arms. The bus stop cover was made of uncolored but foggy plexiglass, not clear enough to see through. My head against his chest, facing the back of the bus stop, I could see the rain running down the plexiglass but not the houses or trees beyond it. I kept watching the water stream down the plexiglass, pretending the drops were racing with each other, noticing the places where they always divided and went around a spot although nothing on the surface seemed to prevent the stream of water from going straight through.

"We'd better go, there's a bus coming," Garth said. As we got up, still holding onto each other, he said, "Are you still my friend?"

"Of course," I said. But I don't know why I added: "Are you still mine?"

"Forever," he said.

Corny stuff happens when you're stoned . . . and you love it.

I wished it was forever instead of two blocks back to the party.

OCTOBER 15, 1979

Why was she here hours before her own show? A quick, by now familiar, undertoned conversation, breaking up when Golden comes in, becoming louder, moving on to mundane topics. We were still in our show, on a newsbreak. She doesn't need to be here for another two hours. I can hardly function with that muttered, sometimes whispered or hissed secret something going on over there.

I shouldn't've tried to ask when I only had three-odd minutes—however long it takes Barry Manilow to drag through "One Voice"—and Kyle doesn't like to cut it that close. But Haley had left and Golden was already on his way back to his booth, and I had to know, risking even the dreaded *It's none of your business* . . . which came in not so many words anyway, making me not realize till now that I got it.

Me: Are you and Haley—
K: We're friends.
Me: No, what I meant—
K: Look, she went out once with Cy a couple of months ago. He doesn't like it if he's not getting enough of . . . the right *kind* of attention . . . that he thinks he's entitled to. He's been here a long time. I still get a one-year contract. I have to be somewhat careful.

Me: Didn't he offer to extend it?

K: Don't get involved.

He was out the door too quickly for me to blanch or step back as though slapped. He hasn't answered my question, though. I never asked it.

If she'd never come to work here, I wouldn't do things like I did yesterday: watching her do part of her show through the glass booth. I think she noticed me, but she didn't actually meet my eyes. Unless for a second. Something hot rushed from the pit of my stomach. But then she was looking away or reading something, those big headphones making her face look pinched, her lips very pale, her hair tousled underneath where she'd put the phones on, then maybe scratched her head or put her hands in her hair. Or maybe someone else did it, teasing her as she spoke over the air, making her voice squeak. What did I think would happen—that she'd come in today and start telling me her problems and secrets because she saw me there watching her?

3 MARCH 1989

I've been sitting here looking at my rubber mouth guard on the window ledge. It's like a fighter lives here. A fighter who may not need it anymore—I'll never get my teeth kicked in a second time. I thought about knocking it out the window, watching it fall, imagining what people would think when they found it.

Should I call my agent? If I want a subcontract, she'd hammer it out for me. She'd also know what might be unwise for me to do, have some guidelines or suggestions. She might not like Garth's idea to use me in a test doing a newscast without any desks, outside in the desert or mountains. It's not that I'm hesitant to call her because I'm afraid she'll say I shouldn't do it. But she doesn't even know I'm here. Not that I was completely clear and level-headed when I left Redding, but enough so to realize that no station, no matter how small, is going to want an anchor back on the air who's had to take several months off after a hysterical panic attack. I told them my mother was dying of breast cancer and had two to six months to live and needed me there till the end and to take care of matters afterward, and my agent got the same message. They couldn't call even if Mom still lived in Scottsdale—they don't know her last name. Which brings up the question: How do I put any work I do for Garth on a résumé if it's done while I'm supposed to be on personal leave from my job? So this is my quandary, which, I admit, didn't stop me from agreeing to go with Garth and do his lame experiment. Am I losing my professional edge?

OCTOBER 23, 1979

Ideas can't be copyrighted.
    But they can be copied.

For whose benefit did he say it? For Haley's? Her voice on the speakers making that female wolf call over some rock singer or movie star. For me? Are my ideas too much like the morning team's in Los Angeles? I've tried not to be influenced by them. I do listen to them most of the time—can't stand Golden and Kyle very long. No matter how alive and spontaneous Kyle's voices are, Golden sounds dead and prepackaged. Watching them is even worse. Separate booths, a glass wall between them, but they seldom look at each other. Have they ever? Not that I've seen. But what's eerie about it is seeing Kyle's face be like a bored old paper shuffler at some bank while he's doing Mrs. Olsen having a cow because the office coffee machine serves Sanka.

5 MARCH 1989

Was that me up on that mountain?

We drove up there yesterday. No snow yet, so no local tourists. The camcorder is light, so I suggested Stonewall Mountain, a twenty or thirty-minute uphill hike to the large flat stone almost capping the whole peak . . . a view of everything in every direction. Isn't that where a news anchor should be—on top of everything?

The background wasn't crowding in on me, not up there. It was everything as far as you could see, but nothing close to me. No trees grow out of the stone on the peak. Bushes are easily avoidable, as was the rusty rail—put there to keep kids from dive-bombing off—and the cracked, dry drinking fountain swarming with ants. I admit, the rail was a good reminder—for me. Standing there with the wind coming right at me, I felt I could lean into it and it would hold me up. Swaying in the breeze. Swaying slowly. Losing weight. Lean a little farther and I'd be flying . . . weightless, powerful . . . capable of anything.

I must've been teetering in the breeze a little. Garth put an arm around my waist and pulled me back. So I sat on the flat stone cap and read some stories—foreign uprisings, local crime, as well as a few human-interest things. Garth had suggested I not spike my hair so it would blow around in the wind. There was plenty of wind. Garth was hidden behind the camera, all silver hair whipping wildly in the wind, a camcorder for a face, but I knew he was in there . . . and even more so, I knew it wasn't just the usual packaged soulless image of the newscaster reflected into his eye . . . I could tell *he* was coming through the lens to where I was. The real, gritty me . . . shivering but sweating as I let go of the papers, lowered my suspender straps, unbuttoned my shirt, and took it off.

The camcorder never stopped. Garth said, "Oh," softly, and kept the thing running. I stopped doing stories, lay back on the rock. The wind was cold, and the tips of my breasts were standing up like pencil points. I wasn't looking, but I felt one with my fingers. When I did that, Garth said "Oh" again.

One fly or bee was buzzing. I said, "There's life on this desolate mountain top." It's really not a skyscraper mountain, but the silence, except the wind and the bee and the camcorder, made it seem far removed and far above.

I had my eyes shut, but he didn't startle me when I felt his mouth close slowly over the tip of one breast. He was on hands and knees, half over, half beside me, the camcorder sitting on the rock beside us, and I could still hear it going.

I said, "You can call your film, 'My Climax at the Summit.'"

He laughed. A kind of groany laugh. He didn't want to move. "Yours too," he said.

"No . . . but it doesn't matter anymore that I don't come." It must've sounded funny. It seemed kind of funny, accompanied by the distant roar of the pine trees when the wind suddenly gusts harder through them.

Going back down the trail to the car, Garth took the videocassette out of the camcorder and put it in his jacket pocket. He said, "I'll keep this forever, hidden away somewhere."

I said it was probably going to be like one of those shaky handheld ads where the camera's showing a guy's shoes or his hand scratching his ankle while he talks about a computer. And, I said, even if this tape was like one of those ads, even if it doesn't show anything at all but the hazy, colorless air off the edge of the cliff, or if he was lucky enough to get his feet or the top of my head in the shot, even if it was a stupid idea, it became a profound piece of work.

"Then I could still show it at the production meeting," he said, *"The News Anchor Working Outside."*

We laughed. I can hear my agent screaming from here. There I am in a few years at CBS and suddenly, one night on *Entertainment Tonight,* a shot of me being fucked through the leg of my leather Swiss hiking shorts. My next job: gofer for Maury Povich. I admit I had a healthy ping of fear when he put the tape in his pocket. But immediately replaced it with an unexplainable giddiness over the tape being in his pocket with his hand there holding it so he wouldn't lose it.

He unlocked my side of the car, then went around and got in the driver's seat, leaned over, took the back of my neck, and pulled me close. I thought he was going to kiss me, but he didn't.

NOVEMBER 2, 1979

Were they arguing? It wasn't really about the gig. Or was it? At first it was *me* arguing, but I got kicked out of the argument quickly, while it was still just a discussion, and Haley took my place after giving me that green-eyed look, finally acknowledging my presence, and . . . more than that? I don't know. But then all three of us were mad and silent, so what was the point of us going along with him to his speaking engagement? I'm not sure. I was there to run the slide projector, I guess. And maybe because I helped him put together his Special Olympics program. In the dark while running slides he did some of his voices, pretending the characters were with him. He had to be good because he pulled it off even though we were all in a funk when we got there.

I was in the back seat with his slides and notebooks like a child with Mom and Dad up front, except Mom was wearing high-heel black boots, a black-and-red skirt, and a peasant blouse off both her shoulders. Some clothes aren't right for arguing in. Her hair is growing out a little, sort of a shag, and the roots are lighter. She was singing with the radio, "What I Did

For Love," her grindy voice covering the singer's clear tone. He looked at her and smiled. She looked back and kept on singing. I got chills. And wanted to die. What would he have said after the song—what would I have said, if I had the guts—if I hadn't immediately said, "I thought Cy told you not to do solo gigs"?

"You mean Mr. Golden?" He looked into the rearview mirror. I could only see a strip of him, just eyes and eyebrows, no laugh-lines, though, and it was only a second. "He *asked* me not to, Miss Jugears. Stop listening to stuff you shouldn't hear."

I think Haley was still humming the tune, looking out the window on her side. She turned the radio off while he was saying that jugears thing. But at that point his voice was still easy, his eyes flashed up in the mirror again, the lines there this time, so his smile was probably what made me go on: "I think he *told* you not to."

"*You* don't know!" The voice got harder so suddenly that it pushed me back, blew me back from where I was leaning up against the front seat. That's when Haley looked at me. I got the full shot from her eyes. I never knew they were green. My heartbeat was a thud in my stomach. But I was crushed and limp against the back seat.

She faced forward, then said, "What'll you do if he does tell you not to?" He didn't answer. I couldn't see if he shrugged. She pulled one leg up, sat on her boot, facing sideways, funny pursed smile: "I mean *when* he tells you."

His hands slid from the top of the steering wheel, down each side, then just held it with one hand at the bottom. He said, "Not do any more gigs, I guess."

"Coward!" That was Haley. I wasn't about to say anything else and maybe get dropped off on the side of the road.

K: No, realistic.

H: The reality is *letting* him bully you 'cause he's jealous.

K: I try to understand how he feels —

H: Bullshit.

K: — this was *his* town.

H: Bullshit. You think I haven't seen bullshit?

K: Bullshit looks different in a rodeo ring. I thought you learned that.

H: Don't try to change this into what I've learned. I've seen what you let him do to you, Warren. I've seen ass-lickers in the rodeo too.

K: I know you have. Not just in the rodeo.

H: Stop twisting what I'm saying. I'm talking about your yes-boss attitude.

K: What attitude do you suggest? He *is* the boss. Next thing you know he'll be program director — without giving up his place on the show, of course. Think that'll be easy on me if I've been trying to undermine him?

H: It's *your* career.

I wanted to join forces with her. He wasn't telling *her* to shut up or stop listening or both. The car vibrating and speeding forward was turning me into lead — immobile, heavy, dead. I stared at my hand on the seat beside me, willed one finger to lift. It did. Which proved I could still move. And I could scream at you inside my head: *If I can see what he's doing to you, so can you!*

But they weren't finished. I'd thought he was going to let it drop, but he didn't. A mile or so later: "We all try to do what's best for our careers, don't we, Haley?" Saying her name like that, while he was already talking only to her, sounded strange.

Her voice practically wheezed, it was so high, hoarse and cracky: "What's *that* supposed to mean?"

K: You know what it means.

H: That date is none of your business.

K: Did it help you in your career?

H: No! I already *had* this job. I went to broad-caster school all summer.

His last word, "Oh," rung in the air the rest of the trip.

NOVEMBER 10, 1979

I was almost proud of how you were such a good sport, Haley, but I guess you could learn that in a rodeo. You don't blame the bull or bucking horse, you get up smiling and wave to the crowd. The difference is: the bull isn't jumping and twisting to *get* your attention but to get *rid* of it. . . . It's pathetic. It's also so incredibly obvious and audacious. And he's just the one I notice doing it, maybe everyone at the station is dancing in rings around you, hoping they'll be the one you point at to come to the center with you. But Golden, he doesn't just wait and hope to be chosen, he thinks he has ways to force you.

Maybe it was those little satiny track shorts you wore that barely covered your butt, sort of fluttered as you walked, and everyone else, except Kyle and one or two others, was wearing sweat pants. Golden was after you on every play, whether you had the ball or not. I was afraid instead of just touching you, he was going to pull your shorts off. And how about his idea last week for a rub-down chain. . . . After every play when you and Kyle would exchange a laugh, a few words, Cy was always there, made sure he was always there. They hardly want to be together in a conference room to plan

their show — now all of a sudden they're a "team" playing games in the park? Since when? Since you. Only
once I saw one of those looks between them, just after
you trotted back to the FM side — everyone screaming,
"*C'mon, Haley!*" as though they couldn't function without you, and Golden and Kyle were walking back to the
AM side, Cy chuckling over whatever it was you'd said
to Kyle, as though you'd said it to *him* too, as though
you'd said it to *only* him. Kyle stared at him and Cy
stopped laughing to stare back, just for a second, then
looked away to shake his head like he thought someone
was really acting stupid.

Maybe you were completely oblivious, Haley. If you
weren't, you might've seen that bucket of water, or
something like it, coming from a mile away. He'd already tried snapping you with a towel. You weren't on
his team, so he couldn't carry you away on his shoulder
like a winged-victory trophy. It wasn't funny, and everything showed through your wet shirt. . . . How could
you play football without a bra? I can hear you already:
*If they don't droop after fifty bucking stallions, they ain't
gonna droop* NOW.

Suddenly, though, you were a different kind of person than that. Hair streaming down, stuck to your
head, your face looked so little, your eyes smudged and
batting, mouth frozen for a second in a sort of shocked
gasp, like, in a way, he'd made you cry. Then you were
hunched over, wringing out the bottom of your shirt,
kind of wheezing, but giggling. Almost everyone out
there laughing. Al slapped his pal on the back. The
bucket thrown into the air like a graduation hat. But
you came up smiling — not at me, looking into your eyes
and holding out someone's jacket for you to put over
your wet clothes — but at Kyle, handing you his own
shirt.

8 MARCH 1989

Remember why Cy said I couldn't play in the football game? I wasn't a personality. You said I could be the trainer. Then Haley said, "I was hoping you'd do my rub-down, Warren." Before you could even smile, Golden was saying, "And you can do mine. We'll have a rub-down chain." Your reaction was: "If that puts me where I think it puts me, no thanks." I would've said no thanks too, because, yes, maybe I'd be rubbing you, Kyle, but I would've had to have Golden doing *me*.

I probably wouldn't have been any good at giving back-rubs then, but now, I'm great. Garth said, "Kathryn always falls asleep after rubbing my back about *ten seconds.*" I like to concentrate on the place where the skin of my fingertips is touching the skin on Garth's back—I think I'm living in that point, that's where I am, and he feels it. I told him his back is like the ocean, like swimming in the ocean, because there are warm spots and cool spots, rough patches, very smooth areas, and I follow the dips and swells. Instead of me getting tired of doing it, he said he felt selfish, rolled to his side, and pulled me beside him, my back against his front, his mouth right behind my ear, our legs tangled. He said, "Tell me a story."

"What do you want to hear?"

"Anything. Just talk to me."

"To keep you from falling asleep?"

He never sleeps at my place. I'd met him at the station and we went to dinner. Sometimes we don't talk a lot—the ebb is just as pleasant as the flow of energy between us. We held hands. But tonight I could tell he was in a peculiar state of agitation, one of those times you can't look around a restaurant or bank without imagining how each person there would do an on-camera interview if, say, the place was robbed or caught on fire.

In my room, he said, "Sometimes making love at night is difficult—it's hard to clear my mind of the day's events."

I said, "You haven't seemed to have too much trouble."

"Do you still need a pill to sleep?"

"Not lately. Sometimes."

"Do you worry about it?" he asked.

"No. My mother did, though. That's kind of how I ended up in California."

"Okay, tell me that story," he said, edging even closer to me.

That story continued from the spaghetti dinner I'd abandoned to go home and take a sleeping pill. My mother started to notice stuff like that. I'd said, "It's not like I'm taking birth control pills or something, Mom," which shows you the level of maturity on both sides of the fence.

Like any good mother, she blamed Libby. But Lib didn't know about the pills. I took them so I wouldn't lie in bed staring at the ceiling, going through endless strings of hypothetical conversations with Lib. And I took the pills because I found out I would sleep heavily all night—even if I dreamed, I might not remember—and I wouldn't rise to the surface so often.

Anyway, my mother had also worried when, at first, I would cry alone in my room over *Marcus* sneaking off to Lib's apartment. Naturally I wouldn't tell Mom what I was crying about, but I stopped the crying and she worried about the pills even more. Maybe worried about the pills *because* the crying had stopped. I stopped thinking about Marcus as I chose what clothes to put on each day, which must've all looked essentially the same anyway. Should I wash my hair? Well, would I be seeing Lib that day? What was I going to do after the two-year-college? What was *Lib* planning to do? My mother had never wanted me to go away to school but changed her mind, thought I should go to California because I had an uncle living here somewhere so I could establish residency. I said California was too plastic unless I could go to San Francisco. Lib had mentioned it. But my uncle was in Southern California. I said no, thanks.

I stopped having to wonder if Marcus ever lied to Libby so he could sneak off and be with me . . . because I'd been avoiding my turn with him. And she, I found out later, was doing the same. He thought we'd finally caught onto his game and had compared notes and were both mad at him . . . when actually we'd been onto him for a year! I don't even remember when he dropped out of school to work full time in the pizza parlor. Was it before or after Lib took me to the club? I can't remember. We were applying to college in Boulder, Albuquerque, Flagstaff . . . but, as you know, I went to San Diego State. When I eventually took off for California, it was *instead* of taking a sleeping pill that night.

The story sort of petered out because Garth listens with his eyes shut, his hand stroking my stomach or the underside of one breast, with his breath steady against my ear, and he chuckles or sighs or moans at all the right times. Last night, after I stopped talking and we were both quiet for a while, he said, "Did you ever think you'd have to go two thousand miles from home to meet someone you'd expect to find in your own backyard?"

NOVEMBER 14, 1979

There was no fast hoarsely-happy voice talking, no breathlessness, no plans and whispers and hacking silent laughter. . . . Compared to that, the room probably did seem depressing. Golden had stepped out, Haley hadn't come in. But she *was* there, for a while, on the radio. She seemed quieter, mellower. But you got up and turned the radio off before saying, "We do a *funny* show, Corinne. Think how much better the show would be if our number-one writer weren't so gloomy. Cheer up! For all our sakes."

Me: You sound like those have-a-nice-day bumper stickers. If you're having a lousy

day, how do you change it so it's *nice* just because a smiley-face on the dirty car in front
of you tells you to?

You: By realizing your lousy day isn't your whole
      life.

Me: I'll keep that in mind.

You: I'm not really trying to peddle you tripe
      about feeling good to be alive and counting
      your blessings and being cheerful through
      adversity and all that crap.

Me: Then what are you saying?

You: [*What a smile!*] You could just fake it, okay?

12 MARCH 1989

So. I never invented that sparkly girl he wanted me to be . . . but
it doesn't matter. *Now* it doesn't matter that *instead* of becoming
a smiley-face have-a-nice-day bumper sticker after I left KIAM, I
was a cold, scaly lizard . . . a *successful* one: my practiced smile
and direct meaningful look only for the camera, or a tool to get
a certain interview, confidences given to me by people I don't
know just because I looked them clearly in the eye, added the
right touch of fraudulent softness, the right half-smile with the
right slight nod . . . *I* got the quotes. But when it came to real
interactions with people, another kind of lizard: who—except
for a few dozen disastrous exceptions—started to avoid any possibility of getting laid for fear that one time, eventually, I
wouldn't ever wake up from the paralyzed coma . . . or the guy
would beat me to death for dying on him—and I'd never know
it. But, Kyle, finally . . . the person I am *now* can be flat on her
back for two days—the past few days—with a thick fever, aching and unable to move, hearing only garbled jabbering voices
on the TV, exhausted beyond mere weariness, my head buzzing

and thunky . . . but still keep this buoyancy, this eager knot of effervescence in my stomach, knowing there'll soon be a night with Garth, and another, and another . . .

When we went out for margaritas the night before last . . . or the night before that . . . I told him I was tired but didn't know why. I felt soggy. But it was good to sit in the amber dark Mexican restaurant, our hands touching, eyes closed half the time, listening to the corny canned Mexican music, no need to speak. Then when we were here afterwards, I was shivering so terribly that he stopped what he was doing, covered me with the blanket, and just lay there holding me. I said I was sorry and he said, "Nothing to be sorry about."

I don't even remember how many times he was here in the last few days. He has to recommend which new weather person they should hire in the next week or so and has had people flying in to interview almost every day, but he still stopped by whenever he could. I dozed and drifted and groaned and half-dreamed all day, until he would come back, calling my name from the sidewalk so I could phone down to let him in. He brought food—orange juice, yogurt, a donut—didn't want to come in and bother me, just stood inside the doorway and let me lean against him, put his face against the top of my head where my hair was matted and greasy. Our first kiss? No. Doesn't count.

NOVEMBER 19, 1979

God, what's wrong with me — I've heard all the words before. Why should I care? And how did it come up at the station this morning? Kyle doing a new voice, a hillbilly without teeth, and Al, hanging around, thought it was a good time to tell how he heard that in Vietnam there was a toothless old lady with a baby in her arms who was forced to give blow jobs to American soldiers.

They might've even started to laugh — Golden and Al — but there was this low moan, which was Kyle. He leaned his mouth on his fist and looked away.

So then I'm lying on my bed like a zombie at about four when normal people are out having drinks or riding bikes at the beach or disco rollerskating or whatever — Haley got skates last week but I haven't seen her wearing them yet. I was listening to my old Moody Blues record, *Libby's* Moody Blues record, mine now . . . phone rings . . . I roll off the bed . . . walk transfixed to the kitchen . . . "Hello?"

"D'you like t'get fucked in the pussy with a big cock?"

My zombie face probably never changed. Stood there. Not even a smart-ass answer coming to mind.

He screamed "Bitch! You bitch!"

But I was without instinct, blank, void, replaced the receiver on the hook, stared at the phone's round face. Why did you ask me that? Now I can't get the answers out of my mind. Do I like it? Not particularly, at least not yet in this lifetime . . . but thanks for calling. But I can't say it, could never say it, won't say it. I can imagine Haley's quick voice: "Hey, baby, not by *you*," then snapping the phone down and forgetting it. Would memories of her father haunt her? Oh god, I don't want to think about *my* old shit . . . this isn't even close to being the same as M & L. Haley barely looks at me. And Kyle? Sometimes it feels like he's inside my head and knows everything. . . . What if he touched my knee under the table, what if Haley came in and asked *me* what I was doing for lunch? You know what? I don't even know if that would be better or worse than how it really is! Sometimes, though, I can go home content, when he looks at me and says stuff like, "Think how it feels when you were a kid coming home from school on the first day of summer. Sometimes I feel like that, don't you?"

Then her voice comes back over the speakers and the air in the room is a little more brittle. Or she comes in the room and the air's cooler, snappier, not so stale. She's not like L. at all.

NOVEMBER 24, 1979

You've been gone three days now, Haley, or two . . . ? We're getting a lot of work done so that Golden and Kyle can work fewer hours around Christmas. Golden wants to take a week off at Xmas and Kyle said, go ahead, he'd work alone over Xmas so he could have his vacation later. But Golden kept saying "What does it say in your contract?" So instead of Kyle doing a week alone, Golden's not going on vacation after all. Golden seemed, or pretended, to recover from the vacation thing fast enough to ask Kyle to go to lunch with him, which Kyle did, and I'll bet he wouldn't've if you were here, Haley.

How can it be that I'm sort of daydreaming about being the one to meet you at the airport tomorrow and at the same time dreading the next time you come into our room to continue whispering your plans for secession with Kyle? Would I mind if you and Kyle left to do a show together somewhere else? If you two were *one* person . . . or if just one of you was thinking of leaving . . . how would *that* be? Should I try to imagine life without one of you? Which should go? If he goes and you stay: You would never come into our conference room anymore. I'd be alone here with Golden. What would he and I say to each other? There'd be nothing to plan for a show he did by himself. He'd tell me to get my ears pierced. To wear makeup. To buy a dress. To stop wearing socks and leather shoes. To let my hair grow. To roll it in curlers every night. To get a padded bra. You'd be off on your rollerskates at the park after work.

But if you left and *he* stayed . . . we might put on tapes with no one's voice interrupting the music or us while we worked. He might not whisper and arm wrestle or go out after work with me . . . but it's possible. At least I'd have what I already sort of have: Sometimes our eyes share an experience behind Golden's back. So it looks like between the two choices, Haley, you leaving would be better. But unless you had never existed, we'd miss you. Like today and yesterday . . . he looks at his watch more often. What's he waiting for? He's not meeting you at the airport until tomorrow afternoon. I tried to imagine what would happen if he got sick or delayed and called me to go get you. Then, since you wouldn't be expecting me, I could watch you come in. You might be tired, pale, your freckles standing out. You'd be wearing a face *he's* never seen and probably never will. Weary, disappointed, maybe confused or unsure of what to do . . . would that really be *you?* I'd come up from behind, put a hand or just my fingers on your back for a second, and say, "Hey, sweetheart." *Why would I call you sweetheart?!*

14 MARCH 1989

It seems like almost every time I've met someone—except Garth . . . and also Alex—I spend more time circling than doing whatever is going to follow the circling. You know, the way animals circle for a while, sniffing, checking things out, sizing each other up, sending body language, then get into their vigorous play . . . or vigorous copulation. Or even a vigorous fight, I suppose . . . and I don't mean just getting popped once in the face without ever knowing what hit you. I mean when both sides *know* the other's there . . . which, it goes without saying, applies to the carnal stuff as well. Fighting or fucking . . . I was a failure. Good thing neither is a requirement to get somewhere in this business.

I went to the station because Garth wanted to show me the tapes of his three favorite candidates for the weather person job. I watched his three picks, then watched a few others because he got a call and was busy on the phone. I liked one guy named Roland Will who he hadn't put in the finals. So when he got off the phone, I said, "What do you think of Will?" Garth didn't know what I was talking about, so he said, "It's sure better than *won't.*" I laughed and he came toward me, also laughing, his eyes squinting shut, saying, "But all the *won'ts* have probably become extinct by now because they *wouldn't.*" Then he grabbed me and we fell together into the easy chair he has in his office, him in the chair, me on his lap.

"I must be the epitome of the sexist bastard," he said, "because when you're around, I can't keep my hands out of your clothes." But I sure wasn't struggling to get away—already breathing hard. I was wearing a black shirt, made of cotton like a T-shirt, but it buttons up the front. He put his finger in between two buttons, stretched the shirt sideways until he found a nipple that was already alert. He rolled it between his thumb and finger until it poked through the little space between the buttons, his other arm holding me firmly on his lap, as though I was going to jump up and run across the room.

"God, someone could knock on the door any second," he said hoarsely, with sort of a laugh. I'm not sure if I answered. He had his chin hooked over my shoulder, watching his hand, then he used both hands to smooth my shirt down tight, the nipple still poking through, and he touched just the tip with the end of one finger, over and over, and said, "Maybe that wouldn't be so bad . . ."

"And maybe this time I'll get it right," I muttered.

"Sounds like you're speaking from experience." He shifted my body so I was sitting across him, so he could bend over me and continue to open my clothes.

I went ahead and started telling him, all in broken little breathless sentences, between moans and groans, and once or twice suddenly realized I'd been humming for I didn't know how long, then remembered to go on . . .

Lib had a friend from high school who went to the university in Flagstaff, and we were considering applying there, so we went to see the school and to visit this friend of hers in the dorm. Her friend didn't look like us at all. She had shorter hair than I've got now—obviously not spiked, though, in 1975. It lay down on her head, her ears poking through, parted on the side and combed over. I forget her name—Melanie? She ran track and played on the tennis team and read poetry.

You know how it is when you get together with two people who have a common past that you don't share, and when they reminisce, you don't know what they're talking about, can't appreciate what they're saying, and, frankly, don't care. Instead, you wish your friend would tell the other person about all the stuff you and she have been doing together lately. They used to sneak out in eleventh and twelfth grades and go dancing downtown. I wondered if this Melanie person knew anything about Lib and Marcus. Or Marcus and me. Or Lib and Marcus and me. Lib didn't bring it up, but Melanie asked about him, saying, "So, do you still know Mucus, or whatever his name is?" I never saw Lib laugh so hard. Melanie took us to a vegetarian restaurant and Lib ordered like she'd known all along what tofu and falafel and tabouli were. She helped me order and Melanie said

"Break her in slowly," as though eating vegetarian food was a big daring step that might frighten me away. Back at the dorm, I went down to the bathroom and took a couple of sleeping pills. The thing is, I'd never taken two before. Although I certainly have since. I didn't hear a sound all night. Lib and I were on the floor in sleeping bags, Melanie on her bed. In the morning, Lib's bag was stretched out along the side of the bed instead of where it had been, parallel to mine in the middle of the floor. I asked Lib if she shimmied around like a snake on her stomach while she was asleep. Melanie laughed, then turned away, making her bed and smiling. Lib smiled too and didn't say anything . . . until later, on the way home, when she told me she'd been awakened up during the night by Melanie masturbating.

"How did that wake you up?"

"Well . . ." Then I wondered if that was all she was going to say. I remember how sharp her profile looked as she drove, as if she was made of paper and might disappear if she turned toward me. Finally she said, "There're a few unmistakable sounds . . . it's a small room. There's . . ." Again she paused for a long time. "There's a, like an instinctive sense we have, an animal sense which we don't admit to or don't consciously know how to use, so, like, with lots of people it's become atrophied."

While I was struggling to tell this story, I didn't even realize Garth was unbuttoning my pants . . .

Anyway, Lib told me how when women live together they ovulate together, the animal sense they have makes their bodies communicate and get into sync, for whatever reason. Garth said he knew why: so when wandering herds of female animals find a lone male, they can all get bred at the same time. If we weren't there on that chair, doing what we were doing, we might've launched into a discussion of matriarchal vs. patriarchal societies, whether or not the male is the object being used to gratify the female's desire to procreate, or the female is the object for the male's desire to reaffirm his masculinity and superiority. But it wasn't the time for a conversation like that. I went back to telling him what Lib said, and how she finally said, "C'mon, Corinne, you're not a virgin, you know what sex smells like." That's what woke her up, she said. At that point Garth pushed his hand into my underwear and stuck a finger into me and I was making a little sound with every breath. And wouldn't've bothered to finish the Flagstaff story, except he said, "Did you find out why her sleeping bag had moved?"

She said Melanie needed to talk. I was dead, as good as dead, no animal sense waking *me* up. Lib said, "You were sleeping like a baby so we didn't want to bother you." I hadn't known what was going on. If I hadn't taken those pills, though, I might've been awake. *Then* what? Maybe nothing. *Probably* nothing. But at least I wouldn't've suddenly realized that for all the effort I'd been pouring out, *I* was the one who slept through whatever happened "like a baby." That's what I felt like. Maybe I looked like her, but hadn't entered her world . . . and she knew it. That was strike one.

There's no way I could've, at that moment, explained all that to Garth. He and I had gone into our own world, together, right after I told him how Lib said she didn't want to disturb me since I was sleeping so soundly. But we knew we couldn't go on for hours . . . in his office, I mean. He stopped doing me with his finger, pulled it out, and said, "If I'd've been there, *I'd* have woken you up."

I said, "So you could breed the whole herd, right?"

He laughed. "Oh, what you must think of me."

He straightened my clothes and we got off the chair. He was sort of just standing there looking around, as though he couldn't remember what he'd been doing before we started.

DECEMBER 3, 1979

Will Haley tell you? If so, what will she say? Will you put two and two together?

I only did it based on your advice, Kyle. "People don't read minds, you know." What was I doing, wishing out loud for a *date*? I doubt it.

It was last Friday. He wanted to know if I'd seen *Kramer vs. Kramer* and of course I haven't. He asked why. A million reasons. Tall people sit in front of me. Air conditioning all winter. Kids talk, I get headaches from staring at the screen, I don't like to go alone. He had easy answers: move to a different seat, wear a sweater, take an aspirin, go with someone else. . . . Well, no one has asked me. Seemed like an honest enough answer. Something I could say to him without it meaning anything else, and we were alone, even though Haley was in the background laughing over her tongue-slip— promoting a concert but saying Long Bitch instead of Long Beach. He laughed too. Then I got the corny advice. *People don't read minds.*

So, of course, she said *no* . . . a boiled-down translation of "I don't really have a lot of time." If I'd said, "Want to go see a movie *tomorrow*?" she could've said she was busy, but that would just mean she's busy tomorrow. So I managed to ask it in the perfect way, for her, so her answer can't be misunderstood, so she can be sure I'll never be tempted to ask again.

God, did she think I was asking her for a *date?* Obviously *he* thought I was talking about Bill, her new engineer who looks about twelve. I had no idea Kyle was going to show up in her studio after his show. I was there waiting to get a chance to talk to her before she started. And he shows up, I don't know why, all he did was sort of joke around about Bill, telling her to call him Willy because he looks so young.

After Kyle left, she never looked at me directly. I stared at her gold starfish earring. Now, remembering back, I want to say she looked up at Bill and grinned, like laughing, after I asked. But I have no idea if that's true.

I don't remember what I was actually thinking on my way back to the conference room, but now it seems like, of course, I was planning to tell Kyle. If I'm so worried that she'll tell you, why would I want to rush back and tell you myself?

I met up with you as you were in the hall filling the coffee pot at the water fountain. I just took the pot from you and finished filling it, then made the coffee without having to say "Let me do that" or "It's my job."

Why *you* were in such a good mood, I'll never know. I don't want to know. How do you do it? For all you know, Golden's figuring out a way to get your name off the show and pretend your voice characters are *his,* and you can still smile like that and say, "How ya doing, Cory? Did I leave fast enough for you? Should I've saluted first?"

Me: You mean because of how I got you to leave
          Haley's studio a minute ago?
You: Got me to leave? You *railroaded* me out of
          the way. Pretty smooth.
Me: Not really—you weren't supposed to know
          you were being railroaded. Besides, it was
          all for nothing.
You: You'll be turned down more than once in
          life. You'll get your share like everyone else.
Me: Not if I never again put myself in a position
          to *be* turned down. This was it, the begin-
          ning and the end.
You: That's a great attitude. Are you sure you're
          not too choosy?

Me: I'm not sure about anything. Except now
        someone thinks I'm really weird.
You: Well, if he thinks you're weird, then it's a
        good thing you know. No use moping
        around about someone who thinks you're
        weird.

And after she tells you it was *her*, not Bill . . . what're
you going to think?

DECEMBER 10, 1979

You must've just forgotten it, Haley. The instant I left,
you forgot, not even important enough to tell Kyle in
your whisper sessions last week. I kept waiting for it,
for you to mutter something in your voice that has a
hard time getting down to an actual whisper—and the
word *she* is far more audible than the rest—and see him
look up at me with an astonished smile on his face, not
a smile that's for me or shared with me, but a gawk *at*
me. But it wasn't even worth the gossip, was it? A relief. So . . . why do I consider throwing an epileptic fit
on the floor beside you, or fainting on the table while
you converse? So maybe even if you don't notice my
comatose body, something will trigger *one* of you to say,
"When we have our own show together, let's ask that
Corinne be hired to work with us." Of course bringing
up my name might cause her to innocently add, "Oh
yeah, she wanted to go to a movie with me last week."
And he'd say, "It was *you*?" So instead of Haley telling
him and his face coming up with an idiotic surprised
grin, he'd tell *her* how upset I was over being rejected,
and she'd cover her open-mouthed smile with one
hand, start that choking giggle, and look at me with
wide popping-out-with-laughter eyes.

Still, I really admired your guts today, Haley. Golden

came in and you and Kyle sort of froze, then Kyle started reading a letter that had been open in front of him for at least fifteen minutes. I could hear myself working on a fingernail under the table, picking at it with the same little rhythm I saw in Kyle's clenched jaw, grinding his teeth back and forth, and the same rhythm of your sandaled foot swinging back and forth, vacant little smile on your face, eyes toward the ceiling. Golden put his stuff down maybe a little louder than usual, turned, and he and Kyle were suddenly eye-to-eye across the table, and he said, "We've got to talk, go wait for me in Al's office."

So Kyle got up and left without another word. Naturally, Haley, you would be leaving then too, but not so fast that it looked like you were leaving just because Kyle did. You stopped to read a poster on the wall under the pencil sharpener. As though you knew Golden would come up behind you and almost pin you to the wall, put his hands on your shoulders, then on your head, stroking your hair back, gathering it together, moving it aside. I thought he was going to kiss your neck. He might've, but your voice came out hard: "I can turn around and get my knee into your balls so fast you won't have a chance to thank me for warning you."

It worked. He practically flew backwards, so fast you almost fell down, but instead of flipping yourself out the door, you stayed to glare at him, giving him the chance to say: "Don't get so cocky, little cowgirl, I hold the reins on your stud stallion."

H: You leave him out of it, Cy.
G: I wouldn't want him along anyway. To-
       night?
H: Sure, and if I don't show up, start without
       me.

15 MARCH 1989

With the curtains open, lights from the city came in and almost flickered in the dark room like candlelight. But the city wasn't very noisy, maybe a distant tinny radio down the hall. Sometimes a booming car stereo from down on the street, like a heartbeat going by. Garth was on his back and I was touching his cock with the tip of a single finger, like I'd done to his fingers earlier in the restaurant. Then he turned onto his side, facing me, and pushed me to my back. He said, "Now it's my turn to tell you a story.

"It was a long time ago," he said. "I was single. I was at a woman's house. She had a friend over too. I'd never touched either of them." His hand was making slow circles on my stomach. My eyes were closed. "Friends," he said. "One had been a roommate . . . of a woman I dated. But . . . we didn't know each other real well. Like . . . I think . . . we'd run into each other somewhere . . . in a bank, a store, and decided, Let's get together. That's all." He pulled my hand from where it was wedged between us, lay my hand on my stomach, traced around my fingers with one of his fingers. I could feel the outline of a hand drawn on my stomach. At the same time I could feel his finger running along the edges of all my fingers. "I didn't know anything about her," he went on. "Or her friend. I'd met her friend a few times before too. We smoked a little. But only a little. For some reason . . . I couldn't go home. Car wouldn't start? I don't know why." He started to run his hand up and down my arm, from wrist to shoulder, slowly. I didn't move. "She only had one bed. Not a double bed. A twin. All three of us fit . . . if we lay on our sides. All facing the same direction. I didn't know anything . . . about these girls. I was in the middle. I reached behind myself . . . took that woman's hand." His hand slid down my arm a final time and lay on top of my hand which was still flat and palm-down on my stomach. He put his fingers in between each of mine. "I brought her hand over me . . ." he said, "our fingers threaded together . . . my hand on top of hers . . . brought her hand over to the woman in front of me. Stroked her breast. Both of our fingers were touching the other woman's breast." He moved our hands together in slow circles on my stomach. Again simultaneously: my skin felt a hand stroking it, and my hand felt itself being sandwiched between my stomach and his palm. "The woman in front," he said, "couldn't tell it was both of us touching her. But then . . . all three of us turned over. I did the same thing. Took the hand of the woman behind me. Threaded our hands together. Reached over to the woman in front. Stroked her breast. But by that time . . . the woman we were touching . . . *she* knew it was both of us touching her . . . because of what I'd done with *her* hand . . . when she was the one behind me. And the woman who'd been touched first . . . by then she *also* knew . . . that when she'd been in front and was stroked . . . it had been me and the other woman *together,* she knew . . . just like she was doing then." He slid my hand, still threaded with his, down into my underwear. "And neither woman pulled away. Neither made a move to stop anything. And none of us said anything. Never acknowledged what we were doing." His fingers were no longer threaded with mine, but his hand still on top. He moved my hand back and forth a little, side to side. "None of us . . . ever mentioned that after a while we *all* realized what was happening . . ." One of his fingers pushed my middle finger into me. I made a sound, and he sort of breathed with a voice in his throat. With the slightest of movements, he was nudging my hand, sliding my finger in and out . . . then suddenly our two fingers went into me together . . . like we were holding hands . . . "That's all that happened that night," he said.

And I think he and I didn't do anything else that night either. I didn't say anything until he got up at 11:30 and I said, "I wish you didn't have to go."

"I know," he said. "Sometimes you put me in a state of . . . I don't know . . . I'm so turned on, but also . . . so comfortable, I just want it to go on forever." That word again.

He sat on the bed beside me for a while, fully dressed, ready to go, then said, "You're so open and strong, but you look so vulnerable lying there . . ." He found his wallet and watch on the nightstand, said goodnight, barely a whisper, and left.

Because of the grass, he hadn't been able to talk in long sentences. And that'll always be how I remember it: those fragments with long spaces in between, hoarsely whispered, words that lay under the surface of what we were doing as he spoke. And I won't remember his story without our movements being part of it—maybe the most important part of his story was how he told more of it without words, and how I listened with my body.

December 19, 1979

Yes, I overheard something. I wasn't listening, I was thinking about something else. Or *was* I listening? I must've been.

K: Maybe I have to be more careful than you do.

H: You think I have something on him? How do you know he doesn't have something on me too?

K: I don't want to hear any more about that.

H: Okay, Mr. Careful. Hey, does he have something on *you* too?

I must've been looking at them. When his eyes hit— wham!—then I was part of it. I knew why I had to help him, or he had to help me, carry some tapes back to the library.

"Uh, I don't know why I should have to tell you. I don't like rumors floating around, especially true ones, because when people ask me, I don't like to lie. You know what I'm talking about?"

"Yeah." I was carrying most of the tapes, reel-to-reels in flimsy boxes.

"I don't like people to ask me what I'm doing with my life before *I* even know. Know what I mean?"

"If rumors get out and people ask about them," I said, "why not just tell them it's a secret? Everyone all day is whispering secrets. What's one more secret more or less?"

"Just tell me what you heard."

"Why?"

"Because . . . just tell me."

"Okay, Cy's going to become program director soon and you're wondering who's going to get fired."

"Good." A sigh and smile, a huge smile, even a hand on my back for a second, saying, "Good, that's wrong, you *don't* know. Oh good. Thank you."

You're welcome—you're welcome—if I thought you were finally appreciating something worthwhile I did for you instead of being *glad* and relieved to think that I don't know your secrets. Yet I can still be such a big help, can't I? We need a jingle. We need a skit. We need a running drama for a few days. I need my checkbook—it's in my car, okay? Coffee ready? Did you bring me a newspaper? Tell me where the nearest gas station is—I'm on empty. Tell me how many minutes short we are. Tell me what was flat in the show today. Tell me when you'll have these letters done. Tell me everything you think you know about me . . . *Good*, oh good, you only know the *wrong* things. Oh good good good. *Thank you.*

How about thanking me for knowing *this*: When you didn't come back with me after taking the tapes to the library—when, instead, you turned off to go straight to your car—I came back and heard Golden on the phone:

"Read me his contract again. It say anything about guaranteeing six days a week on the air? . . . We'll have to start renegotiating a new one soon, right?"

Now where do I run with what I know?

DECEMBER 27, 1979

I must be sick. To wait until everyone was gone, then pick this thing out of the trash. I *felt* it, sitting there while Golden paced back and forth, talking on the phone, and I suddenly kicked the trash can so the diaphragm would fall beneath the loosely crumpled papers, which made Golden stare at me while he said to the phone, "You can't schedule it any *sooner?*"

I said I had tons to do and stayed behind when he left.

Her show was doing an uninterrupted thirty minutes of music, even though halfway through she has to come back on and remind everyone it's an uninterrupted thirty minutes. We heard her say, "Let's start this half-hour set with a little bit of Elton," then within minutes she was in our conference room changing her stuff from her old purse to a new one. We'd been in the middle of something—planning the characters' New Year's resolutions and psychic's predictions (*Dallas* and *Dukes of Hazard* would do a joint two-hour show starring Billy Carter). She said, "Let me know when you hear the Doobie Brothers, that's my cue to get back. Right after Cher." Golden wasn't even here. I suppose it wouldn't even have mattered if we were right in the middle of the best idea I'll ever have—Kyle and I were both struck dumb, as though it was obviously more important to listen to Haley talking about an encounter with an "ex" and how she wanted to prove he had no power over her, couldn't intimidate her or make her feel bad in any way. Kyle pointed out that if she wanted to "act as if" she were not intimidated, or if she planned her behavior so as to *show* him or prove anything . . . then he still *did* intimidate her. She looked at him for a moment, then chuckled, looked into her old purse and said, "But he *doesn't*."

Kyle didn't say anything more . . . he and I were watching her change purses. She looked at each little thing, even explained some of them to him, like a horseshoe nail she found at the bottom, and black nail polish which she left out on the table, saying, "I wonder if I'll need *this* again." Then the diaphragm, without a case, just loose in her purse. "God, I must've been in a hurry!" She had to throw it away twice because the first time she tossed it into the trash it bounced off the rim. The second time, it just sort of balanced on top of the wadded papers.

She said to Kyle, "Pills are so much easier, but look what they do to your boobs."

He said, "They haven't done anything to *my* boobs."

Maybe without the pill it was easier for her to ride a bucking horse, but, of course, she got pregnant.

Kyle had the black nail polish and was dripping it down the outside of his coffee cup. She said that was a better use for it—she'd had to wear it on fingers and toes once. "And black lipstick too," she said, smiling a smile she would probably only use while wearing black lipstick.

K: When?
H: You know.
K: What d'you mean you *had* to?
H: They wanted me to.

K: I don't want to hear any more.

H: Yeah, I know.

K: Why d'you wonder if you'll need it again?

H: You don't want to hear about it, remember?

K: Did you do it *again*? Or are you going to?

H: Do you want to hear about it or not?

K: No.

He left! He suddenly had somewhere to go. She put the nail polish in her purse and said, "Didn't think so." Golden came in, looked at her—I willed him to keep his eyes off the trash—then looked back out the door. He must've just passed Kyle. I muttered "Doobies," and she bolted for the door without a word of thanks.

A little later . . . not much later . . . I was dizzzzy . . . My eyes were closed and my cheek was on the table. Kyle came in and accidentally kicked the table leg, my head bounced, I sat up, eyes still closed, still spinning. My chin fell toward my chest. I wanted to put my hands over my face but couldn't seem to will my arms to move. He sounded almost angry: "You've been so worn out lately, so dragged-out or something . . . have you been getting enough sleep?"

"I thought so." Sleep eight or nine hours and wake up tired. Fight all night, hand-to-hand combat, by myself, wake up exhausted, beat up, bruised.

His voice changed, less hard-edged: "Do you eat enough?"

"Yes." You mean including my fingernails?

"Do you drink enough?" His voice even more quiet and solemn. I looked at him. No laugh lines, of course. Just bluish-grayish eyes which didn't turn away.

"Nothing stronger than water."

"Why don't you see a doctor, have him check you for mono or anemia . . ."

"Oh god . . ." I think I was laughing, or trying to. "I don't have any of those." The laugh joggled me and brought back the dizzy spin, and, Kyle, you looked away, and we both sat there breathing. You didn't even look up when Haley came back on at the end of her set saying she'd get some hoppin' tunes out next so everyone could dance off their holiday pounds. She said, "Clear a space in the center of your office and let's get *down*."

But we didn't move. He was sort of smiling, I think. I had to shut my eyes again. I thought of being sick tomorrow and not coming in, but then I'd miss . . . *every*thing. What would I miss? I don't know what we were waiting for. I still knew exactly where the trash can was, even with my eyes shut. Golden put the phone down: "How d'you like this—I can't get a hold of Shelby because he's with his analyst."

Opened my eyes enough to see the phony wood grain on the table move back and forth. "Maybe that's what we all need, analysts." *My* voice.

First I only heard Kyle say, "I thought you were mine," then I looked up further and saw him pointing to this notebook, except it was closed, and I know he's never read it. I slid it into my lap and said, "I thought *you* were *mine*."

LATER

Haley, I've had to make a decision. It wasn't easy. Actually, once I realized I had to do it, it wasn't a matter of easy or difficult but just . . . *obvious*. I'm sorry it sounds so coldblooded. I don't want it to sound that way. Well, yes I do. I want it to sound that way to *me*, but not to you. Even though you wouldn't care. You might wrinkle your nose and say "huh?" But here's the thing—I have to bail out. I just can't go on caring . . . or trying *not* to care . . . about a life . . . *your* life . . . which hasn't ever actually bisected mine. And I don't know how to *make* it do that. Can anything I do affect you? I don't know. I don't know. All sorts of thoughts and ideas and plans come to mind . . . but. . . . Am I a coward? Probably. But at least I know you won't think that of me. Unfortunately your not thinking me a coward won't be because you understand and agree with what's best for me. It's just that you wouldn't know whether to call me a coward or hero or gutless or confident or smart or shallow. You just don't *know*. Well, now you don't have to know. Hey, the pressure's off, okay? If I'd made the move to get rid of either Marcus or Libby, which one would it have been? I don't know. The point being, Haley, that one of us has to go . . . and I don't think it's going to be me. We both probably knew there was one of us too many, so now no more wondering who'll bow out. It's going to be you. I'm sorry, but we're just going to have to say goodbye.

17 MARCH 1989

Half the time I'm not sure what I was talking about in this notebook, but Kyle, I can remember you and Haley conversing quietly, the way your face looked, often slammed shut or open wide, nothing in between, when you said these things I recorded . . . I remember your laugh, the tension always in the air if Golden was in the room, the tension that lingered if either of us thought or spoke of him when he *wasn't* there. And a different sort of anxiety when Haley was there. The sound of your voice, the glint in your deep-set eyes, the curve of your eyebrows . . . those I can easily remember. . . . But *now* I'm also remembering how worried I was that you were planning to leave the station. Naturally it wouldn't be the first thing in my memory, because if I didn't remember anything else, I'd still know that Haley was gone first, then me, and then you ended up being the only one who stayed . . .

So . . . it says here that *I* decided Haley would have to leave, and then she did. How did I get my wish? A little nervous about the answer. Since leaving KIAM, Kyle, and certainly since leaving Alex, I *have* been driven to have a more and more convincingly successful résumé . . . but I've never stabbed any backs. If *that* was how I am, what kind of sleazy thing might I be doing here to get an anchor position in this major market—the girl who has Garth's cock by night and his ear by day? Everything I've gotten, Kyle, I've *deserved.* That's why they do want me back in Redding after a six-month hiatus—certainly long enough for most viewers to forget they watched the news to watch *me.* And I will go back . . . I've no thoughts of moving my life back here. . . this isn't where Garth lives either. Not that where he goes determines *my* course . . . but . . . he's not just a rubber raft to hang onto while I'm here. Not a mirage. *If* he decided not to go back to Chicago . . . well, certain decisions like that can wait a while. Roads are open to me. And to him. I hope he realizes that.

Garth's not satisfied with what he's doing at the station. He says he feels rushed and it's slowing him down further. He thinks he needs more human-interest shit, and wanted to try a lame idea called "What's Your Story?" People are supposed to send in their stories and someone picks out the promising ones, then the person tells his own story on camera. Even without a subcontract, I let Garth do a test tape last night, using me as the average Jane who has a story to tell. He said, "I don't see it actually *working*—but maybe I just want an excuse to hear more about *you.*"

Garth decided we should go over to the house where that party was several weeks ago, the one with the real thick carpet.

The woman who lives there is a news writer . . . she let us use it while she wasn't home. Garth wanted me sitting on the floor leaning against one of the off-white sofas.

I thought I should act as though I was nervous, but he said, "Don't go out of your way," then kept saying, "You're so natural, this isn't how a regular person would speak to a camera, you're too good at this."

"It's my job, Garth," I said.

I have always been good at it, being on the air. That part was never hard work. Put on your makeup. Your hair is fixed. The clothes are right. The light flashes, the finger points. There you are, on hundreds of TV screens. Tonight with Garth, no difference, the easy confidence yet respectable seriousness. The criticism against me has always been "too intense," "not folksy enough," but here's how I've always seen it: I don't talk on the air to make people listen to me, I'm talking *because* they're listening.

The Grand Canyon story, watered down, was exactly the kind they'd want in a spot like this. Lib and I signed up to go to the Grand Canyon with a Christian club—we weren't members—so we could protest the commercial treatment of the canyon. Did we hope for news cameras or reporters? Did we know that without publicity a protest is almost meaningless? It was her idea, her plan, I tried not to think too much, too far ahead. I snuffed out all other thoughts every night with a pill. When my mother drove us to the bus, she said, "Are you sure you've brought the right clothes?" Obviously my mother wasn't aware that I *always* had the right clothes. And what started out as a little chameleon act is now my trademark artform. Lib and I wore our identical navy storm coats and black knit hats like longshoremen. The girls in the Christian club were in pastel ski jackets, white jeans, or even pantsuits.

Lib and I waved and went to claim a whole seat each on the back of the bus to keep the pastel girls away from us. The plan was to steal as many of the natural items in the gift shops as we could, stuff they'd taken out of the canyon and glued to boards or cardboard or painted "Greetings From the Grand Canyon" on, and we were going to stand on the rim and throw them all back down into the canyon. Who'd have thought Grand Canyon Village would have a plainclothesman security guard? We'd only started, petrified rocks, a few arrowheads from a bin. He let us walk out the door and into the parking lot, then said, "Excuse me," polite as you please, "could I see your receipts?"

"For what?" Lib said, her voice strangely high.

"The souvenirs you put in your bags," he said.

"We don't have any souvenirs," she said, and her voice leveled off again, each word clearly enunciated, a little clipped. She looked directly at him. Her eyes were flat brown.

"May I look inside your bags?" he said.

"Don't you believe me?"

The problem was that my hands were in my pockets, clutching a bunch of arrowheads. And it was like I wasn't listening to Libby. My throat had closed off and my armpits were wet, and I knew if I took my hands out of my pockets they'd be shaking. If I tried to answer like Lib was doing, there'd be no voice. Maybe a squeak. So when he turned toward me and said, "What about the things you put into your pockets?" there were my grubby damp palms holding out the arrowheads, which even glistened a little with my sweat. He said, "Come with me, please," and took my arm. I didn't notice Libby marching along beside us until all three of us went through the door of the gift shop, then into a back room, and Lib banged the stuff from her bag down on a desk. I could barely look at her. We sat side by side on a wooden bench against the wall while the guy tried to find out where our group was staying and if there was an "adult" along.

I paused in telling my story, looked a long time into the camera, my mouth sort of slightly open, and Garth instinctively stopped taping, put the camera down on the rug, didn't say anything, just sat down in front of me where the camera had been, his knees pulled up and his arms wrapped around them, knowing, somehow, that the TV part of the story was over, but that there was more story to tell.

I hadn't even been able to lift my head from my chest, not even after the security guard said, now far less polite, "How many other things have you stolen from us?"

Lib answered, "Nothing you haven't stolen from the natural landscape." There was no waver of tears in her voice, no fear, no surrender. But my whole body was sobbing. I fell forward until my forehead was on my knees. And my mind kept repeating the same phrase over and over in the rhythm that bawling makes. *Not*: I've been arrested, I've been arrested . . . but: *I'm not like her after all, I'm not like her, I'm not like her at all.* So when she put her arm around me and muttered, "It's okay," I cried even harder. It was the same voice she used on old people in a rest home we'd visited, *not* the way she'd ever spoken to me while discussing equal-pay-for-equal-work or the significance of Hemingway's Brett wearing a man's hat. She stroked my hair, and when I sat up, she wiped tears from my cheeks, took my hand, and practically led me out the door . . . I never even heard how we'd managed to get off with only a warning. Somehow she'd worked that out. We went back to our room where the group was staying in a motel before camping for a few nights in the canyon . . . but she went out again, alone, and didn't come back until later in the evening after dinner. I didn't go eat. She said she'd done it—had gotten some things and thrown them back into the canyon.

She'd done it . . . while I lay on a motel bed in my pea coat, holding my longshoreman's hat in one hand. It was a two-sleeping-pill night. But it wasn't the end. Yet.

JANUARY 3, 1980

As soon as Golden was gone, she dashed to the restroom to change and I was still here when she brought back these clothes, draped them over a chair, and said, "Let's go!"

It seemed to take Golden forever to leave today, didn't it? He drank the coffeepot dry. He wanted to have one of those conversations where you remember every movie you've ever seen. Haley sort of kept sitting there tapping her foot, smiling but looking off somewhere, nowhere in particular. Kyle just said, "Yeah, I saw that," or "That was a good one." Golden couldn't wait to see Brooke Shields naked in *Blue Lagoon.* Haley snickered and coughed. It's not going to be a blue lagoon for them today—probably cold and choppy out there, the water will be muddy gray-green.

I *do* understand why you didn't want Golden to know you're going sailing, but it's not as though he's being left out of an important ass-kissing trip on Adcock's yacht. Just some old baseball friend. Haley asked: "Think he'll have any grass?" You said it would be more polite to supply it yourselves. She said she didn't have any with her and you said, "That's that, then, we should've thought of it sooner." But she added: "Well, maybe he'll have some."

Haley will probably forget about the cream-colored three-piece suit she left here, still on the chair beside me. The jacket is lined. There's a pale hair on the collar. She tried to dye the tips of her hair to match what was growing out, but it looks just a little faded, sort of windblown dry. Sometimes she wears a hat with a brim. I have one like that too, which I hardly ever wear . . . haven't worn at all since I started working here . . . but it *would* match this suit of hers. . . . Do I have any shoes to go with it? I've always liked these man-style three-piece suits. Maybe I should take it to the cleaner for her, the cuffs and collar are a little dirty. She won't remember where she left it if she gets stoned today. I'll surprise her.

January 4, 1980

God, Haley, I did it . . . I'm still dressed in your suit, most of it, your pants and blouse and vest, *my* hat, my socks, shoes and underwear . . . the only way for us to be together . . . in a mixed outfit . . . but, Haley, it had to be my last night with you. First and last. Hello and goodbye. And the penthouse was the most logical place. I know you went there once, with a friend, you said, an admirer — or two. Hey, it didn't have to happen this way . . . why didn't you see I also *could've* been a friend who brought you there — just to talk, to share secrets and be with each other. You couldn't see it. Or wouldn't. So last night was the end for you . . .

Last night . . . in the cool dark . . . Why need light, why want light, to count how many people were there with me? There was no one with me. Nice way to say goodbye. To tell secrets that mean goodbye. Did I tell you about Lib? The lining of your suit is silk. My wet hand inside the leg of the empty pants, steam rising from the bubbles, I knew it was silk. Strong smell of steamy booze. I couldn't get the bottle from the bottom, under the whirlpool of water. Left it there. I'm trying to remember, but this is all I'm remembering, and you won't be able to help.

But at last I told you about Lib. Didn't I? The exercise machine, black and silver, twisted metal. Cold air on my wet skin, all prickles and goosebumps, until I got your silk against me again. Perfume of a cowgirl. Your

blouse a good pillow. Sitting at the executive desk.
Kneeling in the chair, your sleeves wrapped around my
head, around my ears, face down, I thought I was telling you about Lib but it was only my voice repeating,
perfume of a cowgirl, perfume of a cowgirl. Lib wore no
scent. Once . . . one time . . . that one time she smelled
like clean, salty sand. Right now I smell of smoke. I was
going to say goodbye to Lib, to write a letter, but never
did, but won't have to now with you, Haley, it was *all*
goodbye last night, I knew it, you didn't have to know
it. You didn't even have to be there. It was shadowy,
and a puddle formed around my head on the desk like
a dark pool of blood, and a loud sound of boiling water.
Brandied steam. The chair like a bronc, my head and
shoulders bouncing against the back to make it buck.
Find a strong horse and we could've ridden double.
The horse whinnied. Screamed. The springs in the
chair? Me? No, I didn't cry. My throat is dry, hot and
sore. Was the weed rough? Did I laugh too much? Too
long. Too loud. Someone may've heard it. What did I
ever want from you that you couldn't give? A smile in
your weird-shaped eyes . . . a cracked laugh . . . a light
touch on my shoulder when you walk in the room. . . a
look of knowing conspiracy as you touch my foot with
yours under the table while they stare at your
breasts . . . the sound of your voice with a spark in it
saying my name . . . a quiet feeling that you're listening
while I tell you about Lib . . . your hands and long fingers in my hair while you suggest how I should cut
it . . .

There was a hand brushing my burning face. Over
and over. From my forehead down over my ear and
cheek, squeezing drops of water from my hair. Not
Lib's hand. She barely touched me. I was already on

my way to California, Lib didn't know where I was, couldn't console me for what I'd done . . . she didn't know where I was. Could've been *your* hand, Haley, also on your way to California after your baby dripped down your legs. Could've been your hand or my hand, your face or mine. . . . Fingers ran through my hair until it was dry, and I was dry, and just breathing. Nothing else.

EARLY HOURS OF 18 MARCH 1989

Wolf in sheeps's clothing . . . in cowgirl's clothing.

I think I had always hoped it had just been another halfway-lucid nightmare I thrashed through . . . I'm probably still stoned. . . . This afternoon after I read it for the first time . . . I left the journal sitting here, went across the park to Garth's place. And that's another story.

I almost wish I'd gone ahead and found you this morning, Kyle, when I was prowling around the radio side of the building. Garth had a bunch of meetings. So I went to the station and just walked up and down some halls. And if I'd found you, Kyle . . . then maybe it wouldn't be a strange surprise if I called you now at . . . what, two A.M.? What is it making me restless, unable to concentrate? If I called, if you answered, what would I tell you? The truth about why Haley lost her job? It was my fault. I know for sure now. Maybe instead, I'd tell you about Garth and me getting stoned at the beach, and what we talked about. As if that would explain anything.

God, no . . . I don't want to talk to you.

After lunch, Garth went home for a nap, then decided not to go back to the station. I got to his place about four-thirty or five. He'd just gotten out of the shower, his skin humid and warm, and I was a little sweaty from running across the park, so

we stuck together in bed. Suffice it to say I was a little agitated
from what I'd just read. At about seven we got dressed and went
to dinner. Do you realize how long it's taking to tap each sentence into the laptop? I'm afraid by the time I get to the middle
of a line, I'll forget where I was going. That's how it felt at the
beach, after dinner, when we smoked. Of course it should've
worn off by now . . . so I'm not really stoned. Just stunned. At
dinner he told me about the meetings that morning. Mulling
over new segments for the news, I think. I wasn't listening.
Probably nodding, saying "Uh-huh," and "Oh."

I thought he was going to come back to my place after dinner,
but he said he had a different idea . . . we went to the beach.
Even on a chilly night in March there are cars in the parking lot,
doors open, stereos jacked up, a knot of guys and a gutter full
of beer cans. But there was no one on the sand, and it was a low
tide . . . the water was way out there. It seemed the sand
stretched as far from the parking lot to the water as it did from
the pier to the jetty in the distance. And after we'd smoked for
a while, it felt like we were specks in the middle of nowhere, but
specks with the two loudest heartbeats I'd ever heard. I closed
my eyes and pictured vividly in my mind one of those police
body-outline shooting targets, and the target was me. And in
the middle of the target, where the heart would be, was a flashing strobe light. Each time the light flashed, a circle jumped out
of the center and began radiating outward, like animated pictures of radar, like ripples in a pond. When the radiating circles
reached the edges of the body cut-out, they bounced off the
edge and started back toward the middle. Of course, with a perfect circle radiating outward, certain parts of the outline will be
reached faster than others, so when it had already touched the
sides and bounced back toward the middle, it was still traveling
outward toward my feet and head. Meanwhile, every flash of
the strobe was sending another circle radiating outward. I felt

my pulse all over, my toes and fingers and tongue and gums—everywhere. I don't know how long I lay on the sand, my head on Garth's lap, watching the mishmash of radar bounce back and forth in the target body-outline. Finally Garth asked if I had something on my mind.

And even though I'd been concentrating on the image of myself as a police shooting target, I found myself saying, "I think I found that rape I told you about . . . in my journal, this afternoon. It sure could've been . . . the booze was there, and the hot tub, and. . . . Someone was raped, someone was *fucked.* But . . . it's like *I* was the rapist."

I couldn't hold myself still. I figured the best way would be to force myself to concentrate on putting words together, out loud, being coherent, staying on the trail of one story. But which story? Haley . . . the owner's penthouse . . . creeping home to bathe my slimy, aching body . . . the blue bite marks . . . the sound of the hot tub and clank of exercise equipment . . . it confused me, made such a racket and kaleidoscope of pictures in my head. I shouted, "Hey!" and Garth said, "Huh?"

"Oh," I said. "Okay. Okay . . ."

"What's okay?"

"I just remembered exactly how Lib asked me if I wanted to go to this dance club with her." I closed my eyes again, then opened them and looked up at the black sky, and I pictured Lib and me on the lawn at school, facing each other. I was reading from a book I had on my lap, bent over, my hair swung forward and closed around my face like curtains. Lib leaned in and used both hands to part my hair, so I looked up, and she was right there, her face looking in at me, as though I was inside something, a box or barrel. Her face filled the only window I had. She said, "Hey, I know this real bitchin' place we can go to tonight."

It was a dance club called Diablo's. It doesn't exist anymore. I looked in the phone book when I went back to Phoenix after leaving the hospital here, the first time in four years I'd been back to Phoenix. I wasn't going to go, just checking, but it wasn't in the phone book.

It had once been a house, but the neighborhood had changed, most of the houses had been torn down, but some were remodeled into other things, and near the end of the business district, just before the road dead-ended into a freeway, was Diablo's. It looked just like a house, people on the porch, smoking, laughing quietly, standing close together. It was dark and I couldn't see them. We went in and any resemblance to a quiet neighborhood house with a front porch was lost in the thumping music and spinning mirrored ball over a tiny dance floor where the living room had once been. One of the old bedrooms was now a pool room. The bathroom was still the bathroom, marked "Women" on the door. Lib said, "I didn't know if I should bring you in and let you see for yourself, or try to describe it to you, but I figured, hey, by now . . ."

"By now, what?"

She shrugged and smiled, drank from a bottled beer she'd bought at the bar that ran along one wall of the living room dance floor. There were booths built in along another wall, mostly filled with women in softball uniforms holding lithe girls in track shorts on their laps. Lib said, "They're not all like that . . . the lines are starting to blur." I nodded, not really knowing what she was talking about but not wanting to let her know that. She went out and danced.

If Lib had asked me to dance . . . I don't know what might've happened. I would've danced with her. Of course I would've. I'd felt I'd been walking a thin line since the Grand Canyon . . . I suspected she had other friends she saw when she said she was studying. I wasn't only trying to keep up with *her* anymore, I was keeping up with all the hip women with their shit together who I suspected she was meeting and forming bonds with while

I was at home listening to my mother suggest how good it would be for me to go away to school . . . and make new friends. Competing with phantoms . . . and here they all were, dancing at Diablo's. But she didn't ask me to dance. I held her beer for her while she disappeared into the undulating tangle of bodies and flashing lights.

The lights in the floor and ceiling, flashing in rhythm with the music, made the dancers look like jerking puppets or flickering shadows on a curtain. There were periodic whoops and shrieks, stomping feet, and sometimes all the girls would clear to the edges of the floor to let one couple put on a show: a lewd tango, bold modern jazz, even a waltz in Fred Astaire-Ginger Rogers style. During these, Lib would return to where I stood, take a few swallows of beer, and watch the dancers without saying anything over the head-splitting music.

When four softball players and their dates got up and left, Lib grabbed their table. She waved for me to come over. I sat across from her, holding her beer without realizing I still had it. It was probably her fourth or fifth beer. She reached for it and held onto the neck a few seconds before I let go. "You okay?" she asked.

"Yeah. Fine!" Said loudly enough to make sure the heartiness could be understood over the music. I was shredding a napkin into a fine pile of sawdust. Lib swept it up with one hand, wet from the beer bottle, used another napkin to wipe the shreds of paper from her palm. Then she started to laugh. It didn't sound like a laugh but was the same one I'd heard her use when we were comparing stories about Marcus: how he tried to cover his tracks or the time she'd read a book while he screwed her. . . . That laugh didn't sound happy, didn't sound light or lucky or glad. It was a laughter of serious business, a lawyer breaking a union, a politician reading his own lying propaganda, a used-car salesman getting rid of a lemon.

I followed Lib when she got up and left Diablo's, leaving her unfinished beer on the table. On the patio we both stopped and had some tokes. Then, with me still in her wake, she headed up the street in the opposite direction from her car. There were a few calls, low whistles, and laughter from the porch as we left, but I didn't understand any of them. Lib had stopped laughing. Her face had the same amused, slightly pursed look as it would right before she raised her hand and asked a probing but sarcastic question during a lecture or club meeting. We turned off the business street, walked a few blocks, a few more turns, and went into an apartment building. She had a key in one hand. "Dara loaned me the key to her place," Lib said, her voice level, the same voice she would use to say, "How was the test in poli sci?" I followed her inside.

She had another joint in her pocket. Sat on the floor, put the joint, a lighter, and roach clip on the rug in front of her, looked up at me. So I kneeled, facing her. "Let's cut the crap, Corinne," she said. Then she smiled. "We don't need Marcus. We've never needed him. He hasn't even been around for three months now, and we don't miss him. I only got a boyfriend in high school because the opportunity presented itself and I thought, hey, this must be what I'm supposed to want." She looked down at the joint, then reached across and took my hand. "Sound familiar?"

I thought I could suddenly hear the music from Diablo's, two or three blocks away, but realized it was my heartbeat. She took my wrist with her other hand, let go of my hand, then flattened her palm against mine, fingers lining up together. When she released my wrist, our hands stayed there, propped up against each other. London Bridge is falling. . . . We pulled away simultaneously. She picked up the joint, twisted the already tight ends, then put it down again. She brushed my hair away from where it had fallen around my face, tried to hook it behind my ear, but it was too fine and dropped forward again. She kissed me. My mouth didn't move or open. Hers was thin and cool.

"Boom, boom, boom," she said, because she had her hand on my side and could feel my heartbeat. As she drew away, her hand slid along my tit, her fingers sort of brushed my nipple, like it was an accident. She smiled, and although it was dark in that room, I could still see the simple sincerity on her face, the last expression I ever saw on her . . . because I got up, said I had to use the bathroom, and from there broke the screen in the window, climbed out, ran back to the business district, took a bus home, packed a suitcase, used my mother's car to get to the Greyhound terminal, and caught a red-eye to Los Angeles.

It had become cold on the beach. I got up and sat between Garth's legs, both of us facing water that we couldn't see. His chin was over the top of my head, his arms around me. When he put his hand inside my shirt, he said, "Ah," softly. Then, "Let's go to my place." It was already about the time he would've been leaving my room if we'd gone there after dinner.

As Garth fumbled to find the key to his door, I heard his phone ringing. We looked at each other. "Go ahead and get it," I said, and waited outside. In a minute he came back out.

"They'd already hung up."

"Call back," I said. We both knew there was no one else who would be calling him so late. "Go ahead, make the call. I'll go on a walk."

"You'll leave."

"Make the call, Garth. It's okay."

"Are you going to leave? Don't leave."

"I won't," I said, but until I said I wouldn't leave, I think that's what I'd intended to do. I know he calls her every day, but I've never been near by when it happens, except once, when I was in his office and the phone rang, and when he said "Well hello!" in an unusually high voice, I went out the door and went home. Later he'd thanked me for that but was worried that I was mad at him. He'd come to my door with a single white rose he'd picked up at the corner grocery store.

So I waited in front of the building. A combination of the street light and the porch light made it look like there were six or seven steps from the sidewalk to the door, but I only remembered two or three. I stepped down each, one at a time, then felt for the next one. After two steps, when I felt for the next one, it wasn't there. It still looked like the sidewalk was at least six inches lower than where I was standing. I kind of strolled down the sidewalk to the corner, looking for more things that weren't really as they appeared, feeling like I could get lost if I turned around enough times. Then I sat on a fire hydrant and imagined myself carried to the top of a geyser if the hydrant broke open. I could've gone home right then and slept without any trouble, but now look at me, three or four hours later and still wide awake, not stoned anymore, but my memory still seems to be. I heard Garth's footsteps come down the sidewalk, got off the hydrant, and went toward him. He put his arm around me and said, Looks like there's trouble on the homefront."

"What do you mean?"

"Well . . . she could tell I'd been smoking . . ."

"And you're not allowed to?"

"Smoking can mean other things. It pushes her panic buttons." We were in his room by then, sitting on the sofa. He said, "And obviously she knows how late it is."

"You're not allowed to stay out late? What if there was a party?"

"I hadn't told her there was a party tonight."

"What if there was one anyway and you just hadn't told her beforehand?"

"You don't understand, Erin," he said. My name sounded funny. "That's just as bad. It feeds her insecurity. She's been lonely and it seems like I'm not being supportive."

I got up then and he reached to pull me back, but I moved away too quickly. "You don't have to go," he said. I couldn't tell if his eyes were open.

"Please don't go."

"You don't want me here," I said.

"It'll be okay. I'll call her tomorrow and apologize. It's just that . . . she could also tell I was in a hurry to get off the phone but she wanted to have a regular conversation. She had a bad day and had been trying to get me all evening."

I stood there, then moved a little toward the door. He looked slack on the sofa, but he lunged and grabbed my arm, pulled me back, pulled me down so I was sitting beside him again. "You're right," I said. "I don't understand."

"Well . . ."

I sat up so I could look at him. He was still holding my arm. "Your life's not your own, is it?" I said.

He took a long breath and let it out. "No," he said, "it's not." His eyes were barely open. Then he squeezed them shut, stood up, and led me into the bedroom, undressed me slowly, making love to me as he took off my clothes. All with his eyes shut. And held me very tight afterwards.

He woke when I got up to get dressed. "It's okay," I whispered. "I'm leaving so you can call home in the morning and do whatever it is you have to do." The way he'd been sleeping, I knew I couldn't stay all night: his body jerking and sort of mumbling, and holding onto me, but in a different way . . . almost in fear. He opened his eyes again and said, "Come see me at the station tomorrow."

It's a few hours until dawn. There was no use trying to sleep when I got back from Garth's . . . and found my journal still open to January 4 . . . which I'd never really forgotten . . . I read it again, though. When you're straight, it's very difficult to understand your own stoned story, like a dream where you receive profound, moving, life-changing advice, but when you remember it wide awake, it's not only banal, it's gibberish. And I guess it's no better when you're stoned trying to remember a time you were stoned: it's like being twice as stoned. . . . Any moment of revelation, if there was one, is lost. Maybe there's no revelation to be had. No comfort to be had in any explanation. No way to say I didn't rape her and leave her for dead.

JANUARY 7, 1980

Her voice isn't coming over the radio. Halfway out of his sweater, he froze, looked at me. "Her car's in the lot."

"I know."

Since then neither of us has said anything. Golden out at some meeting. It's a weekend guy doing Haley's show. He hasn't said she's sick or anything. She's no more sick than I am. Some part of me still hears her somewhere. Or thinks it *ought* to. I think he feels the same way. He's listening. But there's only the humming air system and buzzing lights. He turned off the radio a few minutes ago. He taps his foot . . . three . . . four . . . five . . . then stops. My pencil scratches. Is he looking? Will he guess?

LATER

When Golden came back, we actually relaxed a little. That's backwards, but we're pretending . . . *relaxed* isn't the right word anyway. We're just not frozen mutes anymore, sitting here waiting, without knowing what we're waiting for. Did Kyle really choose *now* to ask Golden if they have any power over who advertises on the show? He thinks the jewelry ads are sexist, but since the ads are prerecorded and they don't have to listen, Golden doesn't see what the big deal is. Kyle and Haley had laughed about those ads—"Get her what every woman *really* wants, the ultimate gift for any woman." She had said, "Can you imagine if all your life's goals really started and ended with a diamond ring?"

"Or glamorous stick pin or elegant pendant," he added, using the sleazy voice of the guy from the ad. She bent forward and sort of lay laughing on the table. If I had a choice, I'd take that as my last memory of her. It was pretty and harmless. Golden thinks the ad is harmless.

G: Don't let anyone hear you say that, boy.

K: What?

G: Calling our sponsors sexist. They pay your salary.

K: My name is Warren.

G: Huh?

*Ass*hole. But, Kyle, if you really were serious about getting that ad off the air, you wouldn't have brought it up to *Golden.* Was it really something else you wanted to say? What are we all doing here, silently smoking in our corners?

MUCH LATER

If he hadn't given me that pill, whatever it was, I'd remember what happened. But then it might not have happened. Were he and I on his couch or Haley's couch? I know we weren't here. I drove in alone some time last night and woke up in the car this morning. He didn't want to *talk.* The reason he wanted me with him, even after we left Haley, wasn't so I could answer questions or listen or agree or add anything. Why else would he want me there except to listen to all the sounds far away and up close, knowing someone else was listening to the same sounds at the same time? Whatever it was I took, I certainly got a familiar result—it made me heavy, dull, slow, thick, asleep half the time. If what he wanted, at first, was simply two people feeling soft about Haley together . . . or if that's what he thinks he got . . . that's not exactly what happened.

It *isn't* possible he thought I was Haley. It was as though we watched her disappear together. So, no, we couldn't've still been at her apartment. It was on a couch somewhere. Then on the floor. It rained. It passed over. I remember wondering for a second if we were having an earthquake, a dull, rhythmic one. It was his heartbeat all around me, coming from every direction, and also thudding inside my head, and I didn't know which side of me he was actually on. Only where his hand was—the only part of either of us that said anything. Where was your head, Kyle? Beside me? But turned away.

I was staring at the ceiling. Once I may've turned to look for him . . . yes, I did, but the ceiling turned with me, then turned twice as fast. I had to shut my eyes. His hand knew where I was even if he didn't. Suddenly aware of my mouth open, barely breathing, could feel my upper teeth gently touching my lower lip. But I wasn't panting, and neither was he. How could your hands be there without you, Kyle? Was my body there without me too? But I couldn't stay away very long. Your hands would come and find me and bring me back. The same hands I've seen twirl a pen between fingers while you do Peter Pepper's voice, the fingers that held and dripped black nail polish on the table, the hands that push against each other, fingers tip-to-tip, stiff and spread, tense so the tendons stand out, forming a little cage between your palms as you wait for Golden to say his inevitable something-to-say. Those same hands . . . with me. Not a single finger, no pinching motions, never a fist . . . nothing but the open hand, flat palm and fingers moving up and over where I rise and fall, changing shape slightly to fit where it lingers. That's all I remember: a hand, large, dry, warm, and it knew me already, and anywhere I was it could find me. And knew what I wanted before I did.

There might've been an electrical storm in the mountains. Usually it scares me when the lightning is right overhead and thunder cracks the sky open. When lightning is farther away, thunder rolls in, soft-edged blurry booms. And lightning even farther away makes thunder just a deep pulse, easier to feel than hear. The lightning was somewhere very far away, so far away we couldn't've seen it even with our eyes open. But I could still see the thunder. We were the thunder. Gray light, your earthquake heartbeat, lingering swirls of smoke, muffled movements, my back arching up from the floor . . .

How'd we get there from way back when Haley came howling through the door into the conference room? She was holding her cream-colored jacket, sort of dragging it by one sleeve. It was crumpled and smelled boozy. I thought it was *her* smelling boozy, so did Golden, who said something about her taking a bath in it and later another comment about her new perfume. I couldn't understand her between screaming "Son-of-a-bitch bastard back-stabber" at Golden, wordless open-mouthed crying, and a succession of "No no no no," as she tried to scratch Golden's face with her nails and kick Kyle at the same time because he was trying to stop her from going after Golden. Then she crumpled up sobbing in a chair, leaning against Kyle's hip. Golden was sort of backed against a wall, his hands over his crotch, then he let go and slithered out of the room.

Kyle pushed the boozy jacket and her purse across the table to me, and we walked on either side of her out to his car where he had the pills and gave her one, sort of shoved it down her throat with one finger, took one himself, offered one to me. We sat three-across in the front seat, Haley in the middle, her head back over the seat, her eyes looking like they'd been put on her face crooked, the outside corners higher than the inside. She hardly blinked. I watched her breathe, my fingers feeling the silk lining inside one sleeve of her jacket, then I pushed it to the floor.

What did we do—drive around for hours? Stop to eat? Sleep in the car? Go straight to her place? Within hours or minutes I was digging around in her purse for her keys, and the two of them stumbled in behind me. She continued on into the living room while he found a bottle in the kitchen and looked for glasses. She was kneeling on the floor, looking down at her lap. He put a drink beside her on a glass coffee table. The clink of the drink on the glass was like a signal. She looked up and said, "Everything was going so well for me."

He said, "I know." That's all.

She said, "I wasn't careful enough, was I? Stopped kissing the right asses too soon? What went wrong?" She was crying.

"I don't know."

"They found my coat up there. There was some sort of wild party. They said the security guard saw me. How could he see me—weren't we out sailing . . . ? Somebody fucked me over. What *happened*?"

"Do you want me to find out for you?"

She slowly reached for the glass, took it, held it in both hands on her knees. "No."

"Here." He slid another pill across the table with one finger. It was like his hand could keep going away from his body forever. We didn't look at each other, he and I, until she sort of fell over sideways, and then just that once.

He said, "Let's put her to bed." And I followed them into her motel-furnished bedroom, plaid bedspread and matching curtains, one blond dresser with a mirror, a row of nail polish, a spectrum clear to red, but no black. When I turned toward the bed, his hands were unbuttoning her blouse, slowly, like each button was made of thin china and might snap in half in his fingers. He said, "She's sweating," but I never moved closer to help him. I had my back against the dresser. Her denim skirt buttoned all the way down the front, so he undid it and laid it open, and I thought he could keep unbuttoning or unzipping layers, opening them away from her, until there'd be nothing left lying there, just the empty skins. He had to peel her stockings off. A bottle of nail polish clinked onto its side. Another followed.

It was almost true, there wasn't much left of her, naked, in her underwear, fragile, almost transparent, blue veins on her stomach, shadows between her ribs, flaccid open mouth, sunken cheeks, brittle and bony and almost crippled-looking legs, as though asleep or stoned or unconscious, she couldn't be Haley anymore. It wasn't Haley. Haley was gone.

Still 18 March 1989

Kyle . . . even my dreams only *wondered* if something like that ever happened between us. I still don't remember it. I mean you and me, that night after we left Haley. This could've been about someone else.

I feel stupid and blank-eyed from lack of sleep. Only 8 A.M. now. Can't go see Garth yet—he might still be on the phone with his wife. Shouldn't I be elated right now, finally knowing you and I were together like that? I wish Garth were here. This could've even been a description of the first time *he* touched me.

JANUARY 8, 1980

Kyle's theory about what happened to Haley: Golden couldn't stand her rapport—that's what he calls it—with Kyle. "I have to be more careful," he keeps saying, but won't really explain. There's something I could explain to him, too. That it was me or her. One had to go.

When he first came in alone, I was here, having thought all night about how we would look at each other this morning—what would we see, what would we say and not say? But the first thing that happened between us was just a flash of smile, an ordinary smile, too quick to be anything else, and he took the phone off the desk, brought it to the conference table, sat there in front of it, staring at it, then his hands hovered above it, tense, like waiting to catch a butterfly, or casting a spell. He laughed, looked up, and said, "I know you won't think I'm going crazy."

He was expecting a valuable phone call. Or dreading it, if it came too late, he said. *Too late* meaning after Golden got here, because Golden has already said no solo gigs—together or not at all—and the call would be from his new agent with a gig, some big club holding a western regional convention.Then his comment about being careful. And:

K: My contacts with people here have to be . . . well not fun. Does that make sense?

Me: No.

K: It can't look like . . . You know, Corinne, it's just human nature for him not to want people to prefer someone else over him. So I have to be more careful not to let that happen.

Me: Oh.

So I guess we're going to act like it never happened.

LATER

It almost seemed appropriate, after Golden told us why Haley was fired, then he left . . . we sat here in stupid silence a while longer . . . I got up, I forget why, and he did too, and it was quick but I could spend forever watching it coming: he came toward me, grabbed the front of my jacket in both fists, shook me once, twice, then let go, seemed to laugh, got a cup of coffee, stood looking at the huge wall calendar marked with all the dates of stuff to do besides the show. His call never came. He had gone from that giddy highwire dance hovering over the phone . . . to pushed back in a chair staring at a magazine without turning pages, mouth getting tighter and tighter, the more Golden laughed about Haley.

Golden's version: Haley brought some "dude" up to the owner's penthouse office, broke in sometime Friday or Saturday night, had some sort of wild time—booze bottles broken in the hot tub, spilled everywhere, left her clothes there, crumbs of drugs and cigarette papers and ashes on the desk, a diaphragm used as an ashtray, hair everywhere, even a smear of blood . . . and I sat here with *my* blood pounding in my head. When Kyle finally said he didn't believe it, Golden said she was seen in the hall by one of the night janitors. But I didn't say anything. Except you know what? I laughed, a crazed giggle, when Kyle shook me, and wanted to say "Do it again!" Only harder next time.

STILL 18 MARCH 1989

Kyle, didn't you ever wonder why I seldom joined your deliberations when you mused aloud, wondering why Haley would do something like that? I probably had questions of my own . . .

like when was Golden going to notice that his key to the penthouse was missing. . . and what was it that made me wave to that night man when he called, "Yo, Haley!" down the hall. Maybe that's actually when I changed my name.

JANUARY 12, 1980

You said, "I'm so tired of trying to guess what people mean, what's underneath what they're saying."

But, Kyle, it's no secret why Golden wants to control what you do in contract negotiations. He calls it his seniority. But to Al, yesterday, he called it his "greater worth." You get a good contract—he can get a *better* one.

G: Let's sit down and discuss what changes you should seek.

You: Let me see what they offer first.

G: That's letting them push you around. Go for security. You should demand a clause tying you to me, all or nothing. We can sit down and work out the language.

You: All right.

That. . . that final weak "all right." That's what folded me in half. No, I also folded in half when you put your hand on my shoulder as you said goodbye and followed him out.

But if I were really taking Haley's place, I would've said something to shut Golden up . . . I would've had snapping green eyes and a way of slipping out the door that would've kept you from going with him.

JANUARY 16, 1980

The radio wasn't on, but a tune was running through my head. Elton John—the last song on their show

today, then I turned the radio off. But the song continued and continued, I don't even know the words. I was
tapping my foot and Golden said to cut it out, he was
trying to hear on long distance. If Kyle hadn't been
over near Golden, he'd never have seen the look he says
I shot. All I know is I looked, stopped tapping, let my
head thunk on the table, wrapped my arms around it,
one eye still looking out for a second, then closed my
lids. And didn't move. Golden on the phone: "Yeah,
Warren will show up, wave or something, then get
lost." I didn't realize how crunched up my muscles
were, my shoulders making a fist around my neck, until
he was gone and you were behind me, Kyle, taking my
heavy head in your hand and shaking it, not rough,
while you said I needed to be shaken.

"Yes I do," I said. "You're right, I do."

You said, "I know how you feel," then took your
hands away from my head, went around the table to the
far end, and we sat like rich people at dinner, a whole
roomful of table between us. "But you can't react that
way," you said.

"Because what happened to Haley could happen to
me too?"

"Because his request that he be able to hear on long
distance had nothing to do with you personally. It
wasn't an attack. But you *act* attacked."

"Your going sailing had nothing to do with him personally, but you can bet he was jealous. *He* attacked.
That's what happened."

"How do you know?"

"Good guess."

"Maybe she really did it."

"You *know* she didn't. But why didn't she fight
back?"

"I asked her that when she called before leaving town. She said, 'How can I fight? I never should've taken a job I had to fuck somebody to get.'" You sounded disappointed. I couldn't look at you.

"Why don't *you* feel fucked?" I said.

"That's too strong a word."

"Didn't you hear him? *He's* allowed to make solo appearances, but you're not—"

"I didn't want that gig. It's like an Elk's Club thing. Hunting, money, women, golf . . ."

"But he didn't *offer* it to you either. Wave and get lost. Would he wave and get lost at a gig so you could do it alone?"

"Why're you so upset?"

"Aren't you tired of being used? Just plain tired?"

"Sometimes being tired is good. A reward for working hard. Imagine a powerful colt nosing his way to the front at the wire: the jockey gets his win; the owner collects his purse, his congratulations; the trainer receives his trophy, his bonus, his week off in Tahiti. All the colt gets is tired. But maybe he's the happiest."

"This is different, though."

"Yes," you said, "this is different."

Then you slid your empty coffee cup back and forth between your hands, watching it, looked up at me, slid it toward me down the center of the table. It only came half way. I got up, took it, and brought you more coffee.

20 MARCH 1989

Now I'm trying to figure out if something's underneath what Garth's saying. He was so happy when I went into his office yesterday. He came toward me, held both my shoulders, grinning almost crazily, said everything was all right again at home, he was forgiven.

I said, "Did you have to *ask* for forgiveness?"

"Not really," he said. "She was tired and upset last night . . . and then insecure. She's okay now."

"Why?" I asked.

"Sometimes she feels more insecure than others. She read something in my voice last night that scared her. But this morning we were both . . . back to normal. It's forgotten."

I might've been more scared if he hadn't been pulling me down onto his lap in his desk chair. But he didn't lift my shirt or undo a button or reach underneath it. And he didn't kiss me.

We looked at each other a few moments. Suddenly he gripped both my arms. "I forgot to tell you why she called in the first place . . . besides just wanting to talk . . . she heard about a job opening up in Chicago, like this one but permanent."

In the car, driving to my place, he kept his hand on my leg like he always does. Then he said, "You won't be upset if I don't come in tonight, will you?"

I acted like it hadn't been a question, just a statement, and didn't move for a while. In a moment shut my eyes. Finally, I said "Why?"

"No real reason," he said. "Trying to avoid routine."

His hand was still on my leg, leaving only to shift gears, then to set the brake when he parked by the curb around the corner from my hotel. I started to open the door, but he said, "Wait a minute." I watched his fingers unbutton my shirt, then the top of his head blocked my view. He licked each of my nipples, then buttoned my shirt again, smiled and said, "There'll be other times. We've got lots of time."

We've got just about two months. And I can't sleep. Thought last night might just be an isolated incident of insomnia, so I didn't bother going to the drugstore for pills today. But I'm obviously not going to sleep again tonight.

JANUARY 19, 1980

Remember how you would make Haley say "Hi" and "Bye" to Golden first, or at least tried to get her to say it at all? Well, after you left yesterday, Al said to me, "I noticed *you* were the only one Kyle said goodbye to, the room was full of people and he said goodbye to you."

Full of people: Golden, His-Pal-Al, and a guy with a beer gut they were going to lunch with.

I was sitting down, elbows on the table, my hands over my ears, and I said, "I was?" The words sounded loud in my head, under my hands. I was smiling.

But it means Kyle's not being careful like he said. Like after my Peter-Pepper-Comes-Out-Of-The-Closet-To-Reveal-He's-Been-Raising-His-Out-Of-Wed-lock-Child-Himself story idea, he pretended to grumble, "I think this show needs a *male* writer. This stuff is getting too sensitive, it's making *me* too sensitive. On second thought, though, Corinne, maybe you're still okay—you don't wear skirts so you can probably get into a more butch frame of mind. Okay? We'll just call you *Cory* to make you remember to think *butch.*"

Boy, he got me. I was pissed, but in a sputtering, confused sort of way, and no words came out of me. The next thing I know I'm giggling and he's got my belt loop, jerking me across the room. "I just wanted to see the pressure build until your eyes popped!"

I rose for that bait, but you pulled it away and instead caught me with your bare hands.

JANUARY 22, 1980

So it was a smoke screen, Kyle ... if you're seen getting into a car with me, it wouldn't, *couldn't* mean you were going to a gig—is that it? But all of a sudden, afterward, you must've realized that if having me along would make it look like you weren't going to a gig . . . it *would* look like something else. Would we have stopped for a drink afterwards if you didn't have to give me the talk about how to act, remind me that being careful is being neutral, and that this appearance is not supposed to be a general topic of conversation at work?

"A secret, in other words," I said.

You: Everyone has secrets. It's okay.

Me: I know secrets are okay. But keeping a se-
         cret for you isn't being neutral.

You: Don't get technical. I'm asking you to do
         this for me.

Don't slight him. That's easy enough.

Oh . . . for your sake I should treat him as though I don't do things for your sake?

You put your hands across the top of your beer mug, then your chin down on your hands, eyes closed, said, "I don't know what I'm saying. You're not the problem. But it's too easy for you to *look* like the problem."

Me: What is the problem?

You: [*Smile*] You recognize that we have to keep
         secrets and ask what the problem is?

Me: The *real* problem.

With one of those laughs that's just escaping air, looking down, shaking your head, you said, "In ten words or less?"

Did you know the corners of your eyes actually go down but the laugh lines bring them up when you smile? You had most of that pitcher of beer. Said, "Don't you like beer, Corinne?"

"It's okay."

"I drink too much beer . . . and too much coffee. Maybe they neutralize each other."

"Neutrality is harder to get than you think."

"I know." Long drink. "I'm gonna buy a sail boat. I like it out there. Wind. Water. Sun. I go after the show two or three times a week. Rent a boat. Go out and think. If it's a rough day, lots of wind, high waves, there's no time to think. Just maneuver the boat. That's automatic. Physical."

He didn't ask me to join him sometime, to go not think with him out on a boat. I wonder if he goes out to not think about Haley. I could not think about Haley if I was with him. It should be able to work both ways.

23 MARCH, 1989

My room only has a shower—maybe that's what made him think of using his place: the bathtub. He had the tub running practically as soon as we walked in the door. Everything else sort of faded out . . . I just leaned back against him, almost all the way lying down, while he used his hand to make warm waves that came up my chest, lapped at my neck. He said he'd never made love in a hot tub—the warm water relaxed him too much. . . it was a place to be comfortable and lazy together, he said. He didn't elaborate on who the "together" meant, and I didn't ask. And he didn't have to say, "But this is different," because I could feel his erection under my shoulder.

I had put dish detergent from his kitchenette into the water while we'd run the bath. He scooped the bubbles up from down by our feet where most of them were piled, quietly hissing and popping, and he arranged them in the water over me like a white lace off-the-shoulder dress. Then with one hand he started to push the dress down, slowly, easing it down, stopping when it still barely covered my nipples, and with one finger reached under the bubbles to touch me until the movement of my hips washed the bubblebath dress completely away.

Garth's body heaved underneath me and he said, "Get up, I have to get out." When I started to get out too, he said, "No, you stay, I'm just starting to get too hot, that's all. Makes me dizzy." I lay back full length in the warm water, which was shallower without him in the tub. Garth said, "Roll over and get the front part of you warm." He was kneeling on the floor beside the tub, his hands still in the water. I rolled over and used my hands to hold my head up. My butt was cold, but the contrast of hot and cold felt good.

Garth's hand was underwater on the small of my back, moving down my spine, up out of the water and over my butt, almost between my legs, then he changed direction and his hand returned slowly over my butt, up my back. His hand made that slow trip back and forth, going farther each time. I can picture it now as though I was watching from the ceiling. At the time I had my eyes shut and thought of nothing but his hand, without realizing that the water was starting to slosh around because, like a cat, I was lifting my butt higher and higher as his hand passed over, his finger barely touching between my legs before going away again, following my spine back toward my shoulders, then turning around and coming back. I think my hips moving up and down were splashing water completely out of the tub. The whole floor was wet afterwards. Neither of us was saying anything, except I could hear him groan a little, with a hint of laugh mixed in, as my butt rose to meet his hand . . . and finally I was almost up on my knees, his finger went into me and I was the one moaning, more water splashing, my hair completely wet, my backside going up and down, his finger moving in and out.

We had to change the sheets later because I think we forgot to dry off with towels before getting in bed. He said, "I bet nobody imagined this when they joke about the wet spot in the bed." When we settled down to sleep, one of his arms and one leg over me, he said, "I took a bath last night and thought about you. I wanted to bring you home *last* night."

"Why didn't you?"

"I wanted it too late," he said. "You were already out of the car and gone."

"That'll teach you . . . decide faster."

"But it was good, just thinking about it, thinking about everything I wanted to do with you. There are still some things I can think of . . . but tonight was perfect, I'll remember it forever, rerun it in my head a million times, the sight of you on your stomach in the tub, the way you moved."

He was late going to the station this morning. The alarm went off at seven, but we'd already been awake maybe an hour before that, both of us fuzzy and drowsy, not bothering to open our eyes or say anything, moving very slowly, languid, like a Sunday morning with nothing else to do all day. It was eight when he finally said, "Good morning," and we both laughed.

"I like making love in the morning," he said. "Yesterday's hassles are forgotten and no new ones yet today."

I said, "All my hassles are forgotten no matter what time of day we do it."

"I know," he laughed, getting up. "I love the way you love it. You've got so much energy."

Is that why Erin Haley *exudes a grim sexiness . . . even while delivering the worst news?*

JANUARY 24, 1980

Wordlessly, but still not being careful, he hands me his coat . . . and I, just as silently, hang it on the hook behind my chair.

Golden watching. I don't care.

But when I asked if he'd done any shopping for his sailboat, he shook his head, not meaning, no, he hadn't shopped; meaning, don't bring it up. But Golden had already jumped in with stories about friends who'd bought boats, the hassles, the crooks, the problems getting a slip in a marina—you have to know someone, maybe he could help. Kyle sitting there listening. His eyes steady on Golden, except when Golden paused to sip coffee—Kyle flipped a glance at me. Just his eyes. Didn't turn his head. Telling me I'd betrayed him. His coffee cup was empty. So I got up and filled it. While I was putting the pot back on the hot plate, I heard him clear his throat. Took me a second to get it, but then I picked up the pot again and turned toward Golden. He just held out his cup and started talking about boat insurance. If Haley had poured his coffee, Golden would've patted her butt. Undoubtedly. Would Kyle glare if he patted mine? Or wait til we're alone and suggest I defend myself like Haley did? But Haley was fired, I'll say. I *should* say: We could protect each other, Kyle.

25 MARCH 1989

I'm never sure whether or not I'll see Garth on Sundays. So I wait for cues. How long have I been doing it . . . all along? But suddenly I felt myself doing it tonight when he brought me home and it was obvious he was not coming in . . . again. Motor still running, double parked in front of the hotel . . . I just sat there, then looked at him. He said "Thanks." I wanted to smile, to share in a split-second the memory of what we'd just done in a dark parking area off the freeway. But I didn't feel a smile on my face . . . I felt myself waiting. Yes, we'd just spent over twelve hours together, so why wasn't I ready to come alone into my room and lie in neon-tinted silence? I'm used to being alone. I'm not supposed to be afraid of *that*.

I took a pill. Supposedly in twenty minutes I'll be restfully sleeping. In twenty minutes I may need another pill. Is this what he calls my endless energy? There's nothing specific to keep me from sleeping. True, he didn't come in. But in the awkward moments before I got out of the car, he did finally say, "What'll you be doing tomorrow?" Was he afraid to come right out and say he wanted a break from me tomorrow because we'd seen so much of each other the past several days? So I thought before I answered and said, "I'll decide tomorrow." That's the mature, modern woman who only needs herself to be happy.

He closed his eyes, nodding, then opened his eyes again and said, "I'll be down at the station . . . if you're free . . . you can give me a call. . . . Or maybe you're wanting some down time."

"I'll want to see the tape." I hadn't been thinking about the stuff we shot today, but some part of my mind threw it up there for me to say. Perfect.

We looked at each other a few minutes more, but he didn't kiss me. He put his fingers in my hair, bounced his palm against the spiked ends, then said, once again, "Thanks."

We took the camera on a drive today . . . quit when it was dark and started home from Carlsbad. We'd taken little rural roads out of the city, the back way to North County, then used the freeway to get back downtown. Once he got into overdrive, Garth sighed, released the steering wheel with his right hand, put his arm around me and said, "Move over here." The car he's renting doesn't have bucket seats, so although there's a stickshift, I slid over, and his arm lay across my shoulders, elbow hooked on my neck, his hand reached down to my chest, feeling me through my shirt with his palm. The window fogged up and he had to put the defrost on. I wasn't drunk, hadn't taken a toke all day . . . but there on a freeway, not an empty one, I was feeling for my buttons, opening my shirt. . . . He said people passing us could see, but I said I didn't care, and he didn't stop touching me either. "They'll think about what they saw," he said softly.

Suddenly he pulled his hand away and started changing lanes, took an off ramp. I just lay there crushed against him. I had slumped so low I could hardly see out the windshield but could tell we were heading for the state beach parking area. He said he'd never done it in a car. "Another first," he said. Well, I'd been to the drive-in movies with Marcus in high school—cramped, sweaty, uncomfortable, unpleasant. Were cars different back then? Because there was nothing even remotely uncomfortable in Garth's car tonight. No straining to see my watch, to guess when the movie would be over at last, no kink in my neck, no feeling like I can't breathe . . . although I was panting, and my voice was gone, couldn't even yelp when, suddenly, Garth pulled me up from where I was crushed against the door. He sat back in his seat and drew me down onto him, looking up at me with his little eyes open as wide as they would go. So I rested my forehead against his, not taking my eyes off his, and just moved my hips. His eyes were up-close blurry. He opened his mouth and cried out, but kept his eyes glued on mine, a crazy wild-man look in them, which ebbed away as he calmed, his muscles sagged, his lids drooped but didn't close all the way. His eyes smiled weakly, then he pulled my face down beside his, ear-to-ear.

We stopped to get supper at McDonald's. They only gave him one card for their lottery contest. He said, "Can she have one too?" He was holding the tray with our food on it. The counter person looked over at me, seemed to stare for much longer than I'd expected. With one hand I checked to see if my pants were rebuttoned. She kept looking at me. Then she said, "Only one game piece per family."

"We're not a family," Garth said, smiling.

How long will two sleeping pills allow me to sleep in the morning?

JANUARY 26, 1980

I watched them do the show today. They sit in separate glass booths facing each other without ever looking up. I think Golden only came to one planning session all week, told us what he wanted. Changed a lot of it anyway. He didn't like the staff characters organizing a strike to protest Mrs. Olsen only getting paid half as much as anyone else. In fact he glared at me before wiping it out with a flat black felt pen. It got changed to a strike demanding brewed coffee instead of instant. I thought I heard Kyle sigh—he had to stay late to tape each of the characters at the protest march so that they sound like a crowd all talking at once. If I shut my eyes, it sounded great. But if I watched them—writing something, staring at the ceiling, winding a watch, looking back at me as though not knowing who I was—they were wooden and dull.

I'm not sure how much they've seen each other off the air. Yesterday Golden came in before Kyle, told me that Kyle should put more effort into getting some new ideas or new characters, and spend less time thinking about sailboats. Said Kyle's had people bailing him out, doing him favors his whole life. And he said, "Sure, he's a charming guy, why'd'ya think I wanted him for my partner? But that charisma isn't solid. There's nothing there for *you* when *you're* in trouble."

What does that mean?

26 MARCH 1989

I'm stuck with myself as company for dinner tonight—maybe I'll get a sandwich from the deli on the corner, maybe a half-dozen donuts and undo the ten years of aerobics that help keep me at the anchor desk. Garth will starve himself. Maybe he figures that's his penance when his spouse cries herself to sleep at night. If only crying worked . . . *I'd* give it a try. They could bottle crying for health-nut insomniacs, call it 100 percent natural, no added chemicals. But I don't know how *natural* it is to cry because you're alone. It depends on why you're alone, and even then . . . I'm alone now and not crying. But there's this "I want to go home" repeating itself in my pulse like a tune stuck in my mind. I remember being sick at scout camp one summer. I'd looked forward to camp for half a year—two weeks away from home, campfires, skits, hiking, horses . . . and they let you choose your "camp name," and everyone called you only by that name for two weeks. But all of a sudden I was sick and lying in the infirmary. . . . and all I thought, or moaned out loud was "I want to go home."

But now, am I thinking of *home* in Redding? Pine Bluff, Arkansas? Not likely. Maybe the apartment I had *here* when I worked at KIAM? What comfort did I ever find there? When I think about that era, I can't even picture myself *in* that apartment. I only see myself at the station in the conference room, half-asleep over the table, listening, listening, listening, waiting for you to talk to me, Kyle. Nobody but me was ever amazed at my capacity to come up with plenty of show skit ideas because no one knew how naturally the ideas came . . . it was just *being* there that was hard work. And, inexplicably, I couldn't wait to get back to work the next day. In my apartment, the rest of the time, the rest of my life, I could chalk up the hours of television to research.

I can't be longing for the home I left in Scottsdale, my mother's house, the home I moaned for while sick at camp . . . now remodeled, repainted, refloored, refurnished . . . and home to someone else. The last time I lived with my mother was after she came to the hospital in San Diego and brought me home to Arizona with a wired-shut jaw. For ten years my letters to her have been a series of weather reports and descriptions of the interesting stories I've covered. No stories about me. She knew I was married, but she never met Alex. She knows whenever I move to a new city; I send copies of my reviews, a videotape for Christmas. Interviewing people who've gone through big ordeals, I've heard so many of them say, "I just want my life to get back to normal." That's like "I want to go home," like Dorothy's Kansas and Scarlet's Tara. But do I have a *normal* to get back to? So when Garth says, "I'm not going to see you tonight," and I turn to leave . . . I feel I've been kicked out of something. But you can't be kicked out of your own life.

God, it's Sunday, nothing on television, the weekend news, which Garth says is the least of his worries at the station. Wanna-bes and has-beens reading intern-written copy. Hey— Garth just called from the sidewalk. He's on his way up.

LATER

I'm alone again now, but it doesn't seem to matter as much. We parted with the same "see you tomorrow" that he'd used in his office just a few hours earlier, but of course it was different this time. Why should it be different just because a man stands on the sidewalk and calls up to your window?

When I walked over to the station this morning, I'd called his office from a phone booth about a block away, so he was waiting at the back door closest to his office elevator, smiling, pulled me close during the ride, tried to mess up my gelled hair, didn't kiss me.

Then in his office I said I wanted to see what he'd done to our tape from yesterday. He said he hadn't touched it yet. He'd had a few other things to sort through, he said. In fact, the tape was still in his backpack where he'd put it yesterday. I turned on the VCR while he got the tape out . . . I said I could think of a few obvious things we should do right off the bat, like put all the fruit-and-vegetable signs together. Almost every fruit stand we'd passed had a misspelled hand-painted sign and they could easily go together, as though our narrator was out shopping and trying to figure out what was being sold, from the somewhat decipherable *cheery cider* and *cukumbers* and *letice,* all the way to *grin bins* and *seedles graps.* Some signs would have to stand by themselves, though, like the "busses" sign in front of the university. Garth had zoomed in on the misspelled sign, then backed up and raised the camera to the name of the university on the side of a building fifty yards away, a fat blur, then focused down on it. While we watched, I could visualize it done on the news with the flat voice-over narration, and I laughed. But Garth just watched, one hand over his mouth, his elbow on his desk. When the "Laddie's Dresses" sign came on, I imitated the voice-over saying, "And what is this, a store for transvestites?" Garth took his hand away from his mouth and smiled at me, but turned the TV off. He said, "I don't know about it, Erin."

"That's because you're looking for a breakthrough, Garth, and there isn't going to be one."

"I'm looking for something that'll show I didn't waste my time here, something that'll make my time here an era in my career, not just something I did because I was lucky enough to get the job and I needed the money."

I started rewinding the tape. "Sure this is thin, Garth. It's not an answer, but . . . it's . . . well, you know how when TV news first started it was only fifteen minutes long? Is there more news in the world now? No, there's still just about fifteen minutes of news. filling the rest of the hour barely takes a ninth grade education." Garth was watching the numbers on the VCR count backwards as the tape rewound. So I went on, a desperate monologue spilling out of me.

I wound down and shut up. Garth said, "I'm sorry. I know

I'm awful to be around when things aren't going smoothly. You can be thankful you don't live with me."

I ignored the last part. "What's not going smoothly?"

"I haven't accomplished anything."

"Sure you have—"

"Don't, Erin. I just get worse when someone tries to tell me everything they think I've done well. I'm sorry . . ." He took my hand. "See how awful I am?"

"What happened, Garth?" The blunt question jumped out of me almost the same instant it came to mind.

He was in his desk chair and I was sort of half sitting on the table that held the TV and VCR. He pushed his chair back a little. "Nothing, really. I called home this morning."

"You call home every day."

"Yes, but, some days . . . Kathryn said she was so lonesome and miserable last night, she cried herself to sleep."

This time my first brusque reaction didn't burst out of my mouth: *Oh puke!* Then I also wanted to say: Crying oneself to sleep is the corniest old manipulation line ever used.

He stood and pulled me to my feet, held me and said, "Thanks."

"For what?"

"For . . . I guess for caring about my frustration here."

We leaned back and looked at each other. "If you get hungry later, let me know." And I stepped back away from him, picked up my bag.

That's when he said it: "I'm not going to see you tonight."

My skin prickled with sweat. And I was suddenly tired—not sleepy, sort of weak, like I'd just given blood.

I said, "What color are your eyes?" and smiled, or tried to. I'm sure it didn't look much like a smile. So I let it drain off my face and just kept looking at his eyes, which were averted, staring at a spot on the floor near my feet. What color were they? There was a lump in my throat and a pulse in my palms. Was I scared?

Could I be strong and understanding and a coward at the same time? My voice was wooden when I said, "Well, in that case, maybe I'll see you tomorrow."

So why did he show up eventually anyway? Dinner was quieter than usual. After calling to my window, he came upstairs and said, "You still want to go for an early dinner?" I went, and we talked a little about the cultural differences between Southern California and Chicago. But there was a lot we didn't talk about also, one thing being that we both knew he hadn't changed his mind about not spending the evening with me. He held my hand across the table. He didn't change his mind.

28 MARCH 1989

Please, let's have a moratorium on talking about Kathryn, the doctor or x-ray tech or whatever who cries herself to sleep. She's been practically supporting him for ten years, but besides that, the few things he's mentioned, in passing, about her: She gave him barbells for Christmas. She said she could die happy the day she got her Bloomie's credit card. She has a daughter from a previous marriage who she hasn't seen in five years because of some sort of falling out.

It didn't start bugging me until recently. Every time one of these tidbits has come up in a conversation, Garth asks me something about Alex, as though he's trying to give me equal time, like: What did he get me for Valentine's Day or did he like to watch the news channel where I was a reporter? But I don't answer. I say I don't remember or I don't know.

Garth felt better today, stopped by this morning with two cups of coffee and two donuts. He's going to L.A. some time soon for the California broadcast awards presentation, then driving to Santa Barbara to do a workshop for a filmmaking class at UCSB. I've been thinking of asking him to take me along, but I haven't asked yet. Waiting for the right time, just like I'm still waiting for the best time to talk about a contract for any work I do for him.

JANUARY 30, 1980

What exactly am I doing wrong? It's just that when I heard the way Golden talked about you while you were home sick, as if you were avoiding responsibility, having the nerve to be sick and make him struggle through the show alone, I tried to say something in your defense.

G: There's starting to be too much undue allegiance being paid to the booth on the left. You tell him all ideas are to be okayed by *me* first.

That was how the whole thing had started—me giving him that promo blurb we'd worked up when he wasn't here.

G: I don't like it.

Me: Okay, we'll rewrite it.

G: No. Give it to me.

Me: But Mr. Kyle said—

G: Hey—I don't care who said what. I haven't been here fifteen years to listen to *your* arguments.

I ripped it out of the typewriter. If he was mad at you, he isn't anymore because I deflected it. Is that what you meant by protecting you? So okay, I guess I didn't stay neutral. I'm sorry.

I thought that when you called and asked me to meet you, you were anxious to hear everything. But first you were *dying* to tell me how you'd forgotten your watch, so you were trying to read the time from some guy's watch at the next table in the restaurant, staring sideways, straining. His wife noticed and gave you a dirty

look, so you had to stare even *more* sideways. Then later
when you got up to use the restroom, you noticed the
guy didn't have a hand on that arm where his watch
was.

We looked at each other, laughing helplessly. Then I
told you about Golden crawling all over my butt . . . and
you weren't laughing anymore. "Don't protect me, Corinne. Don't do that. It's the worst thing you could do.
Next time just tell him it's a misunderstanding, or you
just assumed, tell him . . . anything that doesn't involve
me."

I almost didn't tell you the rest, Golden's exchange
with Adcock. I took a mouthful of coffee and thought,
If I can swallow this I won't cry. Finally I asked if you
wanted to hear the rest:

Adcock: You wanted to talk to me about his contract?

G: What about my new carpet in here? What's
holding it up?

A: Isn't your partner more important than
some carpeting?

G: It's the principle.

You became quiet, turned and looked out at the rest
of the coffee shop, rubbed your hand over your mouth.
I could hear your beard. You hadn't shaved. You did
look a little sick.

But, goddammit, Kyle, I never expected you to say
you would make it your job to always discuss our ideas
with Golden and that maybe you *should* invite him to sit
in on your negotiations.

What? *What? WHAT?*

I think I just stared while my mind sputtered in
amazement. And I think he started to look sicker to
me—more worn down, beaten down, nothing left. I
think I looked at his hand curled on the table, I stared

at it like a wild-eyed maniac, almost wishing it would jump up and strangle me or grab a handful of my hair, pull my head across the table, twist my neck.

Tentatively, haltingly, I finally said, "Mr. Kyle, it seems to me you're . . . well, staying in step just to keep him happy. . . . Why?"

"I'm not."

"Then what do you call this?"

"I have to. For a while."

"*Why?*"

"Hey—who makes decisions, Corinne? Do you? Do you control the station? *Who do you make decisions for, Corinne?*"

By that time my face was down, almost resting on my coffee cup, which I clutched as if to keep me warm. It took all I had to raise my head and look at you. Wishing I were made of glass that could shatter and scatter on the floor. Also wishing I could glare right back at you. I think what I did was somewhere between the two.

You didn't start to talk again until after you started the push-pull: With one hand you took the handle of my coffee cup and began pulling it toward you, with your other hand you pushed your beer across the table to me. And you said, "Look—I have no ambition to move. I want to hold fast. Morning AM is what I want. In order to hold fast, I've got to . . . well, some things you won't understand. Someday, maybe Cy will move on and I'll have the morning show alone. That's just a maybe. I don't know."

Then he finished my coffee, made a face—too sweet for him.

It wasn't quite over. Out the door, his car closer than mine, he was two steps in front of me, turned, and said, "Try to have a nice evening."

"Are you kidding? I'll be busy hating myself for all my transgressions."

"Hey—let me do that for you. I'll take over and give you a little break. I've got a little Corinne doll and I'll stick pins in it."

His hand on my tense shoulder could've broken all my bones with one little squeeze. As I was saying, "I know I deserve it," he arm-locked my neck, crunching me, dragging me beside him by my head, rubbing my skull with his knuckles.

30 MARCH 1989

I'll bet Corinne Staub wouldn't—couldn't—do what I'm doing now. I mean, with Garth only having a limited time before . . . things change. Maybe I'm exactly opposite of you, Kyle: You waited and got what you wanted. I've got what I want, I can't wait around *now*. That's probably why yesterday I went ahead, eyes open and head uncovered, no camouflage, plunged in and asked him to take me along to L.A. and Santa Barbara.

His first response was a slow smile, not looking at me, then slowly lifting his eyes. If he'd *laughed* right away or smiled a smile that wanted to laugh, and looked at me immediately, I would've said I was just kidding, then quickly changed the subject. But he said, softly, "It would be fun, wouldn't it?"

"Maybe *my* station manager will be there," I said, "I could introduce you. Maybe he'd hire you for something like you're doing here. Except . . . he'd want to know what I was doing working for a station in San Diego when I'm supposed to be on personal leave!"

Garth didn't say anything but kept smiling, his eyes greener than usual. He was wearing a new green-and-black wool Pendleton.

"And even though it's in L.A.," I said, "it's like getting fresh air. Maybe we can come up with some new ideas."

"I have plenty of ideas for *you*." His eyes were sort of wild and sent a chill through me. We grinned very dirty smiles at each other. The lunch room was crowded and we were sharing our table with other people, so we got up before finishing our sandwiches and went back to his office. I felt boneless and giddy, flopped into his armchair while he checked his messages. Then he came to kneel on the floor in front of the chair. I said, "You have very green eyes with that shirt on. You wear too much red and blue." All I could see was the top of his head. He was leaning forward, rolling my T-shirt up very slowly.

"I love your T-shirts," he said. "You show right through. Not many women go without bras anymore. Maybe you'll start a trend all over again." He had the shirt rolled up far enough so my nipples were still covered, just barely. He put his fingers underneath and touched the tips. I was on fire. He lifted the shirt a little more, just far enough to give each side a quick suck, then suddenly yanked the shirt down. "I'll think about it," he said.

"About what," I groaned.

"The trip."

We both smiled again, but this time his eyes were far back in his head.

FEBRUARY 2, 1980

I want to know if this is the same thing that happened the last time, but I can't remember *this* time very well either. Did you say anything before it started? Did you just continue to talk about your new boat or about ideas for the show or tell me baseball stories? I only remember in pieces. I remember feeling like we were dancing, but sitting in a dark booth in a dark corner. Every time your hand slid into the neck of my sweater, across my shoulder, down my arm, I swayed forward, caught myself before I crumpled into a ball, before I slid bonelessly and soundlessly to the floor under the table, then rose again, and you withdrew your hand. Once your hand went into my loose neckband, down my arm, under my arm, touched my breast. I closed my eyes, let my head drop, like falling asleep in public when you catch your head before it falls off. . . . Was it just once? Or was it *never* and I only thought it happened . . . ?

Another piece I remember: standing somewhere. You behind me. Looking down. Our legs went down forever. Leaning back. Me leaning against you, you leaning against something else. Our legs stretched out in front. All the way to the ground. Your two feet on either side of mine. Way down there. I was staring at our feet. My knees buckled . . . I think . . . and you had to hold me up. How else did I stay standing?

I remember us walking together . . . maybe out to the parking lot . . . as we left the station? To the car as we left the restaurant? You unlocked the car door and opened it for me . . . I got in and you said, through the window, "You're welcome." Then went around to your side, got in and said, "Someone's going to have to teach you to say thank you. Maybe I'll have to teach you."

"Who's gonna teach you?"

Why'd I say it? What should he thank me for? Bringing him coffee? Going to his speaking gigs? Wearing a loose-necked sweater? Not talking about Haley?

Was it just *today* my mother called and told me: I should come back to Arizona? "The coast is clear by now," she said. *Jesus Christ.* Sometimes I still even look for Haley's car in the parking lot. Find myself listening

for light footsteps approaching our door. How *long* till
the coast is clear, mother?

But you snapped me out of it when you came in after
the show: "Did you wreck your car or something?"

"No, just my life."

"Oh, well, *that's* okay." Then: "Come here where I
can reach you." Slugged my arm, not too hard, your
other hand holding my shoulder. "When you get down
on yourself," you said, "you need someone to push you
around—make you tough."

What you were doing tonight could hardly be called
pushing.

3 APRIL 1989

I did get tough, Kyle. I thought. What else would you call it?
But am I losing it now? So quickly?

I guess Garth *wasn't* the first to make me feel that fold-in-half
helplessness. I thought only in dreams. . . . In dreams when I
seldom know who I'm with . . . until it turns out that sometimes, even in the dream, I only imagined the whole thing.
Maybe I thought I was remembering a dream if I ever remembered being with you, Kyle. But of all the seduction dreams I've
ever had or remembered, it's never been you. I've dreamed of
you—but not . . .

Look at me—the keys are slippery under my fingers, my shirt
is stuck to my back, I can't sit still. I've walked to the window
and back between practically every sentence. As though I'm
scared. But haven't any notion what I'm scared of. Scary that I
didn't remember. How could I not remember! If this happened
with you, Kyle . . . what came of it, why was it apparently isolated . . . ? How did it happen and nothing happened *next* . . . ?
Did something happen next and I don't remember that either?

Is that what I'm afraid of? Or maybe I'm afraid some of the other dreams I've remembered were real too: You sitting on my bed . . . you chasing me as I flew by simply flapping my arms . . . you leading the horse that stepped on my face, then disappearing after the kiss . . . Are you the one who beat me up? But how could you have touched me this way and then . . .

Oh God, Kyle, who is this person . . . who just used her beautifully capped teeth to rip three fingernails off, drawing blood . . . ? This person with enough energy to run ten miles but lacking the courage to do more than pace to the bed and back? This person whose heartbeat feels like a hiccup, whose eyelid is twitching, whose ears are humming . . . ? I'm not even the same person I was this afternoon in Garth's office, waiting for him to finish talking to those people who dropped in unannounced, two men and a woman, all in gray suits. I didn't listen. I found an old peppermint stick from that restaurant in the back pocket of my jeans, unwrapped it, and put it in my mouth while I idly looked over the program schedule on the wall. Garth was still talking by the time I'd sucked all the red off the candy. But a hotter sweetness snaked through me when he reached over my shoulder, took the candy, slid it into his own mouth, then back into mine and went back to the conversation on the other side of the room.

After they were gone, he said it would be okay if I still wanted to go on his trip with him. He said he needed to start staying at the station for the 11 o'clock news at least three days a week, so he was going home for a nap and a bowl of cereal. I offered to give him a back rub, he accepted, and he never did take the nap he'd intended. When he dropped me off on his way back to the station, he said I'd made him feel worlds better.

Is it going to rain?

My jaw hurts.

FEBRUARY 5, 1980

But nothing is different. He slid his coffee cup toward me. No different. No "How're you today?" as though today *is* different from other days, no "Sleep okay?" as though there might be a reason I'd sleep differently. Instead it's as though I imagined the whole thing. I thought he might touch my foot under the table — some sort of sign that it happened, that he remembers, that he doesn't regret it. Or was it such a nothing to him that there's nothing to regret . . . nothing to remember? *I* remembered . . . thought about what I thought I remembered . . . all weekend. I wondered if he'd maybe at least call. I thought about when he came in this morning how there'd be a look in his eye for a second when he saw me, like a blast of something that's both cold and hot. But . . . there was nothing different. I was distracted and didn't do anything, really. Rattled papers. Pretended to think. Watching him. Once he said, "What're you doing. Any ideas happening behind that blank stare?"

4 APRIL 1989

You didn't remember by the next work day, Kyle . . . I didn't remember ten years later. I wonder when I forgot. The day I was beat up? Even if you'd done something like apologize and said it would never happen again . . . I might've remembered. When I walked across the park this morning, I felt like some sort of zombie . . . . Is this just lack of sleep—these thudding things repeating in my head? Even with a pill, I only slept long enough last night to have a quick lucid double-layer dream, which is one of the other things I can't stop thinking about now, along with Garth's sudden backpedaling and my jaw, which still hurts—after the pill, I slept on it hard and ground my teeth . . . don't know where the night guard is . . .

I was going to describe the dream to Garth. Sometimes the only way to get rid of the heavy dream-feeling is to hear it in words in thin yellow air over a cup of coffee at a kitchen table. Most people probably don't remember their dreams—I probably don't remember *most* of mine—but the ones I *do* remember are heavy in my gut when I wake up, still feeling everything. . . . But why do I remember *dreams?* I've obviously forgotten real things I might've wanted to keep, but I seldom want to keep dreams. That's why to tell Garth last night's dream . . . to maybe hold his hand against my face as I tell it, would make my memory of the dream also become a memory of real time spent with Garth. To get rid of the way my heart's jerking like a plunger in a backed-up toilet when I think about the dream . . . which I never did tell Garth this morning.

That's not the only reason I had to see him: I wanted to see how he was. I wanted to see him think about touching me. I wanted to be the first thing he was able to smile at this morning. I wanted to *be* that wonderful person he tells me I am. I know which McDonald's he goes to get coffee and a biscuit. Why should I keep staring at the ceiling as though I'll finally fall asleep at 6:30 A.M.? So I got up, grabbed my coat, and cut through the park. Barely had enough strength to pull open one of the heavy glass doors and slide into the empty bench across from him. He did look up from his newspaper and smile. That much was okay. He had the paper open to the weather page, so I said, "My glass jaw says it's going to rain, so you don't need to read that."

"Where'd you get a glass jaw?" he asked.

"It got broken."

"How'd you break it?"

I paused. He didn't sound interested. He sounded tired. "It's a long story," I said, "better for another time. Didn't you sleep well either?"

"Once I got to bed I slept fine." He looked back down at the paper.

"I'll bet you look at what the weather is in Chicago every day."

He looked up, smiling again. Then he folded the paper, put it on the bench beside him, drooped his head over the table, and pushed his hands across the surface to find mine. He sighed, then opened his eyes, like a mole coming up from underground.

I said, "When're we leaving?"

"I don't know. I feel sort of funny about it." He kept looking me in the eye, but every time he blinked, his eyelids stayed closed much longer than an ordinary blink.

"About the trip?"

"About taking you along." He held my hands tighter. Maybe I did start to pull away when he said that. I don't know whether he held tighter first, or whether I started to pull away. "Erin . . ." he said in a coaxing voice, but it wasn't as if he was trying to get me to look at him. I'd never looked away. "I just said I felt funny. It's nothing final."

"Yesterday it was okay," I said, "today you feel funny. What happened?"

"Maybe nothing happened yesterday or today," he said, "but . . . you know in the cartoons, I always loved it when a character would be running along and come to a cliff and run off the cliff without even realizing it . . . he keeps running without falling. Then when he *does* realize he's off the cliff, *that's* when he gets scared."

"What're you scared of, Garth?"

"It's just an image I thought of . . . see how irrational I am?" He put the tip of my index finger against his mouth for a moment.

"But you still feel funny about the trip."

He had my hands clutched against his chest. My arms were awkwardly stretched across the table, I was leaning clumsily forward but the table was stopping me from falling. "Kathryn's been having a difficult time," he said. "Wondering where her daughter is . . ."

"After five years, she's suddenly wondering about her daughter now?"

"I guess stress brings everything back to the surface. When I called yesterday, she sounded so happy to hear from me . . . I just felt . . ."

"God, Garth."

He didn't say anything. He was holding my hands loosely enough, so I pulled them away. He drained his paper coffee cup. "Why d'you tell me stuff like that?" I said.

"I'm sorry. You're so comfortable to be with that I forget how often I muddle around and do or say the wrong thing . . . you're so easy to talk to, I go right ahead, plunge in and muddle."

"How much more comfortable do I have to be to make you not feel funny about taking me on a stupid two-day trip?"

"You see?" he said. "Don't try to make sense . . ."

He asked if I wanted to be dropped off at home or did I want to go to the station with him. I opted for home but arranged to meet him later.

So, Kyle, I don't have anything to do but sit here and tell last night's dream to myself: I was lucid, but my lucid self in this dream was, herself, dreaming. The inner dream was also a lucid dream. I was lying on Garth like on a life raft. That's what he felt like—firm and safe and wholly comfortable, but while I was dreaming it, a lucid voice said, "You're dreaming, and when you wake up, you'll still feel the pressure where you thought you were lying on him, you'll still feel him there but he won't be there because he never *was* there." And that's just what happened, I woke up from that dream but was really still dreaming, and sure enough I felt where I'd been lying on him but he wasn't there. The next part was not as lucid: A faceless man—not Garth, not you, Kyle, probably not anyone else either—and we'd already gotten past all the preliminaries without my noticing it, were already on the ground going at it. I was on my back. The man said, "I wish I could hold onto the ground and pull myself farther into you, I wish the ground had handles so I could do that." I could hear him say it to me . . . but then I could see it from his vintage point, *I* had the view from on top. And I knew what he meant. I *also* wanted to grab onto handles and pull everything closer. . . . Was I either one of those two people, or both? Asking the question woke me up. I lay awake and thought about you, Kyle. And Garth. Garth was the only recognizable person, besides myself, I guess, in any part of the dream. But I don't remember actually seeing him, just feeling him there, and the secure knowledge that it *was* him. Did he actually have to be there for me to feel that?

FEBRUARY 9, 1980

Something's been happening this week. Shouldn't I tell you? What about neutrality? Tuesday: Golden said he liked my outfit. I'd only worn it twenty or thirty times before. How many different shirts can I buy on this salary? That's not so strange, but coupled with "What do you *really* think about this Mrs-Olsen-Goes-Back-To-College skit? It's *his* idea, isn't it." Not a question—a demand.

Me: You wanted some new voices.
G: Let's us say we decided it was sexist and
          trash it.
Me: But—

G: C'mon, Corinne, you can't *like* this sorority
       rush crap . . . isn't it degrading? Were *you*
       ever rushed?

It would destroy his faith in sororities if I had been.

So he changed the skit. Shouldn't I tell you before
Monday or Tuesday when you expect to start the college skit, and it won't be there . . . ? Instead: his idea
about having a manicurist for the staff named Bubbles.

Then Wednesday, after you left, he told dumb-jock
jokes. He said you'd learned and practiced your ability
to do voices while sitting on the bench for some minor
league baseball team. He said, *"That's* this big talent
everyone's making such a fuss about."

Me: The ratings *are* good, aren't they?

He sort of looked at me, then changed the subject.

Then yesterday, during the news, he came out of the
studio to make a phone call, passed me and said, "This
is a piece of crap today. Too many days out on that
boat, not enough energy expended here."

I said, "He hasn't been on the boat since maybe last
weekend." I think.

He asked if I went with you. I mean on the boat, last
weekend. I said no. Then he said to tell you he's setting
up a meeting with Al and Adcock and you and him to
discuss the direction of the show, so don't plan any sailing afternoons next week.

Meanwhile, where've you been all week? Even when
you're here I want to ask, where are you?

LATER

I can never say everything I plan to say. Things go off
in new directions.

Me: Cy's been talking to me about you.

K: I don't want to hear it.

Me: But—
K: Let him tell me himself. If he really wanted
        me to hear, he would.
Me: Then why tell me?
K: You're a good target.
Me: But he wasn't angry, more like . . . trying to
        get me to commiserate with him about how
        you—
K: I don't want to hear it. He knows you'll tell
        me. That's the point. Just step out of the
        way and don't listen.
Me: It's too late now.
K: Corinne, sometimes it's right and expected
        to line up on one side or the other in a con-
        flict . . . but sometimes you don't help any-
        thing by doing so.
Me: But look where I am. I'm right in the middle.
K: You let it happen.
Me: No. How?
K: By letting it matter. Just do your job.

Then when I tried to say something else, don't even
remember what, he said, "This conversation is over."
And it really was. Wouldn't even meet my eyes when
the three of us talked about some skit ideas. The only
time he spoke, it was always to Golden. I wasn't there.
I was a tape recorder on pause and when they needed
to hear what I had to say, they released the pause button. A tape recorder can't line up on one side or the
other. An old battered tape recorder that stays in the
conference room—doesn't belong to anyone in particular, never gets taken home, to the park, out sailing,
never plays music. Unless, in a pinch, some lonely Friday night when you're thinking about Haley. . . . But
you wouldn't want to *admit* to it.

7 APRIL 1989

The last few times I've seen Garth, it's seemed as if I have to tell him something. But I don't. So I feel like I'm hiding something, keeping something back. But what is it I think I want to tell him—that something's happened to me between the times I saw him this past week? But, Kyle, what *did* happen to me?

It was ten years ago, but . . . you crossed the line, Kyle, then you tried to cross *back*. And I guess you succeeded. But left me whipping my head around, looking for you, wondering where you went so quickly, even while my adrenaline was still pumping.

So . . . looking for you all the time . . . wouldn't I have noticed if it was you who hit me?

FEBRUARY 12, 1980

Did you ever need proof that you're alive? I want to talk to you. But it's you I'm not alive to these days. You can't answer someone who's essentially dead, except for certain functions I perform, of which, as of yesterday, getting your coffee is not one. The only thing you said all day, all week? "I shouldn't be having you get coffee for me." That's the pinpoint moment when I was snuffed out.

10 APRIL 1989

What does it mean to feel *funny?* I know he's not just making excuses, not hiding anything, because a phony coverup might at least make sense. Bald lies would be easy for me to recognize. *Funny* is hard to call a lie. He looked pale and worn-out, even the corners of his eyes sagging, too tired to make up excuses. Unusual, but not unheard of, for him to come by the hotel before breakfast. I've been up since 4:30, anyway . . . trying to sleep is exhausting. When he called from the sidewalk and I looked out my window, he motioned for me to come down. I didn't even see his face until we sat down at McDonald's . . . he was already back inside his car when I came down to the sidewalk. I could see it coming a mile away. In fact, I'm the one who finally said it: "You don't want to take me along, do you, Garth?"

"I feel funny about it."

"You felt funny about it yesterday, too . . . but now you've made up your mind."

"How could it be any fun for you," he said, "if I were nervous, feeling peculiar?"

"I don't understand." I was starting to cry, trying not to, but having difficulty saying more than a few words at a time. "You don't feel peculiar about seeing me *here*."

"No, I don't." He examined the tiny paddle they give you to stir the coffee. "We're so good together here. Why go somewhere where it might be no good at all? It would be . . . I would feel . . ."

"Funny," I said.

"I've always been comfortable with you. I don't want to be uncomfortable."

I took the plastic paddle from him and broke it in half. "Why is L.A. different from here? How is it different?"

He didn't answer. He watched me snap the two halves of the paddle into quarters. He held his coffee on the table but didn't drink. He didn't unwrap his breakfast. My fingers were cold, almost numb. I held them in the steam above my coffee. He picked up the styrofoam lid and put it on my cup. "I would still have to call home every day," he said. "I don't mean *have to*, but . . . I call every day."

"So call. I would wait outside."

"How can I ask you to do that?"

"You're not asking," I said. "I'm offering." Actually, it felt like I was begging. My voice unsteady, the strange strained tone of suppressed bawling. Who *is* this person? I can't remember the last time I cried over a man. It must've been *Marcus* . . . hardly even a man!

He said, "She would feel me wanting to hurry and get off the phone."

"You don't have to hurry. I could go on a long walk . . . have a meal . . . sit in the lobby."

"Believe me," he said, "I know what I would be like and you'd be miserable having to be with me. Why waste our time together with stuff like this?"

I watched him start to eat. He chewed while looking down at his hands holding the sandwich . . . not at the mangled napkin in front of me. I kept wiping tears with it. He chewed a long time. Then he said, his voice brighter, "So, what are your plans for today?" As if we'd just met and sat down. I waited, took the lid off my coffee, and looked at the thin oil glaze on the surface. "Or are you going to spend all day being mad at me?" He was smiling.

"I can feel good with you anywhere, Garth."

"Don't turn it into a contest."

"It's like you're telling me I can't exist for you anywhere but here."

"No . . ." He put the sandwich down.

"What other explanation is there?"

He paused, watching his fingers drum the table. "You've become close to me quicker than anyone I've ever known, Erin. If I saw you again after not seeing you for five years, I know I'd touch you as easily as I do now . . ." He held my hand on the table in the middle of all the McDonald's litter. He sighed and shut his eyes. What a McDonald's ad we would've made. My coffee no longer steaming, his sandwich with one bite taken . . .

the litter and broken pieces of plastic, ketchup package, grains of sugar. I watched him until he opened his eyes again. "It didn't rain," he said. "Your jaw was wrong."

I pulled my hand away and touched my jaw.

"How'd you break it?" he asked. "Did you tell me?"

"It got broken when somebody beat me up."

"Who?"

"I don't know," I said. "I can only suspect. Just the opposite of right now: I know it's you . . . but can only suspect you're beating me up."

He didn't go right in to work. He drove into a cemetery and parked on the little winding road that circled among the graves and trees. Ours was the only car there and we were the only people. That's why he chose it, he said, because we could be very alone together. We've been very alone together other times, like on Stonewall Mountain, leaning into the wind, on top of every-thing, on the verge of flying.

On the outer edges of the cemetery, the graves were newer, the stones large and clean, the grass green and even, the flowers plastic and bright, every conceivable color, even blue. But the central areas were older, the monuments sometimes statues of angels or babies, blackened with age, the ground lumpy, the grass tufty or patchy, the graves closer together. Little stones clustered around one big family marker . . . the little stones said *Mother* or *Brother,* or just a name and a date. The trees there were big and gnarled, their roots surfacing and running along the ground over the old graves. Garth said the cemetery was like a city: The outer parts were planned communities with wide streets and maintained parks and rows of identical shops, frozen yogurt and shoe stores. The older, inner part of town has stained buildings of all different sizes and shapes, holding anything from pawned trumpets and golf clubs to tattoo parlors.

We walked through the old, shady part without saying much to each other. Several times we stopped and embraced, leaned into each other, then walked on, our footsteps making mushy sounds. We paused and each put a thumb on the corroded eye sockets of a baby angel. The breeze was like water splashing on my hot, sticky face. I still had the wadded napkin in my fist, still needed it to wipe my nose and eyes. Every time I did, Garth tightened his arm around me. The old trees were filled with birds, mostly mockingbirds, singing every song they'd ever heard. Our footsteps were very alone, but if I listened to the birds, the place seemed full of happy activity. Ground squirrels ran around, sometimes stopping upright on the top of a gravestone to watch us approach. Dark rain clouds drifted in, and when they slid over the sun, everything turned gray and chilly. When the sun came back out, the leaves glittered and the grass was green again.

FEBRUARY 15, 1980

Maybe I have never learned to rest while I sleep. Neither my mind nor my body is getting much out of it. I shouldn't be waking stiff, sore, groaning. My head shouldn't ache, my eyes shouldn't feel rough, my neck shouldn't be sluggish and rigid. My moods hit me like I'm crashing into brick walls.

Dropped a handful of letters and envelopes, everything flew, scattering all over, and I said *shit* like spitting.

Immediately: "Corinne, control yourself."

No joke. Made visual contact long enough to see the whites of his eyes. Pow. Like a punch . . . land back in my seat, hard, my eyesight shimmers like seeing blood on the floor. This kind of hitting I can't take. Torture me, pound me, jump up and down on me . . . just no more sterile punishment sent through this sometimes soundproof, sometimes one-way mirror between us.

11 APRIL 1989

They say an insomniac shouldn't *try* to sleep. Instead, just be awake, be supple and loose—the bed should stop seeming like a piece of granite I'm flailing myself against. If anything, I should be sore from Garth last night. He says he's amazed at what doesn't hurt me. It's been a while since he stayed here so late. Of course he didn't get here until 11:45 . . . fifteen minutes after the evening news ended. It seems weeks ago that he asked why I didn't have candles—asked as if everyone naturally *always* has candles. So I got candles, but for one reason or another we hadn't been here at night to use them. Once last night a pillow almost caught on fire, it got shoved over onto the nightstand. By the time he left, I was on my stomach, still in my socks, my underwear in a ring around one ankle, the sheets a tangled trail on the floor. I listened to Garth get dressed but didn't watch. Then he sat on the side of the bed and stroked my back like I was a big cat stretched out there. He said, "Are you going to be cold? I don't want to put the covers over you yet."

"It's okay," I mumbled into my arm.

He stood up. "Don't move," he said. "I want to remember you just like that."

He's leaving on his trip sometime this morning. He wanted me to sleep till noon. He said I deserved it. "Give yourself a break," he said. But I was up at five.

FEBRUARY 19, 1980

Bad enough all of a sudden that Golden is slashing through Kyle's ideas, changing everything, dumping characters and killing running gags . . . it's compounded by Kyle groveling like a worm: "Okay, fine with me, we'll try it, sounds all right." All in front of Shelby and Adcock who happened by, and Golden switched to high gear as soon as they paused in the doorway . . . while Kyle nodded yes, okay, all right.

Later, when it was just us:

Me: *That* was a show in itself.

K: Do you know why it happened?

Me: I know *his* reasons: Shelby and Adcock. What about yours?

K: What do you mean?

Me: Are you afraid of him?

K: Afraid isn't the right word.

Me: It's so obvious he acts that way because he's jealous.

K: Small is the word for it.

Me: Big difference.

K: Just be perceptive, Corinne.

Me: He's forcing you to do things you don't want to do.

K: You don't know that. Just be perceptive. That's all I'm going to say. Be perceptive. He's your boss — treat him with respect. Do your job. Don't try to change anything.

I could've said, "What would *Haley* say about how you're acting?" But it would've been a mistake for both of us. Besides, his face closed as he spoke until he wasn't looking at me at all anymore. Over my head. Past me. His eyes washed out. Not blue, not green, not brown, not clear, not even really eyes.

STILL 11 APRIL 1989

He isn't going to call. Maybe he thinks it's too late. No, I told him I haven't been sleeping. Maybe he forgot to bring my telephone number. Dear Garth, are you trying to teach me some kind of lesson? You should see me, I'm so restless, I can't sit still. I walk around the room or flop on the bed between sentences, I can't read, can't concentrate, there's so much bullshit in my head. Why should I feel this way just because you haven't called? Like I'm losing you . . . like I've lost you. . . . But *why*—how could it happen so suddenly, so easily? How could I let you become so important to me when you can obviously forget me in a second as soon as you're a hundred miles away? Why should I allow myself to be treated this way? It's okay for you to be with me *here,* and not just in private—at restaurants, at parties, film festivals. But as soon as you leave, I can no longer exist for you. You can't let the rest of the world know you've lived in Oz with me. I can't be taken outside the Emerald City with you, not physically, not even in your mind. How did I let this happen? Smart people are supposed to protect themselves from shit like this. I'm supposed to say: *I deserve to be treated better than this.* I've said it to station managers and engineers, to agents and waitresses and bell hops. I shouldn't *need* Garth!

FEBRUARY 21, 1980

He sat there a long time looking at my outline for skits with new characters. He stared. His eyes stopped moving across the words. Just drilled a hole in the page.

Me: What's wrong with it?
K: I'm just figuring out how to transplant some ideas into someone else's head so it seems like he got them first.
Me: Huh?
K: Never mind. Be perceptive.
Me: You keep saying that.
K: And you keep asking me to explain things. I can't go on explaining to you, Corinne.
Me: Why? I have to work here too.

K: Then be perceptive. When there's no con-
        cern for who gets credit, a lot gets accom-
        plished. When the *main* concern is who will
        get the credit, little is ever accomplished.
Me: But *both* have to be unconcerned. Not just
        you.
K: Not true. If he starts to feel his getting the
        credit will be automatic or a given, *he'll* stop
        worrying about it too.
Me: Where does this get *you?*
K: Not your concern.

They're little kids playing games, he says, before
slinging his coat over his shoulder and leaving without
saying goodbye. He still walks the same, moves the
same, almost talks the same, sometimes, but seems profoundly tired. The laugh lines seldom appear. But
there's something else: the way his eyes almost droop
without those lines. And his mouth turns down, grimness that makes it look turned down, dipped in concrete.

STILL 12 APRIL 1989

Maybe if I think every day about my memories of you, Garth,
then maybe they won't twist, warp, fade, dance in dreams, or
scare me like rubber spiders dropped in my face in a cheap
haunted house. So even if something happens, like a car accident or I get mugged, I'll still remember you, if I concentrate on
you *now,* on the little details . . . like your voice in candlelight
in my room, in my bed, your words sometimes spaced far apart,
your voice so low I sometimes have to strain to hear, the same
way I'm always straining to get closer when you're teasing me on
the outside and I can't wait for the gentle violence of you being

inside me. I can't wait, but the waiting is on the edge of ecstasy . . . filled with the sound of your voice asking vague questions, and my own voice which can only say, hoarsely, *yes* . . .

Or does remembering make it worse? I can hear your voice so clearly, I can taste it. The phone is right at my elbow. My heart jerks when I glance at it, as though practicing for the jolt I'll feel when it suddenly rings. There has to be a reason you haven't called.

You said I kept you sane, but you probably found out when you left, you *are* sane, even without me. What is it I want, anyway, Garth? I don't want to feel this way! Would I have saved myself all this misery today, last night, yesterday, if I'd told you to fuck off sooner, after you first said I couldn't go with you to Los Angeles, or even before that, one of those days your eyes receded far into your head? Maybe I wouldn't have been caught with my emotions unzipped. I always said I wouldn't socialize within the business . . . and I put in so many hours I didn't socialize at all. Emotions banished to the few spooky hours after midnight while I drift in and out of semiconscious sleep. Success measured not so much by salary and air time, but by the fact that things like *this* couldn't happen to *me!*

Why can't I tell you to just take a hike? Get lost. Have a nice life. Haley would do that. Erin Haley should do it. . . . In the first place, Erin shouldn't *need* you to call so desperately. Or else Erin wouldn't have let it happen this way, would've somehow realized from the beginning that maybe, despite all the things you've said, both stoned and straight, drunk and sober, you'll never allow me to become too important to you. *I* should be the first one to say it, scream it: FUCK YOU FUCK YOU FUCK YOU!

Oh god, Garth, do I mean it? If I did, I'd tear the phone cord out of the wall instead of sitting here looking at it with sick sobbing in my stomach. I went crazy. But it's okay now. When I shut my eyes, I'm picturing that day in the cemetery. A storm was coming in but the birds were singing. There was distant thunder, but up close the gentle, harmless rattle of the breeze in the leaves. That day sounded like the way I love you.

14 APRIL 1989

Did you know that when there's no moon at the beach at night, you can't see the water at all? There's just a dark rushing motion, felt but not seen, the waves roaring as though just beyond the end of your arm, standing up and crashing down. And the sand is gray-black, dotted with even blacker spots and pits: the hollows and dents of footprints or somebody's body that lay there in the afternoon. It was cold, even the sand was cold, but with a blanket down between two small dunes to block the wind, the sand insulated us enough that we never shivered.

I'm not sure what time Garth got back yesterday. I walked around downtown, walked and walked and walked . . . bought a cheap jogger's tape recorder and some beat-up tapes, walked in rhythm, let my heart beat in rhythm, breathe in rhythm, think only in rhythm . . . until around dusk I finally picked up my phone and dialed his number. It was busy. Kept trying, every five minutes. It took almost an hour, but finally he answered.

"You're home," I said.

"Hi. I was about to surprise you."

"With what?"

"With. . . . Is anything wrong?"

"No," I said. "Everything's fine. Want to come over? I could meet you at your place."

"I'll pick you up," he said. "I've got a better idea."

We ate first, so it was nearly eight by the time we got there. He did most of the talking at dinner. His station didn't win zip at the awards thing. After the awards were given out, there was a cocktail reception, a perfect opportunity to make important connections, Garth said, but after the station manager introduced him to a few people who didn't seem impressed, the manager disappeared somewhere and left Garth on his own. So, Garth said, he mingled with the drinks at the bar, mingled with the dip and finger food on the banquet tables, mingled with the facilities in the restroom, then left. I didn't ask why he didn't call me, just sat and listened. He said it rained all the way to Santa Barbara, but the workshop had been fine, 180 degrees better than the awards thing, one of the best groups he'd ever talked to.

I felt like I needed to catch my breath before saying anything.

"And then," he said, "I thought about you the whole way back to San Diego."

"Only then?"

"No," he smiled. "Let's go. I don't want to just *think* about you anymore."

We walked a long way on the beach, past the cliffs. There were no people, no dogs, no birds—just us, the smell of seaweed, the sound of waves, and the sand falling away under our feet. I stood hugging myself to keep warm while he spread the blanket. Then he sat on it and held a hand up to me. I moved closer, he took my wrist and pulled me down onto the blanket.

"Are you sure nothing's wrong?" he said.

"Everything's fine." I lay on my back. "Can you see me? Are your eyes open?"

"My eyes are open," he said, "and I can see you."

The air was so salty that in a few moments we were sticky and tasted brackish. Grains of sand blew off the dunes and stuck to us. The fog rolled in so there were no stars, just velvet salty darkness, and I wondered how, without a single source of light, I could still see him . . . or was I seeing with my fingers . . . were we both invisible?

After he finished, I told him he sounded like a lone wolf unable to howl properly without a moon to point his nose. Garth chuckled, still out of breath, then said, "But I'm not alone." He was on his back and pulled me over, half on top of him. I put my face down against his shoulder. He said, "At least I hope I'm not alone . . . tell me you like me."

I lifted my head. I smiled, and I guess his eyes were open because he smiled back. "I never stopped liking you, Garth," I said, "but I have to admit . . . when you didn't call the past few days, I considered telling you to take a flying leap."

He shut his eyes. "I didn't know you expected me to call."

"I didn't know I expected it either. But that really wasn't the point. I wonder why I allowed myself to be treated that way."

I tried to move away again, but his tight grip had not weakened. "Don't go," he said.

"I was just trying to help you breathe."

My arms trembled from holding myself up in order to see his face. All of a sudden he relaxed his hold on me and took a deep breath. I rolled off and kneeled beside him. He groped for me, found my arm and held on again, opened his eyes and said, "Don't leave me, Erin. I'd be a basket case."

As dark as it was, I could see how his cheeks were bluish but his cheekbones were sunburned. His nose was sunburned too and his eyelids looked puffy, as though in another hour or so his eyes would be swollen shut. Sitting upright like that, more of the wind hit my head and the surf was much louder. We kept looking at each other, his hand moved up and down my arm, neither of us smiled. His voice was hoarse, maybe half of it carried off by the wind, but I didn't have to bend closer to hear him say, "I love you, Erin."

I didn't want either of us to move or speak for another two days, but that's not how things work. He asked if I was cold and I nodded, so he pulled me down beside him and wrapped the blanket around us. We lay on our sides, face-to-face, our noses touching. He didn't kiss me. He said, "We need to get some sleep or we'll wake up tomorrow morning when the tide comes in and hits our feet."

But that didn't mean we would both go to his place and sleep together. He wanted to hold onto the intensity of being with me, he said, and the strange combination of utter excitement mixed with serenity. He didn't want to take it for granted or lose it by falling into the habit of sleeping together. Did I handle that okay? I didn't tell him about the equally strange combination of sensual happiness and heart-pounding panic.

"Were you suffocating?" I asked when we got near my hotel.

"Huh?"

I explained that I had tried to lie face-to-face with another person a few times, long ago, but always felt there wasn't enough air between us. But I didn't feel that way lying with him.

He said, "No, I wasn't suffocating either," a little laugh in his voice. Then the laugh went away.

MARCH 6, 1980

Golden says all three of us will go to the meeting or none of us will go. He doesn't want Kyle and me to go alone, then come back and fill him in. Things get warped, he says. He won't get the whole picture. No qualms about his going without us, but that wasn't one of his choices. Apparently the new sponsor told some-one that Golden's presence wasn't desired, so Golden told Kyle not to go, not realizing that the sponsor specifically insisted that Kyle be there. Management's interest in Kyle is deserved . . . look at the ratings, and the show gets mentioned in various newspaper col-umns almost once a week. The radio/TV editor loves it and loves Kyle, describing the characters as if they're real people, and writes stuff like "Warren Kyle is re-sponsible for bringing Peter Pepper and the Golden-

and-Kyle show to San Diego." But without Kyle, there's no Golden-and-Kyle. Golden alone wouldn't last a month, even if His-Pal-Al is program director. And yet . . . it's like the three of us pull and tug and jostle for position; but not even jostling for the *same* position. Kyle struggles to stay number two.

18 APRIL 1989

If I had a selection of tapes from the old Golden-and-Kyle show, would certain routines and bits from the show remind me of what was happening in the background—or foreground—of the planning sessions?

Do you think I'll ever forget this morning's walk at 4 A.M. . . . ? The birds, the lightning, the smell of wet pavement, the night-light in Garth's front room . . . ? It'll take more than a cracked jaw to homogenize these things into a pastel blur. My jaw ached as I walked last night, as if saying: *Go ahead, hit me again, you can't take this away from me.*

Could you put something like that, the whole atmosphere, on videotape, or will the eventual tape of our pilot show carry the sensations subliminally? When we finish, It'll be more than just 23-odd minutes of documentary-style local stuff: it'll be a tape of Garth and me . . . partner to the Stonewall Mountain anchor-with-no-desk tape, which he still has somewhere.

His new idea, he said, partially grew out of our sign-sighting trip. At first he thought it wasn't going to amount to anything, just didn't seem to fit with a news show, but the program director told Garth he wanted to get rid of the sitcom rerun right before the news and lead in with something current and local, so Garth's idea is a documentary-style show with a host or hosts called *San Diego Follies.* Not just embarrassing stuff around town, but also silly stuff, unusual stuff, stuff that doesn't make sense, stuff that no one ever stopped to look at closely enough. Not a heavy scene—no medical waste on the beach or sewage in the bay or any real "issues." He's going to gather as much material as possible, then start editing several shows at once. He got the go-ahead to work exclusively on this project for a while.

When he told me about it yesterday morning, it was like he'd just gotten a shot of adrenaline directly into an artery. Determined, excited, confident, energetic, intense, giddy. . . all at the same time. He says he feels like he's been floundering around for weeks and weeks, and finally he knows exactly how to swim and which direction to go.

"One of the things I know I've got to do," he said, "is to pick your brain as much as possible. We'll see what we can come up with together."

We were sharing a sandwich outside on a bench, straddling the bench, facing each other. He stuffed all the trash into a brown bag and put it on the ground, then scooted forward on the bench toward me, lifted my legs over his, held my shoulders. I had to tip my head back to look up at his face, then he rested his forehead on mine. His voice was very soft, "How quiet can you be? Can you control yourself?"

"I— What do you mean?"

He still held my upper arms, but his thumbs were brushing the tips of my breasts, barely grazing, but even that much was enough to send spears into my stomach. "How quiet can you be when I do this?" he said, then smiled and stopped. "Tomorrow evening I'll be in one of the studios editing tape, can you meet me there?"

I nodded, he scooted back again, and suddenly it was once again early afternoon, outdoors on a bench between two buildings, other people sitting nearby or walking past. He dismounted, took my hand, and pulled me to my feet.

I don't know what I think of his idea, but I asked if he could loan me one of the camcorders and let me do some looking around during the day while he was busy. He hesitated. "Don't you think I could do it?" I asked.

He fixed my collar, folded it down. "What if you wanted to copyright your material . . . what if—"

"Garth, let's worry about things when there are things to worry about."

"But you're a professional, Erin," he said. "I don't want it to look like I'm using you like a student intern."

I fixed *his* collar so it was standing upright. "If *I* don't think you're taking advantage of me, then you're not taking advantage of me."

He pulled a camcorder from under his desk. It was encased in foam rubber in a gray plastic suitcase, like an assassin's gun between jobs. So I spent the afternoon downtown on foot and got a few good pieces. I had to shut off every time some bozo tried to get in the picture and wave to his mother, but somewhere on this tape are some good pieces of a small pickup truck with the entire bed filled with stereo speakers hooked to the car stereo, and the driver wearing an airport noise-protection headset. When the guy parked and shut the system down, it was like stepping off a battlefield into a peaceful mountain meadow, even with the rest of the downtown noise—car horns, a jackhammer, truck engines—all around.

Garth didn't get a chance to see my tape. He wanted dinner. Afterwards we went for a drink, a place chosen at random, conservative, no one under fifty, high fluffy hair and sparkling jewelry. Garth was amused by the looks he said I got from some of them, in my leather miniskirt, black nylons with lace patterns like racing stripes up the outsides of my legs, a red T-shirt cut very low in back, and my calf-high leather boots. On one side of my head my earrings were all black studs, on the other side all fish hooks. I didn't notice any stares, but Garth said one woman looked me up and down twice over with an ugly frown.

"If the blue-hairs glare, I've succeeded," I laughed.

"Is that the crux of your wardrobe philosophy?"

He walked me back to the car with his hand on my bare shoulder, but as soon as we were in the car, I started sweating . . . somehow I knew it was coming . . . I checked my hands to see if they were visibly shaking, then stuffed them between my legs, picking at a fingernail. The next time I saw my fingers the nail was bleeding. But that wasn't until after he said, "Remember our date tomorrow evening at the station."

"What's wrong with tonight?"

"We've *had* tonight."

I put my bleeding finger into my mouth, took it out and said, "There's lots more of tonight left."

"I don't want to start feeling like we're on a regular routine," he said, "it becomes expected instead of . . . you know . . ."

"Spontaneous."

"I hate to sound like a broken record."

"We haven't had a chance to become spontaneous yet tonight, Garth."

"I knew all day we weren't going to spend the night together."

"Why?"

He ran his fingers around my ear, played with the dangling fishhooks. "There's a lot more to what's good about us than sex."

I put my hand over my earrings so he stopped fooling with them. "Maybe that's what makes the sex so good, Garth."

"Maybe so. . ."

In a moment I blurted out, "Did you call home earlier? Do you have to call home or something?"

"Whether or not I already called makes no difference," he said, smiling, or trying to smile. "If the phone rang while you were there, it would be awful . . . for me, for you . . . for Kathryn . . ."

"This again." I put my seat belt on. "Okay. Take me home."

I sat silently until we got to the hotel. I started to get out without saying anything else. He stopped me with a hand on my leg. "Don't leave that way," he said.

"What way?"

"As though I've let you down."

I took a deep breath. My own heartbeat felt like nausea. "*You* haven't let me down, Garth."

We sat that way for a long time, not looking at each other, his hand still on my leg. Probably that's when I was getting the idea that saved me. I was the first to move: I leaned back in my seat and looked at him. His eyes looked shut, but I knew he was looking down, at the floor or my boots or something down there. All the excitement over his new project was gone. I put my hand over his on my leg. He looked up at me. I said, "Are you afraid to sleep with your door unlocked?"

"Why?" But when I didn't answer, he said, "Well . . . I am, I guess."

"Okay, better idea: Let me borrow your extra key."

So that's why at 3:30 this morning I was up. Actually I was *still* up. I knew I wouldn't be able to sleep but didn't want to take a pill and not make it over to Garth's. I washed my hair and just left it limp and loose, put on jeans and a sweatshirt, and cut through the park to his place. I've been awake at that hour plenty of times before, staring at a dark ceiling, at the pages of a book I'm not concentrating on, watching the flickering light of an old movie on TV . . . but I've never been outside when that hour of the morning is *happening*. There were birds singing at 4 A.M. I passed tree after tree where I couldn't even see the birds, but obviously it wasn't leaves filling out the branches, it was all birds. No breeze, but the trees fluttered. And far off on the horizon to the east, over the mountains, lightning was flickering, sparkling in the sky. I could feel the thunder in my stomach but couldn't hear it.

Garth's front room was lit eerily by a little night light in one corner. The furniture all seemed to lean crazily toward me. The doorway to his bedroom was black and silent. I moved toward it slowly, not wanting to step on or kick anything. In the doorway, I dropped my sweatshirt and jeans, stepped out of my shoes, then shuffled across the rug, feeling for the bed, not knowing which side he would be on. I think he was right in the middle. When I sat on the very edge of the mattress, he made a sound that wasn't really "Hi," more like "Ah," hooked an arm around my waist, and drew me onto the bed beside him.

When he dropped me back here on his way to work, he said I could keep the key.

MARCH 10, 1980

I tried to forget all about last Sunday until he brought it up today. Some race the station sponsored for March of Dimes. Golden, the MC at the awards ceremony, and all the related bullshit. Kyle was only allowed to hand out trophies, shake hands, and carry the poster child up onto the little stage so Golden could "interview" her. Kyle started to join the conversation in Betty Boop's voice, but he didn't have a microphone—no one but Golden and me could hear him. Golden ignored him and plowed ahead. Meanwhile I was gofering but was halfway crazy. Then that night slept twelve hours, 6 to 6. Full of panting, confusing dreams: Lost something and can't find it, have to be somewhere in five minutes and can't find the door, have to go on the air but left my copy at home and can't find the parking lot.

But today, we almost had an actual conversation— just like we used to have before . . . what changed us? . . . the day he started getting his own coffee. Anyway, he was going on about authority being the ability to get people to do what you want. "Willingly," I added. Or did I ask? But I remember him saying outright, "Do what he says because he's the boss." *Because* he's the boss. That's not a good enough reason.

Maybe I was trying to have my own good-enough reason for why I have no respect for Golden's so-called authority, so I asked if Golden treats females subserviently.

K: No. Not really. What do you mean, anyway?

Me: You'd know if you were a female working for him.

K: Ask yourself if that's a cop-out explanation.

Me: For what?

K: For your problems dealing with him. If he doesn't treat women well . . . and you're a woman . . . bingo: ready-made excuse.

Me: You're saying it's me, then . . . it's specifically *me* that's the problem.

Silence. I guess it wasn't such a grand conversation after all.

You know, authority figures sometimes have a weapon, some form of punishment they can dole out if needed . . . so you respect their authority out of fear. I don't think of Kyle that way, but if I were going to respect Golden, it *would* be that way . . . even though being fired doesn't seem a big enough threat. He has no punishment scary enough to get me to have even a child's respect for him.

Once again I should've but didn't—couldn't—bring up Haley.

Sometime during the day I sat watching him tell me a story about his boat dragging its anchor, being taken by the waves and tide toward some rocks that would smash the hull. He had to pull the anchor up, then start the motor with a crank generator before he hit the rocks. I watched his hands as he spoke. As he does so often, just the tips of his fingers touched each other, all five on both hands, like caging a soap bubble. Instead of laugh lines there were creases between his brows. "You have to know before it happens," he said, "that you're about to go onto the rocks."

19 APRIL 1989

Now I can't sleep out of sheer giddy exhaustion. I want to keep it forever . . . the hour or two hours—or two *minutes*, it seems like now—of mute electricity in the editing booth with Garth. Like a silent scream. Here's how far I've come from when I would lie comatose with a man in bed: I was on my feet, or sitting upright on the counter, or upright on him.. . . . We stared crazily at each other, panting through open-mouthed grins.

I didn't get there until around 8 P.M. Practically had to tie myself to my bed to keep from running to the station as soon as the 5 o'clock news was over. I waited . . . and paced . . . I thought I could kill some time talking on the phone to an old friend, but realized, without a thunderclap from the blue, that I've burned so many bridges I don't have an old friend to call. I could've called my mother. God, she'd probably listen to my voice for ten seconds and say, "Corinne, are you about to go fuck someone in an editing booth at a TV station?" I watched TV. I watched the news and the national news. I watched people through the camcorder from my window. I showered, gelled my hair, dressed in jeans, T-shirt and thongs, changed my earrings to black and green studs in every other hole, then took off.

The door to Garth's booth was open and he was talking to someone, an engineer or technician. He was rewinding a tape, the screen of his monitor crackling and hissing with violently moving static. When a break in his conversation with the other guy came around, he said, "Hey Erin, wanna see what I've done to our sign tape?" I came into the booth, the guy left, Garth shut the door and said, laughing, "What took you so long?"

"I thought you wanted to get some work done first."

"I *tried*. I sat here watching the damn thing, wondering where you were. I haven't looked forward to an editing session this much in . . . ever." The VCR clicked off. He started it again and the static on the screen shifted into our sign-hunting trip. I saw the first thing we'd taken, a bumper sticker—"Welcome to California, No Kids, No Pets," then Garth turned me around and boosted me up so I was sitting on the shelf beside the TV monitor. The tape was silent. I tried to be. God, I tried. I also fell backwards a few times so my head thunked on the wall. We could hear people walking past the door, having conversations in the hall. Then other voices. At first I thought it was the TV, then realized it was him, whispering, "Tell me what you want, what fantasy have you always had that I could give you now?"

Dreams of flying . . . isn't that the fantasy that was answered tonight?

But at the time, when he asked, I could hardly answer except to mumble, "This, this, just this . . ." And then, groaning, "It's a fantasy while it's happening."

"That's what I want to give you," he said into my ear. "I want to give you what you've always wanted, and I want to surprise you with it. Tell me what you want."

"This. This." But I felt him hovering, as though waiting, teasing, holding back, holding his breath . . . "You," I said.

His laugh was a sigh, or his sigh was a laugh, a very quiet one, and we didn't talk any more. He came into me slowly but with all the energy of a thunderstorm. His eyes wider than I've ever seen them, and we stared at each other. The monitor flickered light onto his face, zapped by lightning, but the flash lasted minutes . . . *hours* . . .

MARCH 15, 1980

K: Can you take an instruction and keep your mouth shut?

Me: What?

K: I guess not.

I sat staring at him. No smile. No lines. He just looked down, scowling. Then, after Golden left:

Me: You think I'm trying to make or change decisions?

K: No, I don't think you do that.

Me: Well, lately you've seemed to imply . . . that's what you think.

K: I've felt the need to attack you lately because I've been in meetings where I hear, "I'm having trouble with Corinne," and "I'm also having a problem with her," then they look at me. Well, I can't sit there and say, Hey—I'm *not* having a problem . . . tell them that I'm the *only* one not having a problem.

But there *is* a problem. Is our conflict really that I don't pay sufficient homage to Golden? Or is our real conflict over your invention of a conflict so it won't look like you're *actually* having a conflict with Golden? Know what our conflict is? . . . it's your lying down and rolling over for Golden, then wanting me to do the same.

LATER

Golden paced a three-step area. Kyle sat watching. It almost seemed the table came up farther against his chest than usual. He didn't have any coffee, but I didn't make a move. Closed my eyes and it was like a cue for Golden to say, "Tell them they're trying to take advantage of a dumb jock. Tell them you'll talk to Golden and get back to them. We'll go over everything before you sign anything."

My eyes opened, just a slit, Kyle's throat working up and down, looking at the tabletop, but he didn't answer. He needed someone like Haley. But neither of us has someone like Haley anymore.

MARCH 19, 1980, 2 AM

I think I have a fever. I'm also thinking that I know far down in my bones that Kyle can never be a friend. When I become a TV writer or news director or on-air celebrity or publish a book . . . when lots of people know who I am and respect my work highly, give me grants and prizes . . . probably then we can be friends. Not until. Why do I know that's what it'll take? Because when I wake with a swirling fever, I think of him, even groan his name aloud . . . a cosmic drug, a magic tonic, a cool gentle hand . . . as though he'll actually appear, sitting on my bed, cover me with himself, kiss my neck, breathe in my ear, allow me to tell him without words . . . how phenomenal he is. And as though he won't be gone, a night-time apparition, when I wake.

20 APRIL 1989

Amazing how that wretched feeling in my stomach always disappears with a single unexpected yelp of my name from the sidewalk. I hadn't even gotten to the point of cursing out loud. The old stare-in-the-mirror routine, one eye watching as the other gets rubbed with a finger. Flung myself on the bed. Turned on the TV, turned it off, rolled to my back, rolled to my stomach, turned the TV on again. Walked around the room, considered cracking open my videotape over the back of the chair, stringing tape all over the room. Glad I didn't . . . I've got some okay stuff. We went over it today and decided on at least one show theme: apartment hunting, to go with that first bumper sticker, *Welcome to California, No Kids, No Pets.* I told Garth we should probably find or manufacture one of those older stickers that says *Welcome to San Diego, Now Go Home,* to go along with this stuff. I found one rudely painted wooden sign outside an apartment: "Section 8 OK." And another, even better sign that had first been professionally painted, Something-gardens or Something-heights, and listing all the features. But "plush," which used to preface "carpets," had been painted over, and "drapes" had been whitewashed altogether. And I found a singles' apartment with a Taj Mahal facade painted shocking pink. Garth liked what I'd shot but hesitated. Wasn't responding. Reservation hovered around him like a cloud of gnats. Finally he said, "Making fun of someone's home could be dangerous. This isn't news, so we can't just use—and abuse—people without permission. Signs are okay, but how far can you go with that?"

I said, "The sign part of the show can be done like MTV."

He stared at the screen, a freeze frame, shivering on pause, of the apartment sign that no longer offered plush carpets.

"It also keeps the repetition from being boring," I added. "You snap from item to item with the song. The rhythm of the song and the changing images are captivating—and a familiar song is also a hook."

"That's a good idea," he said slowly. He didn't sound any happier.

But when I'd first come in, he had pushed his chair away from the monitor, pulled me into his lap, slipped one hand into the neck of my shirt, saying, "A little memory of yesterday," and we'd laughed together in silly exhaustion, especially after I told him I knew for a fact that if we were in Arkansas we could be arrested. "Acts against nature—worth up to five years in prison," I said.

"Five years for *each* act?" he asked.

"We've piled up some hard time."

When he first started watching my tape, he still seemed up-beat. In fact, before we watched my tape, he said he had a short tape to show me. Flipping around on the TV, he'd found a Roadrunner cartoon, recognized what was about to happen, grabbed a tape, and jammed it into the VCR just in time to get a running-off-the cliff scene.

"It's the only thing I remember from any cartoons," he said. "To me, a character running off a cliff is what cartoons are."

The coyote ran off the cliff, sure enough, ran halfway across the chasm before he realized he was suspended in midair. Looked at the audience, turned and tried to tiptoe back to the other side. Didn't make it. With a desperate leap he grabbed the lip of the bluff with his fingernails, heaved a sigh of relief . . . and the edge of the cliff broke off in his hands. We played the cartoon scene backwards in slow motion, then forward in slow motion.

"Would you ever make a cartoon that did it differently?" I asked.

"What do you mean?"

"I don't know," I said. "What if when you suddenly realize you're standing on thin nothing, instead of frantically scrambling through air, trying to get back to the edge of the cliff . . . shouldn't you just arch your back into a swan dive and float . . . or flap your arms and *fly . . . ?*"

Then we watched my tape. I wish my graffiti series had been more complete, but he liked how it's developing. Day before yesterday I had found a blank, newly painted side of a building, surrounded by fences and other buildings already marked with gang graffiti. But this blank side of a building *did* have something painted on it: *Your Ad Here.* Hoping for a paying customer. Then I went back yesterday before going to the station, and already a gang slogan was dripping across the center of the blank area. I'm going to go back every day and film it with the new additions until it's filled with the new "ads." We can blur the different shots in editing so that it looks like a slowly evolving wall, so you can almost see the new words as they're painted.

But something *was* dragging at Garth. He finally turned off the TV monitor and sat staring at the blank screen. His shoulders slumped. I stood behind him and put my hand lightly on the back of his neck. He let his head hang forward and shut his eyes for a second, then got up and faced me. "I'm sorry, Erin, I shouldn't let you get tangled in my frustrations, I'm insufferable to be around when . . ."

I sat in his chair and pushed it backwards, rolled myself six or eight feet away from him. He remained leaning back against the monitor.

"I'm spoiled, I guess," he said. "I'm used to getting a grant, then going ahead with a project. Now they're stalling on giving me a date to premiere these shows. I got the initial go-ahead but can't seem to get any support. Then there are a million meetings interrupting every large block of time I have. . . . When I get like this. . ." But he wasn't looking at me. How often have I watched him talk to me without him looking at me? "I need to work alone for a while," he said. "Why don't you go on home. You shouldn't be working like this for me anyway. Maybe I'll see you later."

By the time he finished *that* little speech, I was already to the door, saying, "Okay, goodbye."

He caught the door handle so I couldn't shut it as I was going out, then grabbed my arm. "Don't leave like this."

"I have to leave in order for you to work alone."

He looked at his hand holding my arm, slid his hand down and held my fingers loosely for a second, then let go and said, softly, "Yeah," and softer, "Bye, Erin."

But was it Erin who jammed the headset over her ears and

stomped home? Was it Erin flopping around her room, unable to focus, unable to pick up the camcorder and go out, unable to open the journal and read, unable to make her bed or pick up her clothes or listen to more than three words on any of the talk shows on TV . . . ? Where was *Erin* hiding for that hour or two after I left the station, and did she return just because her name was called through the window by this man? Then I heard him taking the steps two at a time, and he came through the door, hooking an arm around me and bringing the two of us crashing onto the bed.

"Are we going to rack up another five years?" I said.

"Why not, we've already got life sentences, don't we?"

MARCH 20, 1980

All that delirious sentimental crap last night, and today you treat me like a piece of shit . . . not worth talking to except for the sarcastic, pointed one-liners: "You know better than to weigh mommy against daddy," and "When you're sent to jail by the warden, only the warden can get you out."

A phenomenon? Look what I wrote! More like the warden's best boy. How many days are you going to stay late, taping show promos and station ID spots alone? How many times are you going to let him laugh and say, "You'll learn, Mr. Jock"? For that matter, why'd you let him add that new voice, ex-jock, surfer-type, dumb as wood . . . didn't you see the obvious put-down? After all, he calls your boat rich-man's-surf board. But all you're concerned with is keeping your-self out of trouble, keeping on Golden's good side, not venturing to say one word that goes against anything he says. *Yes sir, yes sir*. . . you make me sick. Talk about lack of character! And you have the nerve to say, "The real test of a person's character is how they act when they don't get their own way." Maybe a better measurement is when a person doesn't even *try* to get his own way: just follow, follow, flow with the current, don't splash, don't even try to swim. Gutless sonuvabitch.

25 APRIL 1989

I don't think about time when I'm *with* Garth, but when we're together the seconds tick away twice as fast as when I'm alone. And when I'm alone . . . that's when I have to pump heavy metal into my ears or burn miles of tape with the camcorder—every inch of tape I use is something I'll want to show Garth . . . if it takes him forever to watch all of it, even better. Distract myself, distract myself . . . but lately even the journal can't distract me much longer than the time it takes to read the words. This journal is made of days passing, and I don't want days to pass. Dates on pages . . . I've tried to not look at calendars . . . but I feel it out there—that square white day that showed up when Garth flipped a page on his wall calendar to check something scheduled for next month. There's a flight number and time written in red ink on a day somewhere up ahead. And a few times lately he's started to wonder aloud—wistfully?—whether or not he'll be going home to a new job. Now it's doubtful Garth will get this show up and running before his contract runs out, but he's going to go ahead with it anyway, make the first tape, and at least can use it as part of his résumé package. He says it's like the last two or three weeks of school—they don't expect him to get anything done that will make a difference, so they're just letting him float to the dock. Maybe he mistook an idea-swapping session for an actual *Let's do it.*

I guess I should see to my own arrangements, contact my station and tell them my mother's fading fast, the end is near, so I'll be coming back soon . . . or else I'll look for something else.

My mother has my tapes—I could get them and start sending feelers out. Milwaukee's near Chicago, I could try there . . .

I've stopped looking for you at parties, Kyle. Maybe you're fat and married and don't go anywhere anymore. Last night's was at a bar, a general-announcement party celebrating someone's promotion or someone's new job or someone's departure or someone's new baby or who knows. It reminded me of when I met Alex in New Orleans. And I got just loose enough on pink wine last night to launch into that story on the way home. I even started with how after I got out of the hospital, left KIAM and went back to Phoenix, I spent a long time looking like a boy. Well, I'd dressed like a boy in high school and college too, but always had that long drippy hair. This time no long hair. But funny things started to happen . . . men were *interested* in me. I went through a period of about a year when lots of men were interested . . . some of them titillated by androgyny, but some—a few—actually looking for *boys*. I never tried to fool anyone one way or the other—it never occurred to me to supply my gender when making small talk at a rock concert or dance club. But after they found out, felt under my shirt or slipped a soft goose between my legs, sometimes they got mad. One guy popped me . . . not hard enough to break anything, but I decided to go in and have my jaw checked. He hadn't hit me on the same side, but I had it checked anyway. While I was there, I decided to have my nose done different—not a tilted up model, something classy but feminine, I told him. That's also about the time I started to get my ears pierced. Started with the customary two holes. I wore hoops or seashells or peacock feathers. By the time I was in Pine Bluff, I'd added a hole. Then every time I wanted to add one, I had to add two to keep the sides from being even. I think I had two on one side, three on the other about the time some of us from the station in Pine

Bluff went to New Orleans for a weekend. Alex was in New Orleans that weekend also.

Anyway, last night's bar party was in the lounge side of that restaurant that gives out peppermint sticks, so I grabbed one on the way in. I admit that this time I consciously used the peppermint stick to get to Garth when he was trapped in a gaggle of people, mostly women. I recognized one as a reporter who sometimes anchors the noon news. At first I was kind of standing next to Garth, but they started telling makeup and hairstyle horror stories, so I edged away toward the happy-hour free food bar. Garth's eyes flickered up at me several times as I drifted away. Then I didn't go back to him but stood opposite him on the other side of his group. I don't know whether this one woman was talking about her desk chair or her car's brakes or her eyelash curling tool, but she said, "It just gets real cranky if it doesn't get greased fairly frequently."

"Yeah," I said, without knowing I was going to say anything, "Garth gets cranky if he doesn't get greased pretty often too."

His face exploded in laughter, and we stood there, looking at each other through laugh-squinted eyes, across this group of people—as if we could feel that way forever and never get tired of it.

When everything quieted down again, I took out the peppermint stick. Garth watched me suck on it for only a few moments. He began to edge toward me around the group of people. I didn't watch him, just waited, and got that surge of energy that makes you feel you could fly away but at the same time makes you think you're going to crumple to the ground, and suddenly he was behind me, pulling me up against him with one hand, grabbing the peppermint stick with the other, saying "Gimme that, you!"

Later he said I was lucky he didn't retaliate by telling everyone I could suck the chrome off a door knob. We were both pretty loose from the wine. I said, "Oh, I wish you had. It's good to have *some*thing you can be proud of." Did I really say that? God, Erin.

He said, "I didn't because I thought you might get mad. I forgot what a good sport you are . . . you always seem to fit in every situation without having to change too much." There've been a few times, a few people I should've, could've, changed a little for. Alex was one, although not the most important.

I might've never noticed Alex if he hadn't been standing next to Wendy, who I never saw again after that night. She had short, dark, wavy hair, hair I would call alive because it wasn't in a particular style, just sort of flying around. Like Garth's, I guess. A lot like Garth's, except dark. She wasn't much taller than me, wearing baggy canvas pants, a loose camp shirt, her neckline very tan, no makeup, her eyes deep set and dark but laughing out at you when she talked to you. She *did* talk to me. A small mouth, nice teeth, muscled arms, and really dirty fingernails, which Alex teased her about, except it wasn't dirt—She was a photographer and had been toning prints without gloves. Her laugh was sort of raw and squeaky, her voice nearly hoarse. Probably what originally caught my eye—rather, my ear—was her voice, like Haley's . . . *better* than Haley's because there was no *cute* in it, just the edge of husky tone, almost raw, but somehow comforting, a voice I felt I already knew. And, very unlike me, I approached these two people I'd never seen before, Alex and Wendy, wearing my usual for that time: tight, faded, nearly white jeans, thongs, white turtleneck or midriff T-shirt, depending on the weather.

Alex was making no secret of his desires. Amazing that he hadn't ever had what he seemed to want most in the world, but Alex probably never got his two-women-at-once experience because he picked women—or in this case, *one* of the two women—who weren't *at all* interested in men. But the reason it's so hard to remember my first impression of Alex is that when

I remember this, it just seems familiar, just the *usual* Alex: As I approached, he nudged Wendy and said, "There's one for you. I mean for *us*." He went back to my motel with me, he said later, because I smiled when he said that. I was probably smiling at Wendy, at the look on her face—patient, a little pitying, yet also thinking "what-an-asshole." She ditched us later.

MARCH 23, 1980

He's the boss—your theme song lately. Let's put it to music and use it on the show. Aren't they the words you sang to yourself when he handed you that article about the actress who demanded a grip be fired because he wore a T-shirt with a nude woman on a fishhook and a caption that read, *Mount Your Catch* . . . ? Golden: "Work up a skit on this ballbuster actress."

Did you really hate my idea about having the characters give you the silent treatment, but talking among themselves, accidentally leaving their mikes live? You didn't say you disliked it when you read it yesterday. Why did you have to *wait* until you'd showed it to him, *wait* until he flipped it back at you with, "No way, what'll *I* be doing while this's going on?" before you came back to me, in *front* of him, to say, "Not good enough for us, Corinne"? Just to be sure he'll continue to say, "Let's go for a beer, Champ"? And you always go. There's a lull lately . . . you must've signed the contract he wrote for you.

26 APRIL 1989

It seems to be ending with a whimper, Kyle, you and me, just dwindling away from each other. Will I somehow discover I actually turned in a simple letter of resignation, then tripped and fell down the stairs all by myself on the way out of the building?

People part ways all the time without fanfare . . . God, I can't even distract myself anymore. . . . What did Garth mean, yesterday: "I'll remember you forever . . . maybe with a reminder now and then." He said he wouldn't need anything like a videotape to remind him. Does he mean we'll see each other, that it doesn't have to end when his contract runs out?

We lay there like unraveled ribbons draped across each other. Even though he was still with me and wasn't making a move to leave, after he said it, I started getting that panic, that invisible jittery buzz, that agitation. But this time without hopping up, walking around the room, leaning out the window, turning on the TV . . . I'd been planning all day to mention that I was considering looking for a job near or in Chicago. Lying there, that's when I *could've* said something. Before that it was never the right moment, not after he gave me the tape back. And not after we made love, slowly, peacefully, like a long sigh before drifting off to tranquil sleep. During the gentle lull afterwards he said what should've been a beautifully mysterious thing about remembering me forever. But all it did was remind me about how he'd given me the tape back earlier that afternoon. So the soft fall into sleep snapped off abruptly. It was like *fear* I was feeling. If I said anything or moved, he might've detected a stranger in the room.

He said, "Tell me you like me," and I told him I did. Had he maybe felt my panic and misread it as boredom or restlessness? By the time we went to dinner I had everything back under control. But I never really stopped thinking about the videotape he'd given back to me. When I got home after dinner, I saw it still on my desk, on top of the opened journal. *Not* the sign tape, not the tape I've been working on with his camera—the steadily growing *Your Ad Here*—but the tape he said he'd keep *forever,* the one of me undressing on top of Stonewall Mountain. That day . . . I could've flown that day, I just know that was the day I could've breathed deeply, spread my arms and found out they were wings . . .

He said he'd never watched the tape after rewinding it, didn't know if it showed us making love on the mountain peak, didn't know if the lens had been focused and on us. He said, "You watch it and find out." I've hardly touched it. Just once, to move it off the journal. It's still sitting here, beside my elbow. I can nudge it farther away, but why bother?

He'd said, as he tucked it into my shoulder bag, "I'll remember you just as well without it. It's probably too dangerous to keep it."

"Dangerous?" I said. "Just as dangerous for *me* as for you. Anyway, I thought danger was . . . good foreplay."

"Maybe too good!" he laughed. Then quieted, "Kathryn might find it."

"How?"

"You know how it is, not snooping or anything . . . just . . . she'll be cleaning up, straightening up." He sat in my chair and held out a hand to me, but I didn't take it. He leaned forward, still extending his hand.

I backed up, saying, "She cleans up your desk, your studio?"

"Just picks stuff up, comes to get the dirty dishes or whatever." He half-stood up, stepping forward, caught my wrist, then sat again, bringing me back toward him.

I said, "And the tape would accidentally fall into the VCR and accidentally get turned on . . ."

"Curiosity." He smiled.

I just looked at him. He didn't try to pull me any farther toward himself. He said, "Why don't you tape some more San Diego anomalies over it?"

"Because . . . it's the best San Diego anomaly of all."

He laughed again, getting up to hold me, and I slumped against him as though my bones had all suddenly splintered.

MARCH 28, 1980

Everything blew back open. Blew wider than open. Everything blew the same way the door exploded when he came in, as though he was knocking a hole in the wall. Half an hour after the show ended and neither of them had come in yet, then, *boom* —the door opens, the doorknob cracks against the inside wall. He turned and used his foot to slam the door back, made the windows rattle, the coffeepot croak. Why he didn't smash that record to sand against the table I'll never know. After the noise, he stood there looking at me. Not with that sullen grimness of the past few weeks but certainly not smiling either. The air system stopped blowing like the last of the explosion dying away. Then he handed the album to me:

Cy Golden's Greatest Hits
featuring
Peter Pepper
Mrs. Olsen
Professor Patches
Jimmy Hoffa
Cher
The Tidybowl Man
many others
(character voices by Warren Kyle)

He didn't reach for it when I tried to hand it back. He blinked, turned and stared at the phone, laughed in his throat, then groaned, worked the dial without picking up the receiver, came back to the table, sat down where I'd placed the album on the tabletop, held it in the middle with one finger, and spun it around.

K: Want to hear it?

Me: No.

I expected him to pick it up and throw it like a frisbee, but he didn't.

K: I went to see Adcock. Golden was plugging this on the air. Did you hear?

Me: No.

K: Well, I went to see Adcock. I'm fucked, that's all.

What he found out: His contract gave the station permission to tape and use, any way they see fit, anything that is on the air. Golden somehow bought tapes and rights from the station for little more than dirt, then produced his own record. Kyle gets a name credit. That's all. Not even a big-name credit. His actual normal voice never appears on the record.

But at least the puppy is gone. The best boy is gone. The worm is gone. He stood and turned away, then spun back around, leaned over the table, hands on the back of a chair, shot upright again, saying, "I've gotta get outta here. I've *got* to. No . . . I've gotta get *him* outta here."

I didn't say anything. I couldn't've. Everything was still in my head, everything from the past month. My eyes felt like I'd been crying for several weeks. You weren't really talking to *me*, Kyle, right? Maybe I expected you to close everything down between us again, your eyes to go flat. Instead, your brows stayed two diagonal lines pointing in and down, you didn't do that thing with your fingertips touching each other, you even grabbed my wrist when you said,"Want to hear my theory? Now it's also my *wish* — I want him and Al to get *caught* doing it. My theory is they're in love but can't express it to each other so they like to share a woman."

Me: Do you *know* this?

You: It's a theory. Based on . . . well, my theories

aren't just guesses. I don't care *why* they do
it, I just want them to get *caught*.

Me: But it's not illegal.

You: Some people may not care about that. If I
knew when, I'd have no second thoughts
about ratting on them. I've had enough. I
tried. God, I tried. Didn't I try?

Me: Yes. You tried.

We looked at each other. My back ached. It was
bowed, my shoulders still slumped. Like I'd survived
some sort of war but surviving was only a token reward, not worth much.

Until you said: "Do you want to get me some coffee?" And I nodded solemnly.

Before I handed you the cup, you said, "What's bothering you, Corinne? If it's personal, I don't need to
know, but if it's me and the show, tell me."

It's personal. And it's you.

Me: It's . . . everything.

You: What is it?

Me: I don't know. I don't know what's been happening. It's as though something's been happening to *me*.

You: Probably the same thing that's been happening to me.

If it's the same, why did it seem so different?

You only took one sip of the coffee I gave you, then
stood. I thought you were going to the phone or to get
sugar, but then an arm-lock on my neck. The back of
my chair was crushed between us, but I could feel you
crashing around me.

"I need to pretend to beat you every day . . . so I can
fake being mean at least once a day—for the sake of
being well rounded. Then you can go on enjoying being

a victim. That's what we both need, right? It's the only time all day I have actual *physical* communication with someone."

"Me too."

The laugh. I mean, you really laughed. And said, "So we need each other."

27 APRIL 1989

It probably does change a person to find out they've been screwed by two or three different people at once. After that, we laughed, sometimes, didn't we, Kyle, when frustrations made you growl and twist imaginary crowbars in the air with your hands? You *were* that angry, weren't you? What can people do if they're angry enough? I don't think Garth was really angry today, but can he be? I don't think he's the seething type. It seems like, if something's wrong, Garth-the-filmmaker reduces the sound, reduces the contrast, slowly turns the lens, and loses focus while the camera backs up. Everything swims in gray fuzz, becomes light gray fuzz, becomes snow . . . everything's too soft for anger . . . everything just becomes neutral static. Or like a fogmaking machine, he throws up smoke and disappears into it.

"I'm insufferable when I'm like this," he said, for the hundredth time. You should want to get away from me, no one would want to be around me . . ."

He seemed okay at first, even laughed at my little present for him. But before the present, I had more stuff on my *Follies* tape to show him: a billboard, standardly ugly—a huge picture of a tostada and a burrito, the colors sort of faded so the beans are purplish, the lettuce yellowed with age, but on top of the billboard there's a light, so you won't have to miss seeing this gorgeous Mexican dinner if driving past it at night, and on top of the light there are two antennae parallel with the top edge of the light, mechanized to keep turning around and around, like slow helicopter blades. I didn't know what it was for at first. But luckily it fit perfectly with something I'd already shot. The rotating wires are there to keep pigeons off that beautiful billboard, but pigeons don't need billboards—they nest in the stoplights. Sometimes you're sitting at a red light, and when it changes to green, what shows up is the black silhouette of a bird on a nest surrounded by the green glow. I think all Garth said was, "Keep getting as much as you can so we'll have a lot to pick from." I was standing behind his chair while we watched the monitor. I was stroking his neck. He let his head fall forward and said, "I could let you do that all day."

"Okay," I said.

He stood up, faced me, put a hand on the back of my head, smiled faintly down at me. His eyes were puffy, sagging a little like a hound dog. He pulled my head against his chest and held me there for a moment.

"I have a present for you, Garth," I said.

"Oh no."

"You're scared of a present?"

"Depends on what it is," he said.

"Is anything wrong, Garth?"

"No . . . what's the present?"

"Here." I handed him the sack. A plastic grocery sack, clear, with the name of the store printed on it. It was full of the Stonewall Mountain video, all unwound, a bag of balled-up tape. "Isn't this a nice gift?" I said. "It's even *safer* like this."

"Erin . . ." he said, warningly . . . or pleadingly. But still that faint trace of a smile.

"Really, Garth," I said seriously. "I don't want you to have the slimmest of thoughts that if something happened I would use this tape in the wrong way. I don't want that kind of fear to creep in and ruin things, okay?"

"Okay." He hadn't even taken the sack yet. I put it on his desk. He looked at it, opened it and looked into it, shaking it. Then he looked up at me and laughed a little.

"Do you have time for dinner?" I asked. "An early dinner? Or do you want to work longer and have a late dinner?"

"I had cereal," he said.

"Cereal! Wow!"

"I may never eat again," he smiled. "I'm starting to look like the Michelin Man."

"You're not fat."

"Soft. And I've gained five pounds in the last month. I thought I would try to control myself."

"Are you feeling out of control, Garth?"

"Yes, a little." He was still smiling. "Kathryn's buying us a membership in a health club. I'm going to have a lot of work to do when I get home to get back to the lousy shape I was in when I left!"

I was putting on my coat, backing toward the door, hardly aware I was doing it. "What prompted that?" I said, meaning what made him tell me . . . but he didn't understand.

"A birthday gift," he said.

"And all I gave you was a ruined videotape."

"I'll cherish it."

"But you don't want me to take you to dinner."

He caught the door before I closed it. "Admit it," he said, "I'm horrible to be around, you'll be glad to have a nice dinner by yourself somewhere."

"Choosing to have a nice dinner by myself somewhere is a lot different from what's happening right now, Garth."

He stood there holding the door. I tugged on it a little to see how firmly he was holding it. When he did let go of the door, he grabbed two handfuls of my hair and tilted my face up toward his. It didn't hurt. He could've kissed me, but didn't. "Come back in a couple of hours," he said.

"And you won't still be full of cereal?"

"I'll probably love sitting down with you in a quiet place with a glass of wine."

He smoothed my eyebrows with his thumbs, tickled my dangling ear hoops with one finger, then released me.

APRIL 9, 1980

Was he drunk? Had there been enough time for him to *get* drunk? Maybe he'd been gone twenty minutes. A half hour. Came back for his coat. Grinning, then grimacing. Staring blankly, then laughing. But his eyes never met mine. As though we *couldn't* look at each other, a force field keeping our eyes apart, staring at the phone, fixed on a chair, on the doorknob, on the cold coffeepot, on my stack of tabloids. Forgetting what he came back for, picking the coat up, putting it down, forgetting it again. Wiped his mouth with the back of his wrist, then again with his palm, and stared afterwards as though expecting to find blood smeared on his hand. Maybe five minutes of crazed silence. Then he grabbed the *Enquirer* from my hands. No sound of paper ripping, just a loud snap.

Me: What's the matter?

K: You crazy girl, you have to *ask?*

Me: It's finally getting to you?

K: *Getting* to me? I think I've been gotten. I'm *past* gotten. I'm . . .

Me: You're finally *angry.*

K: Too simple. I'm . . . Jesus-fucking-Christ, why don't *you* quit this job?

Me: Me? Why?

K: Before you get into trouble.

Me: How?

K: What're you doing working *here* . . . with your college degree . . . shouldn't you be starting your career as a . . .

Me: An intern at a TV station? Welcome to my life.

K: An intern? Ha!

Me: Well, that's my pay status.

K: Fuck your pay status. Quit this fucking job.

Me: Why? Are *you* quitting?

Pause . . . he turned slowly. Finally managed to look right at me. Looked, then smiled, then let the smile just go away.

K: No. I'm not quitting. I'm going to do something about it.

Me: About what?

K: I'm going to do something about *him*.

Kyle, you leaned forward, bent over, your hands on the table. You let your head drop, hang there, your hair falling down enough to hide your face. Then the way you stood up was like uncurling: pushing away from the table with your hands, rolling your shoulders back, straightening your back, and, last, lifting your chin.

29 APRIL 1989

He said, "Tell me another story. I'm too lazy to go to a movie or read a book. You're more interesting. I want to lie here and hear fascinating things."

We were on my bed, yesterday afternoon, after lunch. We'd pulled the blanket up because, after making love and everything got quiet and still, we got chilly . . . the heat wasn't on, and we were damp.

"Tell me a secret." His voice was muffled in the pillow. "I love people's secrets. Tell me more about your husband."

"Not much of a secret," I laughed, even though I've never told anyone much about him. The only secret I could think of at that moment was the dream I'd just had the night before.

Maybe because Garth curls around me so I can feel his breath and heartbeat and every little puff of silent laugh or tiny groan as he reacts to everything I say, I try to keep a story going as long as possible.

I told him how Alex visited me the weekend after we'd met in New Orleans. He came to Pine Bluff as a surprise. Then he moved his tree-trimming business from Shreveport to Pine Bluff. And we got married. Men who score in a bar don't usually marry the babe. Maybe if they were drunk enough and it was the biggest night of wild abandon they'd ever scored. But our night in New Orleans wasn't like that. Neither of us had brought any grass and I was dry as leather . . . and tight. Every little push hurt, he went soft, so I took care of him the only other way I knew how. That could be what got to him—I didn't just cry or blame him. I knew whose damn fault it was. He said he wanted to be the one to do it for me. That's what he said when he called the next weekend—"Has anyone done it for you yet?"

"Actually, no," I answered, "they haven't."

"I'll be right over."

I managed to let him wiggle all the way in that time, had enough grass to force myself to say *oh-good-good-good* and hold onto his back, despite feeling paralyzed. I don't think he was fooled. Or if he was, that one time, it didn't take much longer for him to figure it out after I no longer had any energy, with or without grass, to say *good-good-good* or anything else . . . couldn't even *move*. I just lay there.

Every time was worse. Maybe we got married for taxes. Or because I liked his motorcycle. I loved his motorcycle. He tried taking me for long, fast rides before bed. I thought about the motorcycle while he pumped away. On the bike I was upright, feeling the motion, moving somewhere . . . just *moving*, that was enough, not getting away or getting toward, simply feeling myself in motion. I liked the hardness of his back muscles, leaning together into the turns, the mystery of our heads closed away behind separate helmets, our bodies together but not our minds. But in bed I was shoved deep into the mattress. *He* was in motion, but I was buried. He probably never watched me on television. I didn't get home until after midnight, and he had to get up at 6 A.M. He slept a few hours before I got home, then usually wanted some action, then slept again. I could tell the evenings when he'd gotten his rocks off somewhere else—he wouldn't move when I got into bed.

I wasn't scared of him. Or of his gun in the nightstand. Or his chainsaw. If I'd been afraid, I might've tried harder not to do the thing that made him so angry: Every time he touched me, started anything, I was suddenly as doped-up as I remember being in the hospital with the broken jaw. Not that he was the first one I'd ever *died* on. I don't mean languid and relaxed, I mean moribund, the mythical seed beneath six feet of snow, stoned and glassy-eyed, wrapped like a mummy, buried in sand . . .

Garth murmured something about how hard that was for him to picture.

Alex and I went by motorcycle to New Orleans about once a month. Seems like every time we went I got another ear piercing, but it couldn't've been that often. Maybe I only got my ears pierced whenever Alex found someone for some action. He said I could do the same. Man or woman, he said. Might improve me, he said. Might help me figure out what it took to get me off.

"A miracle," I said, "that's what it'll take." I think he almost hit me. Maybe I wanted him to . . . for an excuse to not be turned on by him. What other excuse did I have? Especially since by then my dreams were running rampant. I didn't really lie when I told Garth I was inorgasmic, but even as long ago as Pine Bluff, I was coming to little peaks in my dreams. The peaks almost always woke me up, dashed apart any illusion that some kind of real lovemaking had been going on. It was just me, humping the mattress, pressing hard and rumbling inside. One night as it happened, Alex stirred and mumbled, "Are we having an earthquake?" I pretended he'd woken me up, muttered "What? No, I doubt it."

Lots of times when he picked up another chick, he invited me along. But I remember one time the most: Three wouldn't fit on the bike. She had a car and I could've ridden in the back seat. But I took the bike. They probably never missed me. I'd never ridden the bike alone before. Took it out on the interstate, then back into the city, bought some leather leggings and was waiting for him out in front of her place with the bike and the leggings, wearing my black helmet with the tinted visor. He didn't know it was me at first. Then he wanted me to drive home so he could ride behind me with his hands in the crotch hole of those leggings. But I said no. He tried to take my head off with my helmet, but I held on with both hands. I only held onto him with one arm, though, while we drove back to Arkansas. With the other hand I just kept unbuttoning and rebuttoning my jeans through the crotch hole of those leggings . . . the whole way home. I never wore them again.

Garth was almost humming in my ear, not really moving, sort of just slightly rocking against me. *"Now* I'll tell you a secret, Garth. A real secret. A dream I had last night."

"Okay."

"I was sort of living in a shack like this room, except it was detached from any building. Like it was a shack in the back yard of a bigger house. I knew who lived in the bigger house, but you don't know her."

"Have you told me about her?" he asked.

"No." It was Haley, but telling him would've meant a sidetrack. The dream had been on my mind all day because I don't know if I'd ever dreamed about Haley before.

"Anyway," I said, "you would come and visit me in the shack. I would wait there for you. And *she* knew you came to see me there. And she knew what we did. And she was waiting for a time to come to the shack herself, she said, but it had to be just after you left. She wanted to touch me right after you left, she wanted to feel how soft and puffed up and supple I would feel down there after you had been in me."

He had his hands there while I told him, as though I was narrating what he was doing instead of the dream. "Oh god," he gasped. "Oh god, I can't help it."

At least now I won't ever remember that dream without remembering I told it to him.

I was still as confused after I left Alex as after I'd run from Lib. But at least I realized the confusion was sapping usable energy, and that if I redirected it, my career would start to happen. It did.

APRIL 11, 1980

A month ago you felt you needed to publicly attack me to prove there was no preferential treatment going in either direction . . . now you flaunt this lunch thing in their faces.

And what exactly *was* there to flaunt? Sitting at your stilted kitchen table on extra tall stools, a giant's furniture, eating a concoction of cheese, fruit, salad, and thick, obscene-looking sausages, we both stared down at our plates, then looked up simultaneously and laughed, reaching for our wine glasses. Not an easy laugh. Then your eyes went one way, mine another . . . but I came back first and watched you gazing off into the living room . . . model of a yacht on your stereo speaker, a window three stories up framing the top branches of a big tree. You tapped the rim of your wine glass with one fingernail and flexed your jaw muscles over and over.

Were we there to think about Haley, silently, together? Is that what you really wanted—someone you knew could think about her with you . . . without saying anything? Someone who knew the laugh light in her green eyes, someone who'd heard the urgency in her voice, even at a whisper?

But why *today?*

As soon as we went through the front door, I could feel she'd been there. Imagined her looking up, parting her lips slightly as she held out a glass to be refilled . . . just like I was holding out my own glass.

What did we talk about, Kyle? We must've said something.

I guess you told me you'd finally decided to name your boat *Peter Pepper.*

We made up more boat names. That's what we did. *Slow Roller to Third,* baseball announcer's boat. *Strike Out, Looking,* pitcher's boat. *On the Air,* DJ's boat. *Grounded,* electrician's boat. We had to hold our heads up, laughing without looking at each other. None of the names seem that funny now. Except maybe the ones we didn't say out loud, like when you said, *"All Hands on Deck,* a sculptor's boat," I *didn't* say, Or a boat for someone who likes to finger-fuck.

The first bottle of wine had been half-empty when we started. You wanted dessert and stood in front of your cupboard listing everything there—graham crackers, pudding, Jello, cake mix. Behind all that you found what you might've been looking for in the first place: the $75 wine, only enough left for an inch in each of our glasses. You toasted me, you toasted the future, toasted good sailing days, professional independence, *Peter Pepper*'s long life, your glory days (a week) in the big leagues, how I make the show's material *sing* . . . but you didn't toast *us*. Neither did I. How could we have made that kind of gesture—we were just two people sitting at a ridiculously high table sipping expensive wine with the taste of spicy knockwurst grease still in our mouths. Your brazen annoncement, "We're going home for lunch" to Al stunned him to silence for once, and it still rang in my ears: I could still feel where your hand rested lightly on my lower back as we passed him . . . but the word *us* just wasn't in the air when we got to your place, not present in the room, so I couldn't have used it, in any context. No *we*, no *us*. You ate lunch in your apartment at an eye-high table, and I ate there too. Only a how-do-I-look airhead wouldn't have noticed the puffy dark skin under your eyes, your eyes the color of a foggy morning, drifting off between boat names to stare out the window, way out there, or at the floor, way down there, your throat working up and down, your fist so tight on the stem of the wine glass I thought you'd pop the bowl off. But I couldn't even ask you what was the matter—the lunch was your idea. And you wanted to keep naming boats.

30 APRIL 1989

Maybe that lunch was an offhand, awkward apology for all those days of silence. But maybe just looking right at me and saying you were sorry would've been better. I remember that lunch but remember it as isolated from everything before and after it. Was it my going-away party?

There's going to be a farewell party for Garth in just a few days. He doesn't know exactly when he's leaving . . . his plane ticket is "liquid," he says, can be changed to any day he wants. So they planned the party early. He won't talk about it directly. He says stuff like, "We're both going to go on to glorious careers." But a going-away party is like a dead-end—You can turn off before you get to the sign and avoid coming to the end of the road. But once you pass the sign . . . what can you do? In the meantime, you can try to distract yourself.

We'll be lucky if we get just one show of *San Diego Follies* finished. I told Garth that, with a project like this, you can go on planning it forever. What needs to happen is: Decide to do it, then *do* it. I asked him if maybe PBS would be interested in a series like this . . . with maybe the possibility of extending it to include a feature for each of a number of other cities . . . Cleveland, Atlanta, Dallas, Denver. It would be such a *trip* for me to get a grant, leave the newsdesk for a year, and do it. He laughed. Did he ever answer? And what's wrong with me?—the idea's not even that good.

He was stacking things on his desk. Moving stacks from one place to another.

"Is this what you want to do this evening?" I said.

"Got any better ideas?"

"Yes—let's go dancing!" Surprised the hell out of myself too.

Turns out we went to a place where only one person dances. We were a stunning pair in a place full of military lowlife. He wore a gray wool pullover, blue jeans, and white tennis shoes. I was in black parachute pants tucked into my black ankle-high boots, a white sleeveless undershirt, and my black leather jacket with big brass zippers on the cuffs. Garth said he didn't need to go to a strip club, my shirt was enough for him. I took off my jacket in the car. He touched me without pulling the shirt up or reaching inside it. Then when we got out of the car in the parking lot, he said, "Keep your jacket on in here—you'll show as much as *she* does."

There was just a tiny stage in the corner for the girl. In the center of the front of the stage was a pole, like a brace holding the ceiling up. It was the dancer's only prop besides mirrors on the two walls. She was a tall girl, well muscled, powerful, an athlete. She danced barefoot, in a G-string. She climbed the pole, hung on with her legs, and let her head and shoulders hang backwards, touched the floor with her palms, released the pole with her legs, held the handstand for a moment, then somersaulted onto the stage floor, rolled over, her body humping rhythmically in the flashing lights imbedded in the stage. All the lights went out except for lights outlining her G-string, still blinking . . . the G-string was on stage, but the girl wasn't in it. She came out in a robe for applause, then went back into her dressing room to change costumes.

Every dance was basically the same except for different colored costumes. She flung herself around the pole, humped it, even managed, somehow, once, to get the pole inside her G-string, which made the sailors and marines howl.

Garth grinned at me through light suddenly all blue for a slower, but still bouncy, ballad. "Want to buy her for my birthday?" he said. I laughed. The girl was looking at us. We were sitting on stools at the bar, Garth in front of me. I pulled my stool up close behind him, leaned against his back, put my chin over his shoulder. Garth had one beer, I had wine, which I drank too fast. The music was so loud we couldn't really talk. But we smiled wildly at each other.

Every once in a while, a guy approached the stage and the dancer slowed down, leaned forward with her hands on his shoulders, still moving her knees forward and back but keeping her feet on the stage, and the guy would carefully put his hands on her waist for a second, then tucked money into her bikini bottom. Then he had to let go and back into the crowd again. By the end of the dance, she had bills sticking out around the top and leg holes of her G-string. Garth said it was degrading for her to stand there while some guy pushed money into her clothes. I said, "It's degrading for both of them . . . that baby sailor who stands there tucking the money in, in front of everyone, his loneliness broadcast . . ."

"He doesn't *have* to," Garth said. "No one's forcing him."

"That's the trouble," I said. "He doesn't even know how pitiful he looks standing there, like a kid at the blackboard doing arithmetic while the rest of the class watches, not knowing he's adding one and one and getting one for an answer."

"Very profound," Garth smiled. "How much have you had to drink?"

We laughed again, then the song ended and the dancers changed. The next one was a dud, not athletic at all; she wore high heels and just pranced around. The tall athletic dancer stood at the bar near us in a robe and track shorts, talking excitedly to the bartender. I was just about to get Garth to give her some money, hand to hand, like regular people, when she turned suddenly, faced me, and said, "What're *you* laughing at?"

I was dizzy and took a quick breath, but she didn't wait for an answer. "I saw you laughing at me," she said. "You think something's funny, say it to my face. You think this is an easy job, bitch? You wanna try supporting three kids by yourself?"

"I didn't come here to discuss sociology," I said. "I came to have a good time . . . and that's probably why I was smiling. I didn't know there was a house rule—"

The girl had turned away while I was speaking, sort of flounced away, her long arms looking longer because of the sweat bands on her wrists, her strong legs looking stronger because of the white crew socks and running shoes over her nylons. Her movements were big, nothing subtle, like her exasperated sighs and audible under-her-breath curses. But before I'd let my last sentence trail away, she swung back toward me, fists raised.

"Don't try your bullshit on me, what're you doing here—
don't think I didn't pick you out the second you walked through
the door . . . chicks like you only come to laugh—"
I felt Garth's hand on my shoulder. When I started to duck
out from under his hand, everything happened at once: she
poked me in the shoulder with a strong finger, saying, "Just get
the fuck outta here!" and I slapped her hand away. She caught
my wrist, I grabbed her arm, tried to pull my other wrist away
from her. She kicked me in the legs once and I tried to swing at
her, but I had no leverage because Garth had me off my feet and
was half-carrying me toward the door, dragging her along because she was still holding onto my wrist, cursing and spitting,
whipping her head around. Then she let go of my arm, turned
and kicked a table, upset it and shattered several beer glasses on
the floor.

Garth was laughing. "I'm going to harness your energy . . ."
But he never said what he would use it for.

April 17, 1980
Why are you going back to being the puppy who only
growls after the thief is gone? God, sniveling milksop!
"It's best not to fuel the jealousy fires, Corinne . . . one
date with him won't hurt . . . maybe for *my* sake you
should go ahead. . . . You wouldn't *mind*, would
you . . . ? It's not as though you and I are ever going to
be—"
Do you have any idea
I wanted to
I couldn't *think* it made me so pissed at you
After all, it's not as though you and I are ever going to be—
Know what I thought you would say when I told you
he'd asked? I thought you'd be sitting there, as you
were, folding that old envelope into as small a square as
you could, trying to press it down with your coffee cup

when it was about two inches wide, and when I told you that His-Pal-Al asked me out, I thought you'd look up with maybe a surprised, that's-funnier-than-shit smile, throw the folded-up envelope, and say, "Fuck that crap, Corinne."

But no. You kept folding the envelope. One last fold—it was just *bent,* and you pounded it with your fist but it sprang back, then slowly continued to open, like a clam underwater, and you watched as if seeing a miracle of nature, and said in a nothing voice, "Yeah, I figured that's what he was getting at."

"Getting at? What does that mean?"

"He's been dropping questions about you since we . . ."

"Since when? What questions?"

"Oh, he started some time last week. Then again a few days ago. Meaningless questions."

"Like what?"

"What're you so paranoid about . . . maybe he's interested in you . . . so he asked you out. Big deal. Maybe you'll have a good time."

"*If* I go."

"Why wouldn't you go?"

"Why *would* I?"

He snapped the envelope with his finger so that it skidded across the table and off the other side. The phone rang. I counted it. Twelve rings. During the seventh through twelfth rings, we looked at each other. Then when there was no thirteenth ring, it was like a breath I'd taken but never let out.

Until he said, "He was just hinting around about . . . you and me, you know, wanting to know if we are, you know . . . So I told him, no. We're not. Nothing wrong with that. It's true, isn't it?"

Kyle, you didn't have anything to hold. Even your coffee cup had slid out of range already, so you did that finger-to-finger thing, made the little cage out of your hands, held it up to face level but didn't look through it, you looked *into* it, and said, "I told him it was okay, go ahead and ask you."

"And you think I should go?"

"Why not?"

I didn't answer that time. I guess they're only *my* reasons, not yours: Because someday you'll put your hand in my sweater again . . . and this time look me in the eye to tell me you know it's me. . . . Isn't that a reason why I shouldn't go?

You flattened your hands together, palm to palm, fingers pressed together, still in front of your face, then put your mouth and nose between your hands, holding most of your face in a prayer mold, one eye on either side. Your voice inside your hands: "For *my* sake . . . maybe you should go. One date won't hurt. But it *might* hurt if he thought you and I are. . . . Don't want to fuel the jealousy fires, Corinne. . . . It's just one evening, not forever . . ." Dropped your hands, a loud slap on the table, stared down there, at your hands spread flat on the tabletop, and: "It's not as though you and I are ever—"

I wanted to tip the table over on you. But just left instead. And left the door open. And went straight to Al's office.

2 MAY 1989

This is sick, nightmarish . . . reading it is like a surly lucid dream where I know some dreadful thing's going to happen, but don't bother to wake myself up . . . or if I do wake up, I still have all that queasy apprehension . . .

How many other times have I stood in a bus terminal and checked the list of destinations? But this time—just these *two* times, twice in two days—I didn't choose one. I went yesterday . . . and I just got back from going again. Still the same: the indecipherable bored voice chanting departures over the loudspeakers, the plastic chairs with little televisions attached to the arms, the incessant roar and reverberation of the buses and the smell of diesel fumes. People who smell of urine and vomit . . . people eating donuts and coffee . . . people with paper bags for suitcases, sometimes stuffed with bread from Mexico . . . people planting all six of their cracked vinyl suitcases in the first spot in front of the departure door, sitting straddled on two of the bags, each hand resting on a bag on either side, touching the remaining suitcases with a foot or knee. The departers look at the ground as they walk, at the suitcases they're bumping with their legs . . . the arrivers keep their heads up but don't focus on anything, eyes red or crusty. But whether you're arriving or departing, you walk without lifting your feet, shuffling along, dragging whatever you own at the ends of your arms. I just stood there, maybe ten minutes, maybe a half hour . . . but I came back to my room. Is it because Erin Haley isn't really the type to study the Greyhound schedule, standing there in the depot with only her wallet in her hands? Corinne never showed up at the depot without her suitcase already packed. Maybe it's the best thing to do right now. Why wouldn't it be? Maybe I should be the one to leave first. Garth's farewell party is tomorrow night. Maybe I should be gone when he comes to pick me up.

Yesterday he said, "What's going to become of us, Erin?" He was smiling, almost shyly. Any answer I could've come up with started with *Someday* . . . I didn't say it but thought it. *Someday . . . someday . . . someday . . .* we'll plan to meet at a crowded convention in New York . . . we'll plan to cross paths on Route 36 in the middle of Kansas . . . we'll be on the same connector flight from Dallas to Los Angeles . . . he'll look up from his desk and discover I'm the new anchor hired at his station, wherever he is . . .

"What's going to become of us?" He said it after we spent a few hours in the afternoon at his place, when I got back from the bus depot. He never knew I'd gone there straight from his office after he told me things were coming from every direction and he was rattled and wouldn't be much fun to be around, so I'd better spare myself the trouble and find something pleasant to do instead of trying to improve his mood when it wasn't improvable.

"And there's no indication when this will pass?" I had asked lightly.

"Probably not soon."

"Okay, I'll leave you alone."

"Please."

I think it was that last word that sent me to the bus depot. Maybe that on top of the queasy fear of reading even one more page of the journal. I left the camcorder in his office, just lowered it from my shoulder to the floor, and left it sitting there.

When I got back from the terminal, I called his office, knowing full well a secretary would answer because it was five minutes past noon. I made her take the message down exactly, word for word: "I'm sorry for being one of the things coming at you from every direction. E.H." But when he called, as I knew he would, my energy didn't rush back to me like it usually does. My voice was flat and weak. He said, "Everything okay?"

"I guess."

"I'm taking a few hours off. Want to meet me at my place?"

"Okay."

"Everything okay, Erin?"

"Yeah . . ."

"That doesn't sound very good," he said.

"Well . . . Garth, if you keep pushing me away then pulling me back, I'll get stretched out of shape."

Then he laughed, but I didn't join in. "I'm sorry," he said. "I always do this, flail my way through relationships, always manage to do or say exactly the wrong things . . . I don't know what I'm doing . . . so I'll just slowly say . . . I love you."

We drove to Chollas Lake and walked slowly around the jogging trail. The ducks were sleeping. There were no kids fishing. Runners and walkers rushed past us. I told Garth about the end of Alex. Trying to distract myself from . . . the journal, and . . . everything. One minute we were walking along, holding each other, and the next thing I knew I was saying, "I remember the last time I saw Alex."

We'd gone to Dallas for a football game. I'd already gotten word that they wanted me for the job in Las Cruces, but I hadn't accepted yet, and I hadn't told Alex. Somebody had given him a ticket for this game and I'd gotten a ticket through the station. He'd taken his tools out of the shell of his little pickup so we could stop at rest stops on the way to Dallas and get into the back . . . he thought we could see if doing it more or less in public would help turn me on. I guess it didn't work. I remember him pulling me out of the back of the truck by one arm and sort of throwing me back toward the passenger door. We didn't speak the rest of the way to the game.

It was crowded. We went through the turnstile, passing over our separate tickets. I went through first and he was behind me, but I heard the ticket taker call him back: "Sir, this ticket is for last week." I was already inside. They opened a little gate and sent Alex back through to the outside. I was standing between two sets of turnstiles behind a wall of bars that kept people from going in or out. Alex walked away, crumpling his no-good ticket and tossing it over his shoulder, walking upstream against the current of the crowd that pressed into the stadium. I knew he wouldn't stop. He was going to go out to the parking lot, get into the truck, and drive back to Pine Bluff. I just stood there, moving closer to the bars, holding on with both hands like a cowboy-movie prisoner, watching the people surging outside, imagining Alex pushing his way through. When he got to the truck, he would cut a wake through those people as he burned rubber the wrong way through the entrance lanes where they collected money for parking.

I went back to Pine Bluff by bus, got there the next day, packed my things while Alex was at work, then went back to the bus depot. It was a long bus trip. But traveling like that, it's a sense of movement while you're dead. You sit there, staring straight ahead like you're doped or in a coma, you don't move much, your legs get stiff like rigor mortis, you see without noticing anything, hear without really listening to anything, everything blows past without changing you, but at the same time you know you're getting somewhere. At least it feels that way.

Once around the lake the story was over, the walk was over. We stood and embraced . . . held each other for a long, long time . . . but maybe it was only a matter of minutes.

Am I ready for what comes next?

April 20, 1980

Shit . . . 4:15 A.M. I can't remember. God. But there's a feeling of something I'll never forget.

The hot tub. The steam. All my clothes still on. Really? No, my clothes were off. Had to be. A sleeve with silk lining? No. Hot boozy water boiling around me in the dark. Absolute dark . . . ? No. . . . Alone, again, *this* time? No.

But my clothes *are* wet, in a pile over there. I had to

put them back on that way. Cold and clammy, but better that than wearing any of their clothes and have them come around asking to get their shirt or pants back. What the fuck was Cy doing there? No one told me it was a double date, but with only three people. Or were there more? Was Kyle there? Or was it a whole-station party? No. No. No. Someone strung red and blue Xmas lights all around—they were plugged into a thing that makes them go with the music. I was watching. Figuring it out. One string was the bass. One the vocal. All mishmashed. I was staring up. I was being fucked. Wet pants still tangled around one ankle. Wet shirt under my back. Glass of wine poured out over my face. *Wake up, little girl!* Who said that? An open-handed slap. *Do it, show it!* The Xmas lights going haywire like a special show to greet Santa as he climbs down the chimney. His grand entrance. Someone lifting my head. *Watch him do it.* My neck ready to snap in half. Holding someone's ankles, one in each hand, on either side of me. Then turned like a pancake. Like a Polish sausage on the grill. Being pulled up by my hips, like a cat, like a rag doll, my head and shoulders heavy on the floor. Someone laughing. The carpet smelled like wet wool. Someone singing happy birthday. I waited through all the endless happy-birthday-to-you verses to find out whose birthday. Happy birthday dear _____ (your name here). Did I ever find out? How many to-you verses are there? My arms in wet shirt sleeves. My shirt thrown over my head. My back cold. Where was that silk-lined coat? Even colder down on my butt. Something wet . . . and cold. *What is it what is it what is it?* Someone's crazy voice wouldn't shut up.
 Shut her up.
 Just frosting for the cake, sweetheart. Wanna suck?

Nipple in my mouth filling me with whipped cream.

Oh . . . It was *Haley's* coat, not mine, but that was another time . . . not so long ago. . . when her cowgirl scent from a coat wadded around my head overpowered that same smell of booze and smoke . . . If I'd had the coat last night . . . could it have also overcome the woolly smell, their slimy sweat, the grass, the smell of pussy on someone's hand, the cream in my mouth . . . ? Spitting sound of whipped cream sprayed into the air, then landing around me with the soft plopping sounds of wet snow falling from trees.

How's that feel?

Like I gotta take a shit.

Someone thought that was hysterically funny. Someone holding my butt cheeks apart. The whipped cream melting and running down the crack. Someone shaking the can. Someone kneeling on my hand. Someone fucking my asshole. Someone slapping my thighs. How many of them were there? Lying on the floor feeling like I had to take a dump. Did I ever go into the bathroom? Once I did . . . a long time ago . . . another different time . . . after he said I looked like a boy . . . I don't remember ever being on my feet. Did I crawl around all night, slide on my stomach, slither out of the hot tub like evolution? Or was I dragged from place to place by one ankle? Probably not. I don't have rug burns. But a few bruises. And dried blood. Blood turning black around the corners of my eyes, in my ears, and, mostly, in my nose. That's where it had to come from. But I don't remember how I got the bloody nose. One of those spontaneous combustion bloody noses?

Maybe if I try to remember the beginning . . . never should've had those joints by myself before I even got there. Met Al at his office. Working late, he said, so just meet him at the station and we'll go from there. No ride in his sports car, though. Instead: the elevator upstairs. All the way. To the penthouse. The door already open. Did a dozen people jump out and shout *surprise?* It was someone's birthday, wasn't it? Or was that just Al shouting as we came through the door? Golden already there, sitting in the huge swivel chair. When did I say *okay?* When did they ask? There had to be a moment. No one held me down. We passed the weed among the three of us until I lay flat and they finished it together, over me, silently, just the music, the only music I remember, The Doors from six or eight years ago, *Light My Fire.* What were they looking at? Not really me. But my eyes were shut most of the time, opened to slits now and then. Their faces flickering blue and red. In an hour I'd probably already drunk more bourbon than all the other booze I'd ever had in my life. Maybe an exaggeration. Felt like it, though. One of them touched my shoulder, his hand rough like sandpaper, made me feel I was velvety smooth . . . and he was scratching the delicate surface of me. But when did I get undressed . . . or lose my clothes . . . my wet clothes . . . who took them off? Nothing was ripped. Not a button missing. I probably did it myself. Between hits of the joint. Possibly forgetting they were kneeling on either side of me. Forgetting they were there, except to take the joint from their hands when they passed it . . . until I just receded, faded back, and I was already undressed.

The music ended. Someone went to find a new tape. The other stayed, the rock-rough hand still on my shoulder, my upper arm, and he said something like, "You can really be a woman, twice the woman, tonight, if you want." I do remember the *if you want*. I remember saying, "I'm not a virgin." When the other came back, the one who'd stayed said, "Let's go." And they bent over me, each taking a nipple and sucking.

All that after I'd already been in the hot tub. Did I trip? Fall in? How much had I drunk before that? What happened before the tub—before the drugs and whipped cream and fucking . . . did we talk? I want to feel like I didn't say anything.

I also never said anything to Haley. It's not necessary to talk to say goodbye . . . as long as you both know you're saying it . . . I'm sorry, Haley . . . I admit it, you didn't know, I fucked you over, maybe I deserved this . . . but we did have to say goodbye. Not saying it is the best way. I mean not out loud. Meaning it, showing it, that's different. Goodbye can be soft, slow, warm-water smooth, weightless, graceful, gentle as a first touch if you don't try to say or explain it. She would've understood . . . wouldn't she?

But I landed in that hot tub like a crashing cinder block. Shouting. Yes, I guess I used my voice. Just "Hey—" The music was so loud. Maybe every time I said anything, none of us heard it.

Oh shit, I remember something else:

Al said, "Kyle says you'll go along. Won't kiss-and-tell. You want to get somewhere here, don't you?"

God, did you say that, Kyle? *Why?*

And Golden: "You and *Kyle*? I knew it, dammit, the lying bastard. You're fired!"

Got a promotion, then was fired . . . all in ten seconds. But Al said, "Wait, she'll atone for that. He couldn't offer you a party like this, huh, sweetheart?"

Is that when I went into the tub? Or when I got the bloody nose? And what about this nail polish? Black.

fingers and toes. One did the feet, the other worked on my hands. Not very steady, the polish all over my cuticles, smeared on my knuckles. Done after the first bourbon bottle had been emptied, probably. Or was that the bottle that got spilled in the tub? Or . . . did the tub smell like hot whipped cream? Maybe the nail polish is smeary because I was shivering. Or maybe because I kept jerking my hands and feet away. The one at my feet pounded on my leg with his fist, then turned around, sat on my knees. I could still rock my feet on my heels from side to side. Laughing. Was I laughing? Or gasping. *Where'd you get this, where'd you get this, it's—* Haley's. Black nail polish. The acrid smell of it taking the place of any cowgirl perfume that might've been lingering for months in the red and blue air. Didn't I once lay my head on the breast of her coat and cry? When was that?

I did cry. That's right. Because I lost my contact lenses in the hot tub? Or when the burning end of the joint they were passing fell onto my stomach? Or when I opened my eyes and saw Cy's purple face screwed shut, his white hair, and realized it was his dick in me?

He'd finished the polish on my feet. Then they almost had a fight. With him still in me. Al wanted to put a black nail polish mustache on me. And started to. But Golden didn't like it. He said, *Whadda ya think I am, a goddamn fag?*

Keep your wig on. We're just playing around.

WE? She ain't doing shit. You gotta real dud this time.

I heard she was better than this.

Well, at least she's gotta couple'a holes. Make the best of it.

Sweetheart, wake up. Is she dead?

Corpses don't moan. Listen to that. She likes it.

Let her like me for a while.

Let me get a squirt, will you?
You had one.
Hours ago. God, listen to that juice. She loves it.
Sweetheart? Honey?

Sweetheart, honey, sweetheart, baby, bitch, cunt, darlin, honey, sweetheart . . . never once my name . . .

3 MAY 1989

I want to get out of here, I don't know where . . . fly somewhere. . . . Can I get to the bus depot through the window? Or the police . . . should I go to the police? But when they ask, "What happened?" what'll *I* say? I was raped . . . and hurt . . . and there was blood . . . at one time there was blood, but it must've gotten washed away. Now my body just aches. Like a white-knuckled fist that can't be pried open. . . I have to tell the fist to relax, I have to instruct each piece of myself separately . . . relax, toes . . . relax, knees . . . relax because we have to go to a party soon, Garth's party. . . . How can I go to his party when this has just happened to me? I can picture myself swinging a baseball bat in a circle and bashing everyone's head who's too close to me. There'll be party conversations, loud enough to hear but far away, voices in a black cloud, making me unable to see who might be speaking to me:
    What's new?
    I think I was raped.
    You *think?*
    Well, you see, it was ten years ago, and I may've said yes. If I did—I raped myself. Maybe I didn't completely know what I was saying yes *to.* Not to what they did . . . not to *them.* Never to *them.* . . .
    But what if I did say yes . . . dirty pig, fucking *whore* . . . No. I'm not, I didn't, I couldn't have . . . not Corinne Staub . . . you

knew me, Kyle. Did I know what would happen? I wouldn't've said yes . . . but did I say *no*? Why not? What kept me from saying no? Could I have said *no* with a broken jaw? Where's my broken jaw? Is this when it was broken? Why didn't I feel it as I was writing it all down right afterwards? The way I feel it now— it's my jaw I hear crying . . . it hurts . . . *hurts.*

Of course, look outside, you fool: It's raining. And you're grinding. You're not even asleep, and you're grinding your teeth. Maybe Corinne needs to be put in rubber headgear to keep her from hurting herself. To keep her from saying *yes.* Ever again. To help her bounce when her head hits concrete. I kicked the night guard under the desk a few weeks ago. Every time I see it, I think: "A fighter lives here." Not a very good one.

Why me, Kyle, why'd they want *me* at their party? They'd never done more than shove empty coffee cups or lists of crossed-out ideas at me. I was part of the woodwork, the plastic tabletop, the newspapers and tabloids stacked on a chair. But *now* what am I?

You're a successful news anchor . . . and you're Garth's lover. . . . Are you both at the same time?

And remember, there's a party tonight.

Will you be there, Kyle? Will you be one of the ones I smash with a baseball bat or one of those I stare at with moronic eyes as I cling to Garth's arm and wonder what the hell will happen to me when he leaves? I knew it would happen eventually . . . I knew I wouldn't run away from it. I thought . . . what did I think? What the hell was I *thinking*?

MONDAY, APRIL 23, 1980

Déjà vu. Kyle on the air alone. No sign of Golden. No His-Pal-Al hanging around. One thing is different this time, though: this note, found it taped to the door with my name on the envelope, saying Adcock wants to see me ASAP. Kyle's handwriting. All the possibilities keep running through my head, but there really is only one probability: I'm going to be railroaded out of here just like Haley was. But I can't go face Adcock until I talk to Kyle.

LATER

Now he says I have to figure out what to do. He said to wait here—Adcock's already gone to lunch, so I have time to think about it. He said it so low and steady, almost calmly, hard to believe we'd been shouting across the table, standing, circling, always keeping the table between us. Only once did his eyes and face show any sign of softness—not when he left but when he first came in and I was sitting here with his note. He said, "I heard about it," and touched the back of my head as he went around the table. That started the fight and ended any comfort I might've gotten from him because I had to know *how he heard*. And he had to know what I'm going to tell Adcock. "Claim rape or harassment, which one?" he said.

Could I claim rape? Was it? I never intended it to happen. Luckily I barely remember, although I can still feel it, sore and chafed, inside and out. But I didn't want to think about what to legally call it. I wanted to cry for a little comfort—don't you owe me that? This thinking just makes it all come back . . . they lapped and pushed at me like dogs, cheered each other on, but how could it be rape? I didn't leave. I never actually said *no* or *stop*.

Still, the legality—that's all he wanted to talk about . . . that and what I would say to Adcock. But my voice repeated like gunshots, and every time it was my turn to speak, I said, *How did you know?*

Finally he said, "Well, I knew about your date, didn't I?"

"And that means you knew what would happen?"

"I knew enough to make a pretty decent guess."

"But you're the one who said I should *go* . . . you said—"

"I tried to call the cops last night."

"Why?"

"To report a rape. So they could come stop it from going on or going any further. I wanted them to be *caught*. But the cops wouldn't come. So I had to let it happen."

"*Let* it happen?"

"Look, Corinne, they're being fired. I decided I wouldn't just keep my mouth shut this time. I called Adcock over the weekend and told him something had happened in the penthouse, told him what was going on and—"

I stood up. "I can't believe this. You *knew*. You *knew*. And all you did—"

"At least I did something. What did *you* do? You went along. Didn't you know what they wanted? Why didn't you stop them? You could've left. Just walked out the door. I thought *you'd* have more self-respect than that! *You* let it happen."

"Me? I—"

"Damn you, if someone thought you were a thief, would that make you steal? When someone thinks you're a slut, do you have to turn into one?"

"I didn't *let* it happen. It just happened."

"You can't tell that to Adcock. What a cop-out. He'll fire you too. Look, they're gone. That's been taken care of. What're *you* going to do?"

"What should I do?"

"Well, think about it . . . yes, you should feel wronged . . . deeply wronged . . . but what if you claimed it was rape . . . you know how awful that would be: a court case, giving testimony, all the rest . . ."

"But I won't get fired if I say it was rape—"

"That's right. You would still be here where you could *think* about it every day. And everyone who looked at you would remember it . . . every day. Wouldn't *that* be nice."

"I don't know, I don't know, I don't want to think about this. I don't even know what happened. I can't know what to do till I figure out what *happened*."

"That's not a good idea."

"Why?"

"You don't want to know. But you know what you *should* do? Don't make *any* statement to Adcock. Just go up there and quit. Better still, send a letter of resignation. Right now."

"Just *quit?* What'll that prove?"

"It doesn't have to prove anything."

"Maybe I don't want them to get fired just for having a drunken party . . . maybe I want them to be fired because . . . because of what really happened!"

"What good will it do? It's over."

"That's all you can say about it? You *knew* about it!"

"I did what I thought was best."

"Yeah, and *you* thought it was a good idea for me to accept that date too! Maybe what *I* think is best is to tell Adcock that you knew so much about it because it was all *your* idea!"

I wasn't even close to the exit, in case I really was going to dash out and run to Adcock with that story. Kyle was closer to the door. His face changed color.

Something drained out of him. More than just color. "You need to think, Corinne," he said softly. "Before you do anything, just think. I'll leave you alone to think."

So here I am thinking. But pretty soon, too damn soon, I'm going to have to be finished thinking and go out that door *knowing* what I'm going to do and what will happen to me.

STILL 3 MAY 1989

Maybe I'll never remember what it was I had decided to do when I left the conference room that day.

Should I start another letter . . . am I ready to talk to you now? Dear Kyle, now's when I should call you. Now's when I should kill you. The journal ends here. My hospital bill says I was released April 26, three days later. That's when I should've called you instead of taping the notebook closed and sealing it in a vault. I remember when they brought me my stuff from the hospital safe—I was still confused, disoriented, and they were still asking me my name and who was the president and what year was it. I nearly ripped my shoulder bag apart to assure myself the notebook was still there, but I didn't open it when I saw it safely tucked in with the tabloids and magazines. Then, the heart-lurching panic when I realized I couldn't go to the bank immediately, had to turn the cab around in midblock and send it back to my apartment where the earlier two notebooks were stashed in a drawer, praying to myself, *Please don't let my mother have already emptied the drawers and packed them in boxes and loaded them in the moving van.* I guess I was mumbling or groaning, clutching the shoulder bag against my stomach, because the driver asked if I was okay, if I wanted to go back to the hospital, but I just said, "Go, keep going," through clenched, wired teeth. Said nothing to my flabbergasted mother, just burst in, blasted back out. She had thought she was going to come get me from the hospital later that afternoon. By later that afternoon, I was dozing in the fleecy warm weight of two or three painkillers, dreamless, numb. I'd known so clearly that I had to get rid of the journals without knowing *why*. Just an instinct, like knowing when to put food in my mouth, to curl up when I'm cold, to sleep when I'm exhausted. I didn't know, though, Kyle, I didn't know. I didn't know what I'd done and I didn't know what had happened. . . . My eyes wouldn't even focus and I couldn't tell left from right. I didn't know if I'd seen you three hours before, three days before, or three months before. Some frantic primal urge just said *Run and don't look back*. You see, Kyle? I was still protecting you. This time from myself.

How many sleeping pills will I need tonight . . . after Garth's going-away party? Maybe he'll stay up with me all night . . . not talking. Just touching me. Barely touching. Like breathing on me. All night. Maybe the sun doesn't even have to come up again. It won't just *end*, Garth . . . trust me . . . whether we see each other twenty times a year or once every ten years . . . how can who and what we are to each other ever change?

5 MAY 1989, 2:30 A.M.

Have I just awakened from some sort of decade-long claustrophobic nightmare? Or is this what it's like to be mistakenly pronounced dead . . . to rise out of a coma and stretch all your muscles, wringing the stiffness and ache away, feeling every soft breeze as delicious refreshment? Or like someone borrowed your brain, long ago, but finally gave it back so you can get rid of the wheezing loaner you've had to get by with?

How many nights ago was the party?

Imagine it, Kyle, there's a station party at someone's house.

Were you there? I thought so for a while. Anyway, you know the large, brightly lit outdoor patio and pool; the family room made from a converted garage with the long buffet table along one wall for the potluck *hors d'oeuvres*; the spotless yellow and white kitchen where the BYOB bottles lined the shelves, melted ice cubes draining into the sink, pools of Coke appeared, got sponged away by the hostess, then appeared again; the airy high-ceilinged, pine-scented living room with unvarnished oak furniture and polished hardwood floors so no one could sink to the floor and sit in close, comfortable little circles with their legs outstretched. Of course they wouldn't have done that even with the plushest of rugs because they were all dressed in . . . well, not formal wear, but skirts and heels and suits and polished shoes and ties. You probably noticed or might've seen, briefly, the girl in white flannel slacks and a black turtleneck, her short hair not gelled but flat and soft . . . eleven earrings, tiny gold studs. No makeup, no boots, she held her hand against her jaw, afraid it was swollen and blue, afraid that everyone would know what had happened to her.

Maybe you didn't recognize her, Kyle, she's had a little cosmetic surgery since you last saw her in a hospital bed . . . a new nose . . . lost weight . . . and she now has sleepless dark eye sockets, like black eyes. To you, she was just the person who arrived with the guest of honor, but that's not how they'll describe her later. The girl who made such a scene . . . the girl who must've been on something. They'll say they never knew what Garth saw in her . . . they'll say a lot of things for a while, and then they'll forget. But they don't know what you know, Kyle, what *only* you and she know.

She might've just held onto Garth's arm like the edge of a life raft all night, not even noticing that the rest of her body was still in the ocean—as long as her head stays above the surface, as long as she can still breathe . . . just hanging on for dear life, not seeing anyone, focusing on him as he tries to speak with each person there who has come to say goodbye to him, watching the side of his face, his sunburned nose, his small eyes glimmering with energy although the lids are puffy and half closed. She might've been okay like that for hours, if he hadn't gotten a phone call and gone to another room to answer it, removing her hands from his arm before he went, saying, "I'll be back, let me go take care of this." So she turned, a drink in her hands that he'd put there before he left, and—how much later was it, seconds? minutes?—she saw you, Kyle. It had to be you, who else could it be . . . and she was afraid—suddenly, desperately afraid—because she was remembering, and there was nothing she could do to *stop* remembering. Her name is Corinne Staub.

Maybe you left right after noticing her. Maybe you went out to the patio and slipped out the back gate to the sidewalk. Maybe you hid in the bedroom, taking off your clothes there and choosing something else from the host's closet, leaving your gray and white sweater on the bed, hoping someone else would find it and put it on so when the wild-eyed girl spotted the sweater again, grabbed the back of it, and swung him around, saying, "Hey, you, remember me?" it wasn't you at all but a stranger's face, puzzled, smiling, until she said, "Where'd you get this sweater?" and walked away, back to the booze in the kitchen.

She held it in her mouth, trying to apply whiskey directly to her throbbing jaw. She kept checking her hands, holding them up in front of her face to see if they were visibly shaking. They weren't . . . the tremble was somewhere inside. She held her stomach—not there. Felt her heart—not there. It was everywhere. Took deep breaths that fluttered in her lungs, searched for Garth, found a bathroom, found a bottle of something in the medicine cabinet, and pocketed it. Drifted to the game room, telling herself, *I'm calm, I'm calm, I'll always have Garth,* remembering how he'd laughed when she got into his car, patted her head, and said, "You're different tonight—soft and silky." She stood in the game room, staring at the balls on the pool table, feeling her eyeballs clack together when the pool balls did, like she was already remembering this ten years later: when Garth had patted her head . . . she'd winced, ducking slightly as his hand approached.

People were laughing, and her eyes rose from the pool balls. They were talking about a TV show that had been on last night . . . and a newly released baseball movie, and the newly begun baseball season, and who should be traded for who, and maybe the baseball general managers should work on trading for the hostages in the Middle East, and what if station managers got together once a year and traded personalities with a cameraman-to-be-named-later . . .

The girl in the black turtleneck backed out of the room, refilled her glass, wandered to the patio looking for Garth, waiting to feel his hand on her shoulder, waiting to be pulled back beside him where she could hang on . . . but nothing was behind her, and she felt her way backward until her shoulders were against the wall of the house, listening to them talk about Michael Jackson's nose, the balding Beach Boys, should Elton John take John Lennon's place if the Beatles did a reunion tour, the latest pranks pulled by the popular DJ team on a rival radio station, the Oscar-winning movies, the overlooked personal favorites.

"Hey," she said, softly. She was talking to you, Kyle. "You were wrong—you said one date wouldn't hurt. But maybe if you'd been honest and asked me, I would have *agreed* to be used as bait to trap and get rid of them. Maybe I could've seen how frantic to get away from him you really were. We could've worked together . . . could've decided to do something about it *together* . . ."

Three women and a man glanced at her, unsure perhaps if she was trying to join their conversation about cats having kittens in their unlocked cars at night. They opened their circle so she could be included, just in case she was listening and trying to participate. She saw them, heard them, could practically smell what they were drinking and taste their cologne in the back of her throat. But she was also seeing, over and over: your face, Kyle, in a swollen second before your fist hit . . . your calm, expressionless face. Her fingernail was stinging from being peeled down to the quick. She wiped a smear of blood on her white slacks. A woman and a man discussing a wine-tasting class watched, then turned their backs.

She set her glass down so hard on a low brick wall beside her that the glass shattered. "What happened, Kyle?" she asked, "Did I make the wrong decision—didn't I come out of that conference room fully intending to tell the owner it was rape . . . just to make it possible for me to continue working there . . . with you. . . ? Isn't that what I would've decided? But that's not what *you* wanted me to decide to do, was it? Was I supposed to keep quiet and take the blame—or the credit—*with* you?"

Muttering to herself, she moved along the wall, away from her broken glass toward the sliding door, kept her back to the wall, edged into the house, almost knocking over a plant on a tall plant stand—caught it, steadied it. She didn't notice the plant again until she saw all the leaves picked off and lying on the floor at her feet, the last one still in her hand. She shredded the last leaf, balled it into green pulp. In that room, two men were describing to a third how to know the right size mountain bike to buy. "Hold onto the handlebars, feet on the ground— can you lift the bike? The bar should be maybe two inches from your crotch when the wheels are on the ground."

She picked at the studs in her ears. "Why didn't you want me there anymore, Kyle?" she whispered. "You could've just *told* me you wanted me to leave instead of hitting me. How could you get so angry?" She pulled on the stud so hard, the back popped off, rattled on the floor, the gold stud catching under her thumb nail. She flicked it out like dirt, went back to her ear to grab another. Two women telling Reagan jokes looked at her, smiling.

"Everyone thinks it's funny, Kyle . . . they're laughing. Probably because there are no visible scars . . . I can't *prove* it was you. Can't prove that I remember it now: can see your fist, your face. And you turned away right before hitting me, so even *you* weren't a witness. So if I called out *Why?* you wouldn't have to answer . . . or did you hit me again to keep me from asking again?"

The next earring also popped apart and a drop of blood must've followed the stud out of the hole. When she put her hand back to her ear, it was wet. She stared at her fingers, now smeared with red. The women's Reagan jokes had changed to comparison notes on airsickness and having to vomit in the cramped, vibrating closet of a jet rest room. They were laughing their heads off.

"I'm the only one, aren't I, Kyle?" she muttered like a crazy person who wanders around the park and sleeps in the library. "I'm the only one who knew, who ever found out how much rage you had in you. Should I feel closer to you? Should I feel sorry for you? Should I have been more sensitive and realized that you did it because you couldn't bear to have me there any-more—always reminding you that you had pimped me to them for your own sake? And you hated yourself for it, and hated me for it too . . . and hated me, and hated me, and hated . . ."

She was stuck, hardly listening to herself anymore, digging the studs out of her ears. She was in the family room, didn't recall going through the kitchen again to get there. That frag-ment of memory—your face, your fist—like a piece of film picked up from the cutting-room floor, now spliced into a loop, feeding over and over through the projector. But the soundtrack was this frumpy party, one man telling a woman that pesto is a thousand times better when made with Italian parsley because there's more bite to it, two men trading college landmark memories after discovering they went to the same school, three other people barely listening to each other as they eagerly waited their own turn to explain where they were when Woodstock happened. So many groups of people buzzing like they were reciting poetry in some sort of world's record marathon, unaware anymore of what they were saying, the words meaningless . . . democracy coming to China, Russia's new human rights, the continuing problem of skunks living in the stadium, another hillside plowed bare by a zealous developer . . .

"Wait," she said, but no one heard her at first. She had her hands over her ears. She was on the patio again. "Wait, everyone, wait, hold it." They started to turn toward her, without breaking off their conversations. Some of the laughter died down, but for only a second, then they resumed it again, reliving old sitcoms, sharing what they thought the first time they saw the mall at Horton Plaza—like *It's a Small World* at Disneyland, someone said.

"Wait!" she demanded. She released her ears, a bloody earprint in the palm of one hand. "Don't you understand? How can you people stand here talking about roller coasters and sports and old jokes and even older rock bands—don't you know what happened to me, don't you know what's *been* happening? Why is it I can be fucked so often without *ever* getting kissed?!"

She spun to leave but didn't see the screen door, ripped through it, fell with a cry to the hardwood floor, hands reached for her but she wiggled away, bolted to her feet, ran through their wide-eyed smiles, down the hall, through a bedroom filled with coats, no one following her. They probably turned to share smiles and raised eyebrows or ask who she was if they didn't already know . . . if they hadn't seen her for the past two months with Garth, in his office, carrying his camera around, sharing his bed after a 4 A.M. walk through the park and never once getting mugged along the way—never once even considering that it was a possibility . . .

In the bathroom, counting the seconds, the minutes, the pills in the palm of her hand. How many would it take to wake up *yesterday?*

Instead, over twenty-four hours later, I woke up at midnight the following night—I rose from the dead just a few hours ago. But I'm sure I woke several times in between, not enough to move, not enough to open my eyes, not enough to think. It was like dreaming about sleeping. I knew he was carrying me to my room, but it felt like flying . . . I felt him untie and remove my shoes, pull my pants off. I felt the bed shift as he sat beside me. I felt his fingers on my face and his breath in my ear. I felt his lips on my forehead and his cheek against mine. Over and over . . . I felt him . . . everything tinted dark violet black. Every gentle caress anticipated for hours, then lasting as long as I wanted it to. The sweetest sleep imaginable. The sound of deep breathing close beside me. My weightless body floating and cradled by something warm, something strong, something . . . someone. I tried to open my eyes and couldn't. He was repeating something. Stroking my cheeks and forehead. He didn't say anything except the name, "Erin . . . Erin . . ." his voice far away, then right up against my ear, and I tried to smile. I knew he would kiss me. The most lucid moment of my life. It was powerful and soft . . . the rush of wind in dry wild oats, heard before it's ever felt . . . or thunder throbbing behind the mountains. I didn't think about anything while he kissed me. Maybe I thought it felt like it would go on forever.

Garth's note, on a blank page torn from my journal, said he'd call tomorrow, but *that* tomorrow is already over. If he tried to call, I never heard it. In a few hours, but still before it gets light, I'll walk to his place.

5 MAY 1989, 2 PM.

Dear Warren,

I'll write this goodbye letter to you. I've already said goodbye to
Garth. Somehow it feels like you would want to know how
things ended with him.

Warren . . . it feels funny typing that name . . . *your* name.
But I guess, in a way, my own name feels funny too. Which
name? Either one.

But I'll be calling my station in a day or two. Erin Haley will
be back on the air. Smiling the slow half-smile, leveling the direct look at the camera, exuding the grim sexiness.

I jumped on a noon bus heading north. No, I couldn't have
stayed there one day longer, not one hour. I didn't know how
quickly I was going to leave town, though, until I came back to
my room, cool and tinted blue at 6 A.M., cold candles on the
nightstand, empty wine bottle on the floor, and knew I would
never get back into that bed where the thin white sheet twisted
like a tornado.

How many thousands of people have stood in an empty
room where once they had a lover? Today I stood in two of
them.

It was almost like one of those I'll-never-get-there dreams:
loping through the park at 5 A.M., no moon or stars because of
the overcast, couldn't see the ground, the trees black and invisible against the sky. The wind was up, not steadily, just slipping
through so the branches and leaves rattled, then dropped to silence. The damp air was heavy with eucalyptus scent. Was the
last spring storm coming in or going out? There was no mute
lightning in the sky over the mountains, no heartbeat of thunder. His car wasn't in its place, nose-up to the front door of his
rooms. My ears were plugged as though the altitude had
changed, my voice thudding against my eardrums: "Garth,

where are you, where *are* you?" but I don't think any words got past my clenched teeth. Gripping the locked doorknob in one hand, the key rattling against the lock. "Please, goddammit, *please,*" my mind screamed. I dropped the key three times, knocked my forehead against the door, beat my numb hands against my sides, retrieved the key and tried again, "Garth, *please . . .*"

So I finally got the door open . . . to an ordinary motel suite with kitchenette. The maid hadn't been there yet. But there was nothing in the front room that shouldn't be there—no blue sneakers between the sofa and coffee table. No wool Pendleton slung on the arm of a chair. No floppy briefcase, no camcorder, no stack of ripped-open mail, no newspapers, no cereal boxes, no balled-up socks, no radio and cheap tapes strewn on the floor. But there was one envelope perfectly centered on the coffee table. A name on it. Erin Haley. And the address of my station in Redding. A stamp in the corner. No return address.

I took the note into the bedroom and turned on the light. Not even realizing I was in the bedroom until long after I'd finished reading the letter. One of my earrings was in the envelope, a unisex hoop with a gold lightning bolt hanging from it. He said he found the earring while packing. That's how his letter ended: "P.S. Your earring was under the bed."

Dear Erin,

Sorry we didn't get to say goodbye. I tried. I hope you understand. That call I got at the party was Kathryn—for two reasons. The first was that I'm one of the final candidates for the job in Chicago. My interview is tomorrow. I'm going home today rather than fly back for the interview and return here for just one more week. Unfortunately, her other reason—she asked who I was seeing in San Diego. I tried to assure her, without directly lying, but I think my coming home immediately

will do as much as anything to let her know her world is still intact. So maybe it would be best if you didn't call or write.
As always,
Garth

As always. No, you weren't *always* this way, Garth. You weren't like this when you called to me from the sidewalk to let you in . . . or in the editing booth . . . or following me down the street in the rain . . . *Please come back,* you said. *Don't leave me,* you said.

I came back, Garth, I never left you. You said forever and meant three months. I knew it was three months but thought it meant forever. Why didn't I leave first? Last week, two weeks ago, or way back when you wouldn't take me to Los Angeles . . . when you wouldn't stay in my room late at night . . . when I first realized you hadn't kissed me yet? Why didn't I end it then?

There is a reason . . . how else can I say it . . . because I loved you. Your name goes here, Garth.

And for a long time, after I read the note, I don't know how long, minutes or hours, I was falling. Not flying, *falling.* Not moving through clear, sweet air that blows around the top of a mountain, but spinning away, dwindling out of sight, surrounded only by a motel room . . . what used to be *your* room. I was on your rumpled bed, lying there as though that's where I'd landed after being hit.

But Garth, somehow, some way, I did the best thing I could've possibly done. I had the most lucid dream of my life. Was I even asleep? I hardly think so. It doesn't matter. Within seconds I arrived at the airport. Avoided all the potential typical dream confusion of wandering endless labyrinthine halls through slow-motion jostling crowds, of never being able to find the monitors that would tell me where the Chicago flights and you were. I needed no information booth, no directions, no frantic dash through the security check and metal detector. I walked calmly into the waiting area and there you were, reading a newspaper, checking the weather in Chicago. You knew I was there and stood. The newspaper disappeared without a rattle, without loose fluttering pages scattering on the floor. You looked at me with your colorless eyes. You said, "I didn't think I'd ever see you again."

I came to say goodbye.

"That wasn't necessary."

Oh yes it was.

We didn't touch each other. Noise surrounded us like clouds, the sounds of boarding announcements, greetings and farewells, children whining, jet engines, murmured telephone conversations. But we were close enough that the fog wasn't even visible. And Erin Haley . . . she was smiling a flat smile, her eyes feeling sharp, not restless, bold, without questions, without fear, capable—most importantly—of seeing the whole picture with perfect clarity. Not just your packed camcorder cases and suddenly wedding-ringed hand stuffed up to the second knuckle into your jeans. Not just the tired apology, the pitiful excuses hanging at the corners of your eyes. I saw your sadness, your weary frustration, your longing stifled by the burden of a nameless responsibility you couldn't remember volunteering for. And I saw that I could neither cure nor take these things from you. We might've flown together. *I* could fly alone. But would you? *You'd* be the one getting on a plane. But *I* was the one who could fly. My smile turned inward for a second. And someone's voice said:

If I'd ever gotten that subcontract I never asked for, what would I have accomplished? What would my job have been? What would I have produced? What could possibly be more important than THIS *moment? I'm the one saying goodbye, Garth. I'm the one saying it's over. I wouldn't want you to go away remembering me as that limp, watery girl who melted out of your arms and into a bed before your very eyes. But it's more than just for the sake of how I'll look in your memory. It's for my own sake, to prevent another decade of wondering whether I was kissed or beat up. This time there're no pills and no abrupt escape. Always before I let myself miss this chance. This time nothing'll stay festering, unanswered, becoming warped and rotten and unrecognizable in my memory. Because I'm here, saying goodbye, and nothing will be left unresolved.*

"But aren't you just having some sort of weird dream or fifteen-minute alternate reality? " you said. "So you're not really facing *this* resolution either?"

Yes I am, Garth, think about it, I'm doing it, I'm facing it, it's over.

Then it was okay to leave. I suddenly found myself staring up at the lightning-bolt earring dangling over my face as I lay on my back on your bed, focused my eyes there until I finally could roll to my stomach, propped myself on my arms and put the earring in one of the empty holes in my right lobe.

It was your plaid bedspread I stared at as I felt for the hole in my ear. You had pulled it up over the wrinkled sheets before you left, just as you'd done every morning. "Why?" I asked once, "when no one'll see the bed except you until you get in it and mess it up again—why make it?"

"It's not made," you'd said, "just covered to keep spiders from crawling in."

"Spiders!" I'd shrieked and stood upright on the mattress. We'd been talking in bed . . . several weeks ago. You pulled on my leg, laughing, sat up to take my hand and get me to lie down again. "To *keep* them from crawling in," you said. "So there *aren't* any now."

And, without thinking, I guess, you pulled up the bedspread the day you left—to keep the spiders out. My hotel was much rattier, but you never worried about spiders in my bed. Will you ever remember the last time you were there, the last time you called up to my window . . . ? The day of your farewell party. When you came up, you had said you weren't ready to face the party right away, led me to the bed, and we lay down together, fully clothed, just lying there looking at each other, holding each other's faces, and you said, "What'll become of us, Erin?" It was the second time you had asked that question.

"I don't know," I said. "What do you think?"

You had your eyes shut, and I closed mine too because you were running your finger along my eyebrow. Your voice said, "Time to start over again . . . for you. For me . . . time to go home."

Where does a person start over *from*, Kyle? Rock bottom. The old cliché. From where the only direction is up. I thought I'd already made the climb, years ago, as I went from intern to reporter to anchor, each market slightly bigger, each audience share squeezing out a few more points. But who was that? *She* came back to San Diego, had an affair, he left her, she cried . . . a story told too many times to wet another eye. Yes, Erin climbed alone to her meager minor-league career success. But she's practically an empty shell. Now, purged, exhausted, cleaned out, next time the bus stops, I'll get off and go back again, Kyle, and this time let Corinne find you, knock on your door or the glass window of your booth, see what the decade did to your pure eyes and turned-down mouth that always wanted to smile. Not to ask *why*. Erin already knows why. She must've known all along. But for *Corinne* to at last have a chance to say, *I left my job with you undone, Kyle, but it's finally over now*. And hope you can recover too. It's time to bring it all back and leave it there with you, where it belongs. I don't need it anymore. Then Erin can welcome Corinne back, recognize that what she's been missing *is* Corinne, not answers. We'd lost Corinne, left her behind, abandoned her . . . because of the one question I didn't want to ask: Kyle, in a way, did I help you plan it?

But before I go back to you, Kyle, before the bus stops, there's one more thing I have to take care of: the plastic grocery bag filled with all the loose videotape I'd pulled out of the cartridge and given back to Garth. I took it with me from his room where he'd left it behind, on the nightstand. He hadn't thrown it away when he left the office that day. He carried it home. Remembered to take it out of the car. Then didn't throw it away in his room. Maybe saw it every day for a week, two weeks . . . didn't throw it away. Didn't throw it away while he packed. Now it's sitting beside me, squished between my hip and the wall of the bus, like a cushion to protect me from the jolts in the road. But I'm going to crack the window open and feed it to the wind outside, loop by loop, inch by inch, let it fly. Somewhere on that tape, Erin Haley sits on top of a stone-faced mountain reading phony news copy . . . lets it blow away in the breeze . . . takes off her shirt . . . smiles at the cameraman . . . who loved her . . . until the tape ran out . . .

COLOPHON

This book was set in Adobe Garamond and Adobe Cochin type faces. It was printed at Edwards Brothers, Ann Arbor, Michigan and smyth sewn for durability and reading comfort.